Never

Quit

By

Graysen Morgen

2016

Also by Graysen Morgen

Never Let Go

Meant to Be

Coming Home

Bridesmaid of Honor (Bridal Series book 1)

Brides (Bridal Series book 2)

Mommies (Bridal Series book 3)

Crashing Waves

Cypress Lake

Falling Snow

Fast Pitch

Fate vs. Destiny

In Love, at War

Just Me

Love, Loss, Revenge

Natural Instinct

Secluded Heart

Submerged

Acknowledgements

Special thanks to my editor, Megan Brady, who worked her magic on the longest book I've ever written! *Muchas gracias!*

A very special thank you to my readers. This is my eighteenth book, and without you, it wouldn't be possible!

When I first started my Coast Guard story idea, seven years ago, I made it to 13,000 words and stopped. I thought about that old story here and there over the years, but never knew what to do with it. Then, I picked it back up again earlier this year and completely rewrote those first 13,000 words, turning the new direction into two extraordinary stories, one of them being the longest that I've ever written! I'm glad I Never Quit on that old story idea!

Dedication

This book is dedicated to the United States Coast Guard Rescue Swimmers. Thank you for doing what you do every day. *So Others May Live*

And to my wife: Who never quits on me.

Prologue

Finley Morris stood in front of the long mirror in the closet, buttoning the light-blue, short-sleeved shirt that went with the dark-blue slacks and polished oxford shoes of her United States Coast Guard, Tropical Blue uniform. The pointed-collar shirt was perfectly pressed and adorned with over fifteen years of service decorations, including her newest rank of Senior Chief, and the gold wings of the Helicopter Rescue Swimmer insignia, a badge she wore proudly.

"I don't think I'll ever get tired of seeing you in this," a soft, feminine voice said.

"Oh, yeah?" Finley mumbled, closing her eyes when she felt hands brush her shoulders from behind. She couldn't believe it had been two years since she'd gotten back together with Nicole Wetherby, the love of her life and mother of her child, after seven long years apart.

"Yes, Senior Chief," Nicole murmured. "But, I prefer you out of it," she added, sliding her hands under the open collar and over Finley's small, bra-covered breasts.

"Nic," Finley sighed, stilling her hands. "I need to get to the base."

"You have a few minutes," Nicole whispered in her ear. "The new class won't start without you."

Finley pulled Nicole's hands out of her shirt and spun around, facing the beautiful, blonde-haired woman with hazel-green eyes. Unable to resist temptation, Finley leaned in, kissing her tenderly.

Nicole wrapped her arms around Finley's neck and pushed her hips against her, heating up the passion between them. Finley pushed her hands under Nicole's shirt above her hip bones and began walking her backwards towards the bed.

"Mom! Are you ready to go?" a teenage voice yelled from down the hall.

"Damn it," Finley muttered. "Rain check?" she asked, looking at Nicole with apologetic, deep-blue eyes before kissing her softly.

Nicole shrugged and smiled. "It's a date. Now, get out of here," she said, glancing at the clock. "I have another hour before I need to get ready for work."

"That's a lot of time to kill...alone." Finley grinned as she began straightening her uniform and closing the buttons.

"I—" Nicole began before being cutoff.

"Mom!"

Finley rolled her eyes and opened the bedroom door. "Caitlin, I'll be downstairs in a minute. Go eat your breakfast."

"I already did. You promised to drive me to school early this week so I can use the pool before first period started. We're going to be late," she said, standing in the open doorway.

"She's right, you did. Otherwise, she'd be waiting to go with me when I leave," Nicole added.

Finley grabbed her garrison cap, tucking it under the side of her belt. "Come on, kiddo. Let's get you to school," she said. "I love you," she added, looking back at Nicole.

"I love you both," Nicole replied, hugging them. "Good luck with your new class."

"Thanks." Finley smiled.

Chapter 1

A group of twenty Aviation Survival Technician training cadets stood in formation outside of the administration office building. The class consisted of sixteen men and four women, all of whom held the rank of Airman or Petty Officer Third Class. They'd all completed basic training at some point and had become members of the United States Coast Guard. Now, they were reporting to AST school to hopefully become Helicopter Rescue Swimmers.

They'd just gotten out of an assembly where the commanding officer of the base welcomed them, talked about the history of the Coast Guard, and the history of rescue swimmers. Then, he introduced the group to the officers who were in charge of the daily operations of the base, as well as the lead instructor and assistant instructor for the swim school.

February in South Carolina was cold. A few of the cadets had begun to shiver in their short-sleeved, Tropical Blue uniforms.

"Class 16-20, listen up," said Chief Petty Officer Neil Denny, the assistant instructor. "When I call your name, fall out of formation and go into the administration building to get checked in. You'll receive your ID badge, uniforms, and swimming equipment. When you've finished, go to the dorm building, pick out a bunk, and drop off your belongings."

4

"Aye-aye, Chief," the group replied. Neil went down the list of names on his clipboard, finishing with the only person left standing in front of him. "Jordy Ross, fall out," he said.

Jordy nodded and jogged over to the building. As soon as she walked in, she gave them her military ID. They took her picture and handed her a cadet ID, as well as a duffle bag with a red survival swimmer vest, black fins, and a black mask and snorkel set inside of it. She tossed the bag over her shoulder and proceeded down the hall to another room, where the rest of the cadets were walking through a line, collecting the t-shirts, shorts, bathing suits, and sweat suits that would make up their uniforms for the next eighteen weeks.

"Don't bother giving her everything. She won't be here that long," one of the male cadets said, making a joke about a female cadet that was ahead of him in the line.

"Hey, maybe you don't need your stuff either," Jordy countered.

"Girls," the guy muttered. "They don't belong here."

Jordy pinned him with a stare and shook her head.

"Move it along cadets!" CPO Denny yelled from the doorway. He'd already changed from his Tropical Blue uniform to the Operational Duty Uniform, which looked like solid, dark-blue Police SWAT fatigues with long sleeves, cargo trousers, combat-style boots, and a matching ball cap with his rank insignia sewn in the middle and Coast Guard written above it. His rank was also sewn on both points of the shirt collar, and his name and US Coast Guard were stitched above the breast pockets. "You have ten minutes to get back into formation," he yelled.

5

"Fuck," Jordy whispered. There were still at least six or seven people in front of her in the line. "Come on. How hard is it to grab the pile with your name on it?" she huffed.

*

The dorm was a chaotic mess when Jordy finally entered, literally running with her duffle bag filled to the max with her equipment and uniforms. The large room had five rows of double bunks on the left and the same on the right. She moved through the crowd, searching for the only empty bunk, which wound up being the bottom bed in the last row on the left. She tossed her bag down without bothering to see who was next to her.

"Hey, you didn't need to stand up for me back there. I can hold my own."

Jordy raised a brow and spun around to see the female cadet from the uniform line. She had dirty blonde hair and light blue eyes. Jordy, who stood about three inches taller, tucked a loose strand of dark hair that had escaped her bun, back behind her ear. "I wasn't. He was being a dick towards all of the girls in this class," she stated flatly, giving her a second look before turning back around.

"I still don't need your help," the other female cadet muttered.

"I have twenty dollars that says he won't make it," another male cadet said.

Jordy turned to see him adjusting the bunk above hers.

"Hey, I second that," another guy added. "Evan McDonald. Nice to meet you."

"Jordy," she said, shaking his hand.

"Rich Webber," the guy bunking above Jordy shook her hand as well.

The two guys were about Jordy's height, maybe an inch taller, with lean builds.

"And you are?" Evan asked the other female who was bunking below him.

"Ericka Burney," she replied, still looking at Jordy.

As they headed outside to rejoin the formation, Jordy noticed Rich had her same rank of Petty Officer Third Class. Ericka and Evan were both Airmen. "How long have you been in?" she asked.

"About a year. I was waitlisted after basic training. You?"

"I'm two months out," Jordy answered.

"Seriously?"

Jordy nodded as she fell in line next to him in the formation of five cadets wide and four rows deep.

"Lucky dog," he whispered.

"Class 16-20, stand tall! Officer on deck," Neil yelled, bringing everyone to attention.

"I know you sat through an assembly earlier today, being welcomed by Captain Ingram, but I'd like to personally welcome class 16-20 to Air Station Charleston. I wish you the best of luck with your rescue swimmer training. Helicopter Rescue Swimmers hold one of, if not the hardest job in the Coast Guard. They are honored day in and day out for the work that they do," said Commander Hill, the executive officer of the base. "And now, I officially turn you over to our Rescue Swimmer School Lead Instructor, Senior Chief Petty Officer Finley Morris. They're all yours, Senior Chief."

Finley stepped to the front of the group, where she saluted him before shaking his hand. She'd also changed into her Operational Duty Uniform, which was the daily working uniform in the Coast Guard.

"Helicopter Rescue Swimmers have their own motto: 'So Others May Live,'" she started. "It has a double meaning for those of us who have the privilege of wearing the gold, winged-fins on our uniform. You will all leave your blood, sweat, and tears behind when you exit this base, but for those of you who graduate, you'll understand the double meaning, and that motto will be forever ingrained inside of you. I personally guarantee it."

Finley walked up and down each line as she continued. "Coast Guard AST Rescue Swimmer school is eighteen weeks, broken up into three phases that progressively get more difficult. This school has the highest attrition rate of all military rescue swimmer schools. Nearly seventy-five percent of you will washout." She moved back to the front of the group where Neil was standing at parade rest. CMDR. Hill had walked away after turning the class over.

"Welcome to Phase One of Rescue Swimmer school," she said, looking down at her watch. "You have ten minutes to get changed into your sweats and report back to muster for your Physical Fitness Test. Dismissed."

"Aye-aye, Senior Chief," the group called out before running as fast as possible to the dorm building.

"I thought you were going to wait until the morning," Neil said.

"Changed my mind." Finley shrugged.

*

Jordy quickly changed from her Tropical Blue uniform to a black, one-piece bathing suit with a gray sweat suit over it that had her rank, class number, and last name stenciled on the front of the shirt. She finished with a pair of Nike sneakers and checked her watch. She had two minutes left. She pulled her dark brown hair out of the bun at the back of her head, shaking it out. The slightly wavy strands touched her shoulders, but didn't hang much lower. She quickly wrapped it back up into a tight bun and jogged out of the dorm.

"I can't believe we have a fitness test on the first day," one of the other female cadets mumbled to Jordy as they rushed into formation.

She didn't say anything as she stood at attention, facing forward. The mid-day sun in the distance wasn't warm enough to make a dent in the cold air blowing right through her clothing. She was too busy concentrating on staying warm, to notice Ericka slide in line next to her.

*

"Stand tall!" Neil said loudly.

Those who weren't already at attention, immediately straightened up.

"Class 16-20, do not bring your cell phones to my pool, my classroom, or my PT course. When you are in my pool, my classroom, or my PT course, you are on my time. When you are in that dorm building or mess hall, you are on your time. If I catch you with your phone while you are on my time, I'll toss it into the pool, where it will stay until you either wash out or graduate," Finley stated sternly.

"Aye-aye, Senior Chief," the class replied together.

"If any of you washout in the first week, shame on the United States Coast Guard for allowing you to even get here. There are hundreds of service men and women lined up behind you, waiting on a list for their name to be called. I suggest you think long and hard about why you are here, and how you plan to survive the next eighteen weeks...starting now!" She nodded at Neil to begin.

"Jumping jacks at the sound of my whistle. When I blow it again, stop and stand tall," he said. *Tweet!*

As soon as the whistle sounded, the group began exercising. Neil watched the seconds tick by on his wristwatch. When the number thirty rolled over, he blew the whistle again. "Jog in place," he said, blowing it again.

The group went through three minutes of warm up exercises before they were brought back to attention. Everyone was warmed up and slightly sweaty.

"Welcome to the Phase One Physical Fitness Test," Finley said, stepping up in front of them. "Hit the deck in plank position."

The cadets jumped down to the ground with arms extended, holding their body up off the ground.

"Down...up...down...up," Finley called, over and over. After thirty push-ups, one of the girls began to struggle. "If one of you quits, we start all over! Do not quit on me!" she yelled.

Neil stood next to her, holding a clipboard and a stopwatch.

"Stand tall," Finley stated. "Back down in the sit-up position. Now!" she yelled. "Up...down...up...down," she continued.

When Neil nodded at Finley, indicating they'd passed one minute, she brought them back to attention. "Burpees on my count. Down...up...down...up!"

Finley watched a couple of the cadets who were starting to struggle with fatigue.

"Stand tall!" she yelled, bringing them back up. "Right face," she called out. "March!"

The group faced to the right and began marching in formation.

"Double time," she said loudly, bringing them to a jog as she stayed on pace beside them. "Pick it up!" she snapped.

*

Jordy had sweat pouring from her pores, running down the sides of her face and between her shoulder blades as she trudged on. She hadn't expected the first day to be so physical, but basic training had been the same way. She was in excellent condition and had been training every day leading up to this point, so she wasn't worried about failing the test.

"Is your tampon slowing you down?" the jerk from the uniform line snickered. He was in the row next to Jordy.

"Is your shriveled dick slowing you down? It is a little cold out here," she retorted.

Hearing chatter in the group, Finley kicked up the pace even faster.

"Idiots," Ericka mumbled, shaking her head. She had no idea why she wanted to be better than Jordy Ross, she just did.

Maybe it all started when they were in the uniform line, or perhaps when she saw Jordy blatantly checking her out. She wasn't an object to ogle. That was part of the reason she'd decided to become a rescue swimmer, to prove to everyone that she could do it, that she wasn't just some pretty lifeguard at the beach.

Chapter 2

By the time they hit the one-mile mark, most of the group was tired. A couple of the cadets were struggling to keep up.

"Stay together, or we go another mile!" Finley yelled.

"Come on, you pansies!" the jerk groaned.

Neil ran ahead, opening the door to a building in the distance. Finley brought the group to the building and stopped them.

"Form a single-file line and double time it inside!"

The strong scent of chlorine filled Jordy's nostrils as she entered. Her lungs were burning from the brisk, mile and a half run in the cold after the rigorous beginning exercise.

"Get your sweats off and get into my pool!" Finley said with authority. "You're going to tread water for five minutes. If anyone touches the edge or the bottom, we start over!"

"Don't touch the wall, ladies!" the jerk sneered as he jumped into the water.

Finley stepped to the edge and knelt down. She pointed to him and made a come here gesture with her finger. He quickly swam over.

"Grab the wall," she said and asked, "What's your name?" She hadn't gotten a chance to look at the front of his sweatshirt.

"Parish, Senior Chief. Petty Officer Third Class Jon Parish."

Finley nodded. "Why are you here?"

"To be a Helicopter Rescue Swimmer, Senior Chief!"

Finley looked at the rest of the class who was treading water.

"What's the one thing Rescue Swimmers cannot go without?" Finley asked.

"Their mask and fins," he replied.

Finley turned her head in Neil's direction. He laughed as he kept an eye on the cadets treading water, as well as the time on his watch.

"What's the definition of team, Chief?" Finley asked him.

"A group of people who work together," Neil answered.

Finley turned back to Jon. "Petty Officer Parish, your team is the one thing you cannot go without. Turn around," she said. "Your team is doing your exercise for you. Every cadet that you see in front of you is treading water an extra five minutes on your behalf, while you stay here with your hand touching this wall," she said as she stood up and walked back over to Neil.

"What about his test?" Neil asked.

"He failed today, didn't he?"

Neil nodded and wrote the letter F next to Jon's name.

When they hit the ten-minute mark, Neil pulled them out of the pool.

"Congratulations," Finley said with a smile. "You made it through the easiest day of Helicopter Rescue Swimmer school."

Neil clapped as the cadets' shoulders sunk.

"Go to your dorm, get cleaned up, and head to the mess hall for evening chow. Be outside of the dorm at six a.m. tomorrow morning for muster in formation and in your sweats. Keep up with your training syllabus to know what uniform to wear each day. Every morning, Sunday to Saturday, you will muster in formation under the flag pole for class inspection. You're dismissed for the rest of the day." She watched as they hurried to the towel bin to dry off and get warm, before she headed to her office.

"What do you think?" Neil asked, catching up to her in the hallway.

"I think we have a good class, but I see four or five of them that probably won't make it through week three," she sighed.

"That asshole is going to be a problem."

"Let's see if they handle him themselves. He'll either learn to be part of the team, or he'll washout. It's that simple."

"Aye-aye, Senior Chief," he said. "Have a good night."

"Thanks. You too," Finley replied as she opened her office door. A stack of manila files containing the service records, background checks, and Aviation Survival Training Center reviews on each cadet, sat in the middle of her desk. She sat down in the squeaky chair and opened the first one: Jordy Ross.

Petty Officer Third Class Jordy Ross had been in ROTC all four years of high school and had almost two years of college completed, before dropping out to join the Coast Guard. She had high remarks from basic training, finishing third in her class, and she was twenty years old. Finley looked at the picture in the corner of the service record and glanced at her stats. Jordy was five-foot-seven with a lean, muscular build, dark brown hair, and brown eyes.

Airman Ericka Burney, the next folder in the pile, had not participated in ROTC and had no college credits. Her background consisted of six years as a pool life guard and four as an open ocean life guard at the beach in Oceanside, California. She was also twenty years old. One thing that stood out was her extremely high entrance exam and ASVAB test scores. Finley made a mental note before glancing at her picture and stats. She was petite at five-foot-four, but strong for her size, with dirty blonde hair and light blue eyes.

Petty Officer Third Class Rich Webber's file followed in line. He had three years of ROTC and had been in the Coast Guard for fourteen months, spending most of those aboard a cutter ship while he waited on the entrance list for AST school. He reminded Finley of the boy next door. He was only five foot eight, but in good physical condition. He also had a nice smile with dimples in the corners, and crew cut, light brown hair.

Airman Evan McDonald's folder came up next. He hadn't had any ROTC experience, but he also had high test scores, which had moved him up the waitlist. He and Rich were about the same build and the same age, and he had buzz cut, auburn-brown hair.

Petty Officer Third Class Jon Parish was the name on the next folder. The picture inside reminded Finley of the guys in the military movies with their high and tight Marine haircuts, dog tags dangling, and an assault rifle in their hands. He was well-built at five-foot-ten with a thick, muscular frame. He'd also been in the Army National Guard, serving two years of active duty and two years of reserve duty in an infantry unit, finishing as a Specialist before requesting a transfer to the Coast Guard, making him the oldest cadet at twenty-three. Finley read over his ANG service record. He hadn't had any conduct issues and had always reported on time, carrying out his duties as requested. She did notice that his reserve unit was led by a female officer, which wasn't uncommon. Closing the file, she moved onto the next one.

*

The large, open dorm room had separate showers and bathrooms areas for the male and female cadets. The men waited in line, taking showers six at a time, while the four women used their facilities simultaneously.

Jordy stepped into the small enclosure, pulling the curtain shut behind her. She was happy to see they didn't have to take group showers like they'd done in basic training. They were given some semblance of privacy. She hung her toiletry kit on the wall hook, and began showering off the sweat and chlorine from the long day. *Day One - Week One,* she thought.

"I almost didn't make it today," one girl said as she stood at the sink, brushing her teeth. "My legs feel like jelly."

"I'm a little sore, but it'll pass. I'll be fine tomorrow. All you need is a good recovery," Ericka replied to her.

Jordy's ears perked up when she heard Ericka's voice. She shut off the shower and pulled the curtain back, waiting an extra second that Ericka took notice of, before grabbing her towel. "If you're hurting now, you don't stand a chance," she stated, stepping out of the stall. "This place is going to be like basic training on steroids, times ten."

"And you're so confident that you'll skate by, right?" Ericka retorted.

"No. No one is given a pass, but I came prepared. That's all."

"So did I. And I'm sure she did too," Ericka snapped as the other girl walked away, leaving them to hash things out alone. "Why are you such an ass? Isn't it enough that we have to deal with guys thinking we don't belong here? Now we have other women telling us that, too."

"I never said you didn't belong, or she didn't for that matter. All I said was, it's going to get much harder. If you couldn't cut it today, you're going to have a hard time going forward."

"We'll see who has a hard time," Ericka sneered. "I promise you, I can do anything you can here, so bring it on," she added walking away.

"Game on," Jordy mumbled to herself. She liked the idea of a little personal competition, especially since Ericka was attractive.

*

The mess hall was half full of guys from her class when Jordy walked in. She passed through the serving line, collecting her meal of grilled chicken and vegetables, with a side of mashed potatoes. At the end, she found the dessert table, full of brownies and chocolate chip cookies, with a few bowls of banana pudding left. She added a bowl of pudding and a cookie to her tray and proceeded across the room towards the tables. She saw Rich sitting at the end of one of them, so she set her tray down in front of him and took a seat.

"It's not bad," he said, referring to the food. "Could use a little salt and pepper."

"There's pepper up there in the line, but not salt," she replied. "What did you think about today?"

"Man, it was brutal, but I expected it to be. It's been awhile since I was in BT, so I'm not used to so much at one time. I think I'll be okay though. What about you?"

"I'm good. I've been training every day since I got out of BT."

"Hey, guys," Evan said, sitting next to Rich. "There's a bet going at the other end of the table on who's going to hook up with Ericka first."

"That's ridiculous," Jordy laughed. "Is that all you guys think about?"

"Nope. I'm here for me," Evan said. "I have a girlfriend back home."

"Yeah, I'm not here to hook up, unless you're willing," Rich teased, looking at Jordy.

"Oh, yeah. I'll meet you in the bathroom later," she joked sarcastically. "It's been real, guys, but I'm going to go get some sleep."

"Can I have that cookie?" Evan asked.

"Nope. It's coming with me." She grinned, walking away.

Ericka was sitting in her bunk, writing a letter, when Jordy walked over to her own bed. "Do people still do that?"

"What? Write letters?" Ericka asked. "How else do we communicate with people back home? We weren't allowed to bring our phones."

Jordy shrugged. She hadn't thought much about communicating with anyone. Her parents had pretty much written her off after she told them she had dropped out of college and joined the Coast Guard, and her brother followed everything they did anyway, so he hadn't spoken to her either. "By the way, there is a pool going around about you."

"Excuse me?" Ericka retorted, setting her letter aside.

"The guys are betting on who's going to hook up with you first."

"That's absurd."

"I know. I put my name in the hat." Jordy grinned, kicking off her shoes.

"Why did you do that?"

"My radar pinged as soon as I saw you looking at me."

Ericka rolled her eyes and shook her head. "No one's going to win that stupid bet anyway because I'm seeing someone."

"Yep. Someone named Toni, right?"

"How did you know?" Ericka squeaked.

"Dear Toni," Jordy replied, pointing to the letter.

Ericka snatched it up and huffed angrily as she went back to what she was doing.

Jordy pulled the cookie from her pocket and sat on her bed.

"You're not supposed to have food in here," Ericka said without looking up.

"Are you going to tell on me?"

Ericka glanced at her and wrote another line in the letter.

"That's a better idea, tell Dear Toni," Jordy laughed.

Chapter 3

It was after 10 p.m. when Finley walked into her house. She hadn't planned to stay at the base for so long, after dismissing the class at seven, however, once she started reading the cadet files, she couldn't stop. She felt better knowing a little bit of back story on each of them ahead of time. With her last two classes, she'd waited until someone had washed out to find out who they were.

"You missed dinner," Nicole said, from the couch in the den.

"I know. I'm sorry. I got caught up in paperwork," Finley replied, leaning down to kiss her softly.

"How was the first day?"

"About the same as all of the others, I guess." Finley sat next to her and bent down to remove her boots. "I can probably tell you the names of the first three or four to washout, and I'd honestly be surprised if I was wrong."

"How do they get in if they can't cut it?"

"Anyone can look good on paper. They don't exactly go through a physical fitness test to get in. You'd think their basic training notes would be able to weed out the bad seeds, but it still lets a few slip by."

"I remember when you were there as a cadet. It was hell."

Finley leaned back against the couch cushion, rolling her head to the side. "That seems like a lifetime ago."

"No kidding," Nicole murmured, reaching for her hand.

"How was swimming today?" Finley asked.

"Pretty good. I got held up late, so she actually practiced after school too."

Finley nodded. "When are we going to have the talk?"

Nicole raised a brow. "And what talk would that be?"

"Nic, she's fifteen and a half. She needs to start learning to drive."

"I know…I just…I don't think I'm ready to think about her behind the wheel."

"Me either, but it's going to happen. Personally, I'd rather her be in her own car and know what's going on, than riding around with her friends. Besides, I think we've drilled drinking and driving into her head enough that she won't attempt it."

"I certainly hope not," Nicole sighed. "Did you eat at the base?" she asked, changing the subject.

Finley nodded. "I need to get to bed. I have to be at the base at five. Do you think you could get Caitlin to school? The rest of the week should be normal."

"Yeah. I better make sure I get up or she'll be pissed. I hope this teenage drama ends soon. I don't think I can take much more of it."

"Hey, at least now her attitude is focused on important things and not you."

"That's true."

"By the way, we're doing a night drill this weekend, too."

"Oh, boy. That sounds exciting." She smiled.

"It is if you're me. Not so much for the cadets though." Finley grinned. "Come on."

"Senior Chief Morris, are you asking me to go to bed with you?" Nicole teased.

Finley stared at her for a moment. Nicole was dressed comfortably in loose pajama pants and an old t-shirt. Her blonde hair was hanging forward over one shoulder, and she had one leg folded under the other. Her hazel-green eyes had a twinkle in them from the TV lighting. Finley felt every bit as in love with her in that moment as she had been the first time she'd kissed her, over sixteen years earlier. Looking at her soft, teasing smile, Finley whispered, "Marry me."

"What?"

"You heard me."

"Finley, we talked about this."

"It's been two years. That's all behind us," she paused. "Do you love me?"

"Of course. I've loved you since I was seventeen years old."

"Then, what's stopping you?"

"You."

"Me?" Finley sat up.

"Do you really want to marry me? Even after everything I did to you...to us?"

"We're back together aren't we? I love you, Nicole." Finley got down on one knee in front of the couch and grabbed her hands. "I've always loved you, and I want nothing more than to be married to you. Caitlin is ours together and has been since before she was born, but I want more. I want you to have my last name. I want to call you my wife. Your mother and Dave Dulinberg robbed me of that a long time ago, but it's not too late." Finley reached up, wiping a tear from Nicole's face. "Marry me," she whispered.

"Yes." Nicole sunk down on the floor in front of her. Wrapping her arms around Finley's neck, she pressed against her, kissing Finley passionately. "I want nothing more than to be your wife," she said breathlessly as she broke the kiss.

Finley smiled and met her lips again as they made out like teenagers. The clock on the wall chimed, letting them know it was eleven. Nicole pulled away.

"As much as I want you right now, you have to be up in a few hours. You need to get some sleep."

"Rain check?" Finley smiled.

"You're going to owe me big time." Nicole wiggled her brow and smiled.

"You know I'm good for it."

"Do I ever," Nicole murmured as she got up off the floor.

"So, how long do you want to wait?"

"To get married?"

"Well, that and to tell people."

"We're older and I've done the big wedding with a long white gown and hundreds of guests. Is that something you want?" Nicole asked, thinking they'd never really discussed it. After her marriage to Dave, she'd be happy going to the courthouse, as long as Finley was the person standing beside her.

"I don't want anything huge either. All I have is my mother. I do have a few close friends in the Guard, but they're scattered around. As long as you're there, I don't care what we do."

"How about a small ceremony when your class is over? That way we can take some kind of honeymoon before the next one starts."

"Good idea. Is that enough time?"

"Yes. I think so."

"What about your parents?"

"They haven't spoken to me in two years. I honestly don't think they'll be there. I'll invite them, but don't expect an appearance."

Finley shook her head. "Well, my mother is going to flip out with excitement."

"I love your mom."

"She loves you too, more than me, I'm starting to think." Finley grinned.

"What about Caitlin?"

"How about we tell her at dinner tomorrow?"

"Are you going to make it home early enough?"

"Yes. I put them through the PFT today, which took extra time, and I wound up reading their files afterwards. I should've just come home."

"What you're doing is extremely important. Do your job. I'll always be here when you get home."

"Come on, soon-to-be Mrs. Morris. Let's go to bed."

"That's how all of this got started," Nicole teased.

Finley smiled and tugged her hand as they headed up the stairs.

*

Finley awoke just before the alarm was set to sound. She took a quick shower to wake up, then dressed in her dark-blue ODU. She wrote a note to Caitlin, saying she'd make it up to her with a big surprise that coming weekend, and slid it under her door. Then, she walked back to her bedroom and into the closet. The coat from her Full Dress Uniform was hanging in a garment bag with all of her medals dangling on the front of it. She reached into the pocket and retrieved a diamond engagement ring, before closing everything back up.

Nicole was sound asleep when Finley bent down, kissing her cheek. She barely stirred as Finley slid the ring onto her left hand and closed her fist. "I love you," she whispered.

Chapter 4

Finley was dressed in a gray sweat suit, similar to the one the cadets wore, and a pair of sneakers. The front of her shirt had the AST badge on the upper left chest: gold fins with aviation wings. Coast Guard Aviation Survival Technician Helicopter Rescue Swimmer encircled the emblem and the word Instructor was written underneath it.

She yawned as she checked her watch. It was precisely 5:30 a.m. "I'm ready when you are," she said to Neil, who was dressed in the same sweat suit.

He nodded and swung open the dorm door. They stormed inside, flipping all of the overhead lights on, and smashing metal garbage can lids together loudly. "It's party time!" Neil shouted. "Everybody up and at it. You have five minutes to dress in your sweats and muster in formation!"

"Holy shit," Jordy muttered as she flew out bed, bumping into Rich and Evan as they all tried to get dressed in the tight space.

"Let's go, people!" Neil yelled, still banging the lids together.

Finley walked outside, leaning against the building as she pulled a black woolen cap over her head and ears to ward off the cold air. She watched as the cadets began filing out, two and three at a time, racing to get into the formation lines.

"Welcome to day two," Finley said, stepping over once the full group had emerged. "Sampson and Gilliland, front and center."

"Yes, Senior Chief," they said at the same time.

"Hit the deck!" she yelled.

Both cadets jumped down into the plank position. "Why were you late to muster?" she asked.

"I ran out of time," Sampson replied.

"Five minutes is not enough time for you?"

"I took too much time brushing my teeth and getting dressed. I won't be late again, Senior Chief."

Finley looked at the young guy on the ground next to her. "Gilliland?"

"I couldn't find my shoes. I won't be late again, Senior Chief."

Finley looked up at the dark sky. "What happens when we get a call out, Chief?"

"We have less than five minutes to be dressed in all of our gear, on the helo with our flight bag, and ready for wheels up."

"What happens if we are late because we take too long getting dressed or can't find our equipment?"

"Someone dies."

"Exactly," she said flatly, staring at the two cadets in front of her. "I'm not here to babysit you. I'm not here to be your friend," she said loudly, addressing the class. "I'm here to weed out those of you who cannot and will not make it as rescue swimmers. I'm here to make those of you who do make it, into the best rescue swimmers you can possibly be. I will not quit on you, but if you quit on me, you will fail." She checked her watch, noting the two cadets on the ground had been in the plank position for close to five minutes. "Stand tall!" she barked. "Fall in."

27

Sampson and Gilliland rushed into their formation positions.

"Fucking idiots," Jon sneered as they passed by him.

"Class 16-20, right-face. March!" Neil called.

"Double time," Finley added, jogging alongside the group. The cool air burned her lungs, but the running felt great. She always made the cadets do her morning five mile run every other day. It gave her the exercise she was used to getting, and it gave them the physical fitness that they needed. She still swam 1600 meters in the pool on the alternate days before she met with the class for the day.

"Come on. Let's go!" she yelled, picking up the pace a little bit after the first mile.

*

"She's physically trying to kill us," Ericka mumbled, starting to pant after the third mile had come and gone.

"What's the matter? You can't keep up?" Jordy razzed.

Ericka gave her a dirty look and kept going.

A few stragglers in the back had started to slow, including Sampson and Gilliland.

"Pick it up!" Neil growled.

Two people fell out of formation, puking in the grass.

"Senior Chief, we have chunks!" Neil called, stopping to attend to the two who were sick.

Sampson and Gilliland began cramping up and both came to a stop.

"Four of your teammates are down, class 16-20. What do you do when your team needs you?"

"We go back for them," Jordy called. "Once a team, always a team."

Finley turned them around and headed back towards the four who were in the grass with Neil.

"Halt," Finley said, stopping the group. "Burpees on my count. Down...up...down...up." She kept them going over and over. "Anyone else need to puke or stretch while we're here?"

"No, Senior Chief," the group replied.

"Are the four of you finished?" she asked, still calling out up...down, to the rest of the class.

"Come on, you pansies!" Jon yelled.

When the four cadets got back into formation, Finley got them up on their feet and jogging again. By the time they finished their fifth mile, all of the cadets were exhausted, sweaty, and hungry.

"You have thirty minutes to get morning chow and muster back in formation," Finley yelled. "Dismissed."

"Aye-aye, Senior Chief!"

"Are you going to eat?" Neil asked, watching the cadets hobble off towards the mess hall.

"I ate at home, but I'm going to go to my office and grab an energy bar. Get them changed and into their gear at Pool Room A when they muster. I'll meet you there."

"Aye-aye, Senior Chief," he said, walking away.

*

"I've never been so hungry in my life," Evan mumbled between bites of food.

"Don't overeat, you'll really be puking. I'm sure that jog was a warm up," Jordy said.

"Is that what it was to you? A warm up?" Ericka mocked, shaking her head.

"No. I'm as tired and worn out as everyone else. I thought I was going to pass out around the fourth mile. I'm simply saying I'm sure there is more."

"How do you know how far we went?" Rich asked.

"I'm pretty sure the route we took was a mile, and we passed the same buildings five times, hence five miles."

"You girls may have lasted that little run we just did, but you'll never make it once we get into the pool," Jon spat, walking past their table.

"Do you hate all women, or just the good-looking ones who turn you down?" Jordy countered.

"You'll never be a rescue swimmer, so you might as well quit. I'm just helping you realize that," Jon laughed.

"Ugh, I hate him. I think if he were drowning, I'd let him," Ericka stated.

"It's only day two. He can't possibly keep this up for eighteen weeks, especially if you don't washout. Prove him wrong," Rich said.

"I don't know about all of you, but I'm not washing out. I never quit," Jordy said, standing up and clearing her tray.

"I plan to be here longer than her as well," Ericka growled, watching Jordy walk away. "I don't quit either."

*

Finley sat down behind her desk, biting into a chewy, cookie dough flavored bar as she checked her cell phone. She had a voicemail from Nicole, simply saying call me, I love you. She checked her watch and smiled. Nicole was more than likely on her way to work after dropping their daughter at school early. She still had fifteen minutes before she had to go meet up with the class for another physical fitness drill, so she swiped the button to make a call.

"Hey, you," Nicole answered.

"Good morning," Finley replied.

"So, I had something mysterious happen to me. I think someone came into our house."

"Oh, really? What was it?"

"I woke up with a beautiful diamond ring on my finger. Any idea how that got there?"

"Nope. Maybe it's that woman you're engaged to," Finley teased.

"It's stunning. I wish you would've woken me."

"I was up before the alarm, so I headed to the base. I wanted to see your face when I gave it to you, but I couldn't wait."

"Why didn't you give it to me last night?"

"I forgot. I was so tired; I could barely stand up. It dawned on me as soon as I woke up."

"I love you so much."

"I love you, too. I need to get going. I'm about to make these cadets swim until their legs fall off. I already ran them this morning until they started cramping and puking."

"Good God, you're going to kill one of them," Nicole laughed.

"Nah, they'll be fine. I've been doing this for over two years and no one has died yet."

"I miss you."

"Miss you, too. Are we still on for dinner tonight?"

"Yes. Will you be out of there at a decent time?"

"Yeah. I'll call you on my way home."

31

"Okay."

"Hey, did Caitlin see the ring?"

"No. She was too busy ranting and raving about breakfast and getting to the pool on time. I thought we were telling her tonight?"

"We are. I was just checking." Finley finished her conversation and slid the phone back into her top desk drawer, before heading over to the pool in the next building.

*

"Stand tall!" Neil yelled when Finley entered the room that housed their large, 50 meters wide and eight-feet deep, pool. It was about the same size as an Olympic competition pool and had black lines painted along the bottom in rows.

All of the cadets were standing at attention next to the edge of the pool, wearing their bathing suits, survival vests, fins, and masks and snorkels.

"Everyone into the pool," Finley said. "And don't touch my walls or the bottom," she added. It was much warmer in the pool room, so she removed her sweat shirt, leaving her in the gray sweat pants and a dark blue t-shirt that had the same logo as the sweatshirt on the upper left chest. She left the cadets treading water in front of her as she grabbed her stopwatch and whistle that were hanging on a wall hook nearby. "Listen up, when I blow the whistle, you're going to swim to the other side, tag the wall, and swim back, tag the wall, over and over again until I blow the whistle once more. If someone stops, we go even longer. We learned the definition of team yesterday, but it obviously hasn't sunken in yet. So, we'll keep going until it does." *Tweet.*

Neil stood next to Finley, watching the cadets swim back and forth, lap after lap. "How long are they doing this?" he asked.

"Until one of them fails and the rest go to his or her aid as a team."

"We might be here a while then," he sighed.

"Keep going!" Finley encouraged. "When you're fighting six foot waves to rescue a crew of ten men on a sinking ship, you don't stop. You never quit. You get them all off that ship and safely in that helo or you die trying! Do you hear me?"

"Yes, Senior Chief!"

After they'd gone over 300 meters, Finley pulled them out of the water. They quickly got into pool formation, which was basically one long line at the edge of the pool.

"Take off your fins and hit the deck for pushups," Finley said. She began the Down...up count.

*

Jordy felt like her body was made of Jell-O as she pushed herself up on shaky arms over and over. Water mixed with sweat as it ran down her nose, dripping to the floor under her. She closed her eyes, concentrating on the Senior Chief's voice as she called the cadence for the pushups.

Ericka wanted to vomit, but she forced herself to keep going as she looked to her left at Jordy Ross, moving through the pushups like they were nothing. *Damn her,* she thought. She wasn't going to be the first to break. All of the training she'd done on the beach, failed in comparison to what she'd been through thus far, and they were only two days into swimmer school.

When Finley told them to stand tall, Ericka's knees started to buckle, but she stood up.

"Don't lock your knees," Jordy whispered.

"I don't need your help," Ericka hissed.

"Fine. Fall over. I don't care," Jordy murmured as they put their fins on and headed back into the pool for another set of laps.

"Come on, ladies. You know you want to quit," Jon called out.

"You first," Jordy growled.

*

"Pick it up!" Finley yelled. "Who wants to quit on me?"

No one answered as the group swam back and forth, lap after lap.

"Petty Officer Parish, what about you? Ready to get out of the water?"

"No, Senior Chief. I'll swim until I die!"

Finley raised a brow and shook her head.

"That's 500 meters," Neil said, looking over at her.

"Everybody out of the pool!" Finley said loudly.

The cadets were literally crawling out of the water. Finley watched as Lynne Sampson climbed out and stood up. Her head lulled forward and she collapsed backwards into the pool with a big splash. Most of the cadets just watched as she sunk to the bottom.

Finley kicked her sneakers off to dive in when Jordy beat her to the water. She swam to the bottom, using nothing but adrenaline as she grabbed the young cadet and brought her to the surface. Neil and Finley dragged the girl out of the pool and knelt down next to her. Thankfully, she'd just fainted and hadn't swallowed any water.

"Am I out?" Sampson whispered, finally orienting herself with what had happened.

Finley looked into the brown eyes staring back at her and nodded slowly. "You didn't quit," she said, wrapping a towel over her shoulders.

Neil helped her to her feet. "I'm going to help her back to the dorm," he said.

"Get her in some dry clothes, then get her some chow. I'll process her out when I'm finished here." She turned back to the class. "Eyes left. I want each and every one of you to watch her walk away." When the door closed, she yelled, "Eyes front! Maybe now you'll realize this isn't a game. I'm not here to break you. I'm here to make sure you can handle the physical and mental strain that comes with being a Helicopter Rescue Swimmer." She took a minute to look at each one of the cadets standing at attention in front of her. "Petty Officer Ross, front and center."

Jordy quickly stepped out of line and hurried over to her, stopping at attention next to Finley.

"Why did you dive in after Airman Sampson?"

"Because she fainted and was going to drown, Senior Chief."

"Yes, but why did you go in? Why not wait for an instructor, or someone else from your class?"

"I saw her in distress and I reacted, taking action, Senior Chief."

"You did the right thing, Ross. Fall back in." Finley crossed her arms over her chest. "I'm trying to figure out why the whole damn class wasn't in the water, trying to save her. When you're a team, you are all in. If one goes down, you all go down, and together, you rise back up. Burney, Parish, Webber, if you'd fainted and fell into the pool, would you want a classmate to jump in and save you?"

"Yes, Senior Chief," they said in unison.

"What about the rest of you? Huh?"

"Yes, Senior Chief."

"I suggest you all take a page out of Petty Officer Ross's book and learn what it means to be a team. Go take a hot shower and get some chow. We muster at six a.m. Class 16-20, dismissed."

"Aye-aye, Senior Chief."

Finley walked out of the pool room as they toweled off.

"She was legit trying to kill one of us," a male cadet said. "I'm glad it wasn't me."

"Really? Sampson could've drowned right in front of us, and that's all you can say?" Jordy snapped, shaking her head.

"We can't all be hotshots," Jon sneered.

"If I'm dying, please don't come to my rescue," Jordy spat.

Jon laughed. "Deal."

"We're not going to make it through week one, much less seventeen more weeks of this shit, if we don't work together," Evan added. "That's obviously what the Senior Chief is looking for."

"I came here for me. No one else is riding through on my coattails. It's not my fault Sampson was weak," Jon scoffed as he walked away.

"That son of a bitch needs a boot to the face," Rich mumbled.

Jordy agreed as they walked together out of the pool room and down the hall.

*

"Senior Chief," Neil said, rapping his knuckles on Finley's open office door.

"Come in," she replied. "I'm almost finished with Sampson's paperwork."

"That could've been serious," he muttered.

"Yes, but it wasn't. You and I were both headed into the water to get her. This happens at least once with every class," she sighed.

"I know. What do you think about Jordy Ross?" he asked.

Leaning back in her chair, Finley answered. "I don't know much about her. We're only on day two."

"She knew enough to dive in after that girl today. We've never had another cadet do that in week one. They're usually scared shitless."

Finley nodded in agreement. "Someone needs to step up and lead this group. Maybe it'll be her." She thought back to when she was there, at the same school, as a cadet. She'd also rose up, taking the lead in week one. "Airman Sampson will be cleared for release after I talk to the Command Master Chief," she said. She hated washing people out, but it had to be done. If she didn't weed through each class, washing out the weak, she'd be going to their funerals.

*

Finley looked up at the overcast, gray sky as she walked towards the command building. The clouds looked like they were holding snow, despite the forecast calling for a clear night. As soon as Neil had left her office, Finley changed into the dark-blue, Operational Duty Uniform that she kept in her office for when she needed to speak with those in command above her.

Command Master Chief Glen Wright was sitting at his desk, dressed in the same uniform Finley was wearing. He waved for her to step inside when she knocked.

"How's it going, Morris?"

"Not bad. Week one is the hardest, right?" She smiled, handing him a red folder.

He knew what it was without opening it. All of the cadets that washed out of Aviation School, whether it was is for Aviation Maintenance or Aviation Survival, their paperwork went into a red file. "What happened?" he asked, opening the folder and signing the papers that needed his authorization.

"She fainted after a long swim and fell backwards into the pool."

"Did you need to resuscitate?"

"No. Actually, another cadet dove in after her. We got her out before she swallowed any water."

CMC Wright nodded. "What do you think of the class so far?"

"The same thing I think with every class. Talk to me in about six to eight weeks. Right now, they're exercising. We'll see what happens when things get real."

"Fair enough." He finished signing the papers and handed the folder back to her. "Airman Sampson is good to go. Have her check in with administration and personnel, so they can get word to her previous command that she is returning on the ready. Depending on the location, she'll get an airplane or bus ticket."

Finley knew the routine from washing out countless cadets in the past two years. There certainly was nothing exciting about it. You're out, pack your bags and get on a bus to go back where you came from, in the middle of the night, mind you. No stops at home to see loved ones or takes time for self-pity after washing out of A school. You simply picked up where you left off. If you weren't already assigned to a command, you'd be assigned to one before the Aviation Training Center released you, If you weren't able to go anywhere with the Coast Guard, you were out completely with a type of discharge called: Entry Level Separation.

Chapter 5

An hour later, Finley watched the lights disappear in her rearview mirror as she drove off the base, towards her house. She'd finished processing out Airman Sampson, and left Neil to take her to personnel. As the lead instructor, she actually did a lot more than she needed to, but she wasn't big on delegation, not when it was something she could take care of herself. She preferred to lead by example.

Multiple lights were on in the white, two-story bungalow they were renting, when Finley pulled into the driveway next to Nicole's Mercedes, something she'd kept in her divorce. Finley put her ball cap on her head as she got out of her SUV, and walked inside. The smell of Mexican food wafted from the kitchen, tickling her senses and causing her stomach to rumble.

"I thought I heard the door," Nicole said, smiling when Finley walked up, removed her hat, and kissed her softly.

"How was your day, fiancée?" Finley asked with a smile.

"Fine." Nicole grinned. "I was so popular; you'd have thought I'd won the lottery or announced that I was pregnant."

"What? You're pregnant?" Caitlin squeaked, coming into the other side of the kitchen on a beeline towards the refrigerator.

"Dinner is ready, so get out of there, and no one is pregnant."

"Oh, thank God," Caitlin said.

Finley laughed. "I'm with you. One is enough."

"I already have two kids, one is just much older than the other," Nicole chided as she swatted Finley's hand away from the stove. "I can't feed the beasts if you two don't let me get the food to the table!"

"Come on," Finley said, nodding at Caitlin. "How's the morning swim practice going?" she asked as they stepped in the living room.

"I've had some pretty good times this week, high twenty-fives for the 50 free and high fifty-fours for the 100 free. My 200 free is still two-minutes or just barely under."

"What is Coach Whitehall saying about the regional qualifier?"

"Not much. We're focused on staying consistent right now."

Finley nodded. "That's a good plan. How did you do on your Chemistry exam?"

"I got a B. I don't think Mrs. Hockley likes me. This is the second time I got all of the multiple choice right, but she took off for the written explanation section. I know I had the formulas correct."

"Well, did you talk to her about it?"

"No."

"Why not? If she's done this twice, then maybe you are missing a part or she's simply looking for something else. If the means of communication breakdown, you can't depend on knowing what the other person is thinking or intending."

"You're right."

Finley smiled as if she'd said 'I told you so.'

"I'll do it tomorrow."

"Dinner is on the table," Nicole called from the dining room.

"I'll be there in a second. I'm going to get out of this uniform," Finley stated.

*

As soon as they'd finished their chicken fajita dinner, Nicole pushed the plates aside. "So, we have something to tell you."

"Oh, my God. You really are pregnant, aren't you?" Caitlin shrieked.

"No," Nicole laughed. "Mom and I are getting married," she said, showing off her sparkling ring. She'd kept it in her pocket while cooking, so she didn't get anything on it.

"Seriously?" Caitlin said. "It's about time! Way to go, Mom!" she added, checking out the ring, before hugging them. "I love you both more than anything. Seeing you happy and together again has been…" Her eyes welled with tears. "I'm so glad we're a family again," she finished.

"We are too, kiddo," Finley said.

"We love each other and we love you. That's all that matters to us," Nicole added.

"Oh, does Grammy know yet? I bet she's excited."

"I haven't told her. It just happened last night. We wanted you to be the first to know, but we also wanted to tell you together."

"What about Grandma Wetherby?" Caitlin asked, referring to Nicole's mother, who hadn't spoken to any of them since Nicole had divorced her husband and gone back to Finley.

"What about the old bat?" Finley growled.

"Finley..." Nicole chided. "I don't know, Caitlin. I'm sure she won't be happy about it, but my life isn't her concern anymore."

"She *is* an old bat," Caitlin huffed. "If she can't see how happy and in love the two of you are, then something is wrong with her."

Nicole reached across the table, squeezing Finley's hand.

"Do you want me to wash the dishes? I think it's my night."

"No, we've got it. Go get your homework finished," Finley replied.

"I'm almost done. I have a couple of chapters to read for History," Caitlin said as she left the room and headed up the stairs.

"She's just like you," Nicole laughed, shaking her head.

Finley shrugged and pushed her chair back as Nicole stood to go the kitchen. Finley tugged her hand and pulled Nicole down into her lap.

"Are you sure you had a good day?" Nicole asked, wrapping her arms around Finley's neck and kissing her.

"I had a kid almost drown."

"Oh, God. What happened?"

"I wore them down until they couldn't move. She passed out and fell into the pool."

"Wow. Is she okay?"

"Yeah. She's fine. I was about to go in after her when one of the cadets dove in."

"That's good," Nicole stated, running her fingers through Finley's short, dark curls.

"It's rare. Usually, the cadets choke or freeze up when something happens, especially in the first week or two. They barely know each other. They are exhausted. And they don't really know the protocol."

"Why did she do it then?"

"Because it was the right thing to do," she stated. "I don't know much about this kid, but there is something about her."

"Maybe she reminds you of yourself when you were there."

"She does actually," Finley said, looking at the hazel-green eyes staring back at her. She leaned in, pressing her lips to Nicole's in a kiss that quickly heated up.

Nicole kneaded Finley's breasts though her t-shirt and Finley had her hands under Nicole's blouse, running them up and down her back as they traded passionate kisses.

The sound of a throat clearing, grabbed their attention and they quickly put space between themselves.

"I leave the room for a minute and you two start going at it like horny teenagers," Caitlin chided.

"Sorry," Nicole said. "When did she become the parent?" she whispered to Finley, who simply shrugged.

"It's okay. I'd rather see you in love and making out all over the house than screaming at each other and crying." Caitlin stated. "Anyway, can one of you drive me to the movies this weekend? I'm meeting my friends. I also need to go to the library or a bookstore. I can't find the book in the school library that I need for my English Composition paper."

Finley looked at Nicole and raised a brow. "No," she said.

"Mom!"

"You can drive yourself," Finley added. "We're going to get your permit and you're going to start driving."

"Oh, my God! Seriously!" Caitlin wrapped them both in a hug. "Yes!" she whispered in the hallway as she headed back upstairs.

"Uh…weren't we going to wait a little longer?" Nicole asked, getting off of Finley's lap.

"If we wait any longer, she'll be sixteen. I'll do it. I know how nervous you get about her driving."

"And you don't?"

"Nic, of course I do. She's our baby girl, but she's growing up and she's responsible enough to start driving."

"I don't like this."

Finley stood and pulled Nicole into her arms. "I don't either, but she'll be fine."

"I need a drink."

"She hasn't even driven yet," Finley laughed.

*

Jordy stood under the hot shower spray, allowing it to massage her sore muscles. She wished she could take an ice bath to help recover her body from the strenuous physical training, but there were no bathtubs. Instead, she switched the water back to freezing cold, hoping the hot/cold method would be sufficient.

When she finally flung the curtain back and reached for her towel, she saw Ericka standing at the sink, staring at herself in the mirror, lost in thought. She dried off and wrapped the towel around her body.

"What you did today…" Ericka murmured, trailing off.

"Anybody could've done it. I simply made it into the water first," Jordy replied.

Ericka nodded, but said nothing as she watched her walk away. *I've spent the last six years as a life guard, pulling people from the pool and ocean, saving their lives and I did nothing.* "Some rescue swimmer I'm going to be," she whispered, chiding herself.

Knowing Jordy was the last of the four female cadets, Ericka had the bathroom to herself. She placed a towel on the tiled floor and began doing yoga stretches to help soothe her sore body and clear her cloudy, judgmental mind.

*

Later that night, Jordy watched as Ericka handwrote another letter, which she assumed was addressed to the mysterious Toni. Most of the cadets were asleep in the darkened dorm room. Everyone was worn down, nearly to their weakest point, in a test to see who would break and who would prevail. Jordy's eyes fell back on the soft light of the book lamp Ericka was using to illuminate her paper. She thought about writing a letter describing her training, reaffirming her dedication to becoming a rescue swimmer, and apologizing to the ones she loved most for being so far away for so long, while making promises to see them soon.

She rolled over, turning away from the light, back to the darkness. She could write letters every single day if she wanted, but there was no one to send them to. No one cared about where she was or what she was doing. Any ties she had with her loved ones were severed the day she dropped out of college and joined the Coast Guard, going against her parents' wishes and ruining everything they had planned for her. Doing this alone, with no support and encouragement from the outside, gave her the self-confident attitude that other's referred to as arrogance, and made her push herself twice as hard.

*

On Friday afternoon, after another long exhausting day of physical training, Finley stood in front of the class. A late-winter dusting of snow flurries swirled around as she began walking up and down each row of cadets.

"As a Helicopter Rescue Swimmer, you have to be always on the ready. No matter what day it is. Whether you are on shift or at liberty, in the back of your mind, you are ready for the next call out. Putting your life on the line to save others, is an adrenaline rush more powerful than any street drug, which is why being a rescue swimmer has been described as an addiction."

She moved back to the front of the group. "I want each of you to write a 500-word paper on what being a Helicopter Rescue Swimmer means to you and why you want to be one. I also want a separate 500-word paper on the word: TEAM. What does it mean to be a team? How does a team function? What is teamwork? Chief Denny will collect them at muster on Monday morning. I expect each of you to look at this weekend as a chance to recover your body. You made it through week one, but it doesn't get any easier. If you struggled this week, take a long, hard look at why that was and what you plan to do about it." She paused and finished with, "Don't forget what I said about being always on the ready."

"Aye-aye, Senior Chief!"

Neil watched her nod at him before stepping away from the group to head over to her office.

"Listen up! The senior chief decides whether or not we train on the weekends. She has chosen to give you a break to recover. This isn't liberty, so if you leave the base, you'll be dropped. I expect you to take this time to rest and write the papers that were requested. If one of you shows up to muster on Monday without both papers, the entire class will pay for it. The mess hall will be serving all meals and the pool room will remain open all weekend. Just because there is no scheduled training, doesn't mean it won't happen. Always on the ready, means always be prepared. You will still muster in formation under the flag on Saturday and Sunday, but at seven a.m. instead of six. Class 16-20, dismissed!"

"Aye-aye, Chief!"

Chapter 6

Finley pulled into the parking lot of a closed school and cut the engine of her Ford Explorer. Then, she unbuckled her seatbelt and slid out.

Caitlin eyed her suspiciously. "Don't I need a license first?"

"We're in an empty parking lot. You can't hit anything but a curb. Come on."

Caitlin got out and walked around the front of the SUV. When she got into the driver's seat, she had to slide it forward one click. Then, she put on her seatbelt and turned the key.

"Alright, before you do anything else, look around you and check your mirrors. If the coast is clear, put it in gear and give it some gas."

Caitlin swallowed the lump in her throat as she followed her mother's instructions. She let out a deep breath as she pressed the accelerator a little too fast, causing them to lurch forward. She quickly slammed the brakes, making them bounce to a stop.

"Holy shit, kid!" Finley exclaimed, stretching her neck. "Easy on the gas. It doesn't take much."

"Yes ma'am," Caitlin mumbled as she tried again. This time, the SUV eased forward.

"See, now maintain your speed. When you come up to a speed bump, press the brake gently until you come to a stop, then roll over it slowly."

Caitlin made a full lap around the parking lot, stopping and starting at each of the four speed bumps.

"Go ahead and make another lap," Finley said. She'd let go of the death grip she had on the door handle.

After a few more laps, they practiced parking in the spaces, as well as backing in. Thankfully, the SUV had a backup camera like most modern vehicles, so that helped Caitlin see what she was doing.

"Alright, I think it's time to go get that permit. Have you read over the book?"

"Three or four times," Caitlin replied as they switched places.

*

The DMV was crowded with young drivers and their parents. Thankfully, Finley had been smart enough to call ahead and schedule an appointment. They'd been seated for maybe ten minutes when Caitlin's name was called, and she was shown to a computer station.

"Verify your name, date of birth, and social security number," the man said.

Caitlin read the screen. "That's me."

"Great. So, you read each question and type the letter: A, B, C, or D, that corresponds with your answer. Then, press the Enter button to move to the next question. You cannot go back, so make sure you pick the right letter. When you get to the end, it will tell you how many you got right and wrong, as well as whether you passed or failed. If you pass, go to window 14 to get your picture taken and your permit printed. If you fail, you have to wait two days to retake the test. Any questions?"

"Uh…no, sir," Caitlin stammered, staring at the screen.

As soon as he walked away, she pressed Enter to begin.

*

Finley waited on the other side of the DMV like a nervous tick. She wasn't exactly happy about Caitlin driving, but she was smart…much smarter than Finley's brother Mike, had been. She wondered if she should've fought Nicole harder when she refused to let Caitlin take Driver's Ed. Nicole couldn't deal with Caitlin driving a car without one of them being in it with her, which Finley understood. So, for the sake of not causing a war in their house, she gave in and agreed. Now, she hoped it was a good decision. Finley hadn't gone to Driver's Ed either. After the instructor at her school had been arrested for DUI, her mother insisted on teaching both of her children how to drive herself.

"Is your kid taking the driver's test?" a woman asked as she sat down next to Finley.

"No. She's doing the computer test for her permit."

"Oh, you're lucky. That's the easy one. My son is out on his driving test right now."

Finley nodded.

"I hope he fails," the woman said, shaking her head.

"Why is that?"

"He did great in Driver's Ed at school, but he gets nervous when he's out driving on the open road. He's just not ready, but I promised when he turned sixteen we'd go take the test. His birthday was yesterday."

A short, skinny kid walked up before Finley could say anything. His looks reminded her of a cartoon character.

"Well?" the mother asked.

"I failed," he replied.

"Aww. It's okay. We'll try again in a few days," she said, standing up.

As they walked away, she looked back at Finley and pumped her fist with excitement. Finley raised her eyebrows, nearly bursting out with laughter. "What the hell?" she whispered, shaking her head.

"Mom!" Caitlin yelled from across the room. "I passed!"

Finley pumped her fist with excitement, just as the other mother had done. "Way to go!" she said as Caitlin got in line to get her picture taken and the permit card printed.

A few more parents sat down, waiting in agony as their children took the tests. "I wonder who is more nervous, the parents or the person who has to ride in the car with these kids?" one father asked.

Finley laughed. "I'd put my money on the person in the car."

He smiled and stared at her. "You look vaguely familiar," he said, trying to place her.

Finley, who was dressed in jeans, sneakers, and a black, zip up hoodie with the Coast Guard Rescue Swimmer logo on the upper left chest, looked back at him. "Maybe we've been in the same grocery store line," she replied.

He shook his head and looked at her again, noticing the patch on her jacket. "Are you a Rescue Swimmer?"

Finley nodded.

"I'm AET First Class Mathew Terrell," he said, which stood for Avionics Electrical Technician Petty Officer First Class. "We've probably crossed paths at the air station," he added with a smile. "I'm AST Senior Chief Finley Morris. I'm the lead instructor for the Aviation Survival Training Center," she replied.

"I've seen you with your classes," he said, offering his hand. He'd actually seen her a few times, but outside of her uniform or swimmer gear, she was nearly unrecognizable. "Maryanne," he said, waving his daughter over when she finished her test.

"I passed, Dad!"

"That's great! Come here, there's someone I want you to meet. This is Senior Chief Morris. She's a Helicopter Rescue Swimmer and the lead instructor at the swimmer school on the base."

"It's nice to meet you," Maryanne said.

"You too," Finley replied.

"She has to a write a paper for school on prominent women," Mathew said. "Senior Chief Morris is a real-life hero. It takes a lot of guts, strength, and determination to do what she does. Her position isn't given…it's earned, and well-respected."

"Thank you," Finley replied with a smile. "Maryanne, I think what your dad is saying is, prominent women come in many forms. They're not just famous people or political standouts. They can be anyone who holds an important job, or plays an important role in society. They are people whom others look up to."

"Thanks," Maryanne said.

Caitlin stood off to the side, listening to the conversation, before stepping up next to Finley after they left. "He's right. You are a real-life hero…to me and to all of those people you've saved over the years."

"Thanks, kiddo." Finley wrapped her arm around Caitlin's shoulders. "Let's see it."

Caitlin held up her new Beginner's Permit. Her face was full of excitement in the picture with a big, cheesy smile.

"Looks great. Now that this is out of the way, let's go driving."

"Right now?"

"Yeah. You want to meet your friends at the movies right?" Finley asked as they walked outside.

"Yes!" Caitlin squealed, taking the dangling keys from Finley's hand.

"Don't tell your mother," Finley muttered as she got into the passenger seat.

*

Finley walked through the front door of the house, depositing her keys and wallet on the end table in the living room, and removed her hoodie, hanging it in the nearby closet. She heard the TV playing in the den and walked in that direction, assuming that's where Nicole was. The room was empty, however. She raised an eyebrow as she passed through the kitchen, kicking her shoes off before heading up the stairs.

After checking their bedroom and Caitlin's room, she found Nicole in the laundry room, humming a tune she'd heard recently, while folding clothes. Finley watched her hips sway back and forth as she bobbed her head to the song she was thinking about.

Stepping closer, Finley wrapped her arms around Nicole from behind, startling her.

"Mmm, I think I like where this is going," Nicole murmured as Finley pushed her hair to the side, placing light kisses along the delicate skin behind her ear while her other hand slipped under Nicole's t-shirt, fondling her bare breasts.

"Think?" Finley whispered in her ear as she moved her hand from Nicole's hair, down to the crotch of her form-fitting, yoga pants, circling her center.

"No..." Nicole mumbled, laying her head back against Finley's shoulder.

"No?" Finley paused her hand.

"Not thinking...like. Definitely like," Nicole corrected, turning her head to meet Finley's lips in a hungry kiss.

Finley felt the soft material of Nicole's pants begin to dampen as she continued rubbing her fingers back and forth. She cupped her breast with the other hand. Nicole moaned and rocked her ass against Finley's crotch as Finley squeezed her nipple.

Reaching up, Nicole ran her hand into Finley's short curls as Finley's hand finally slipped under the waistband of her pants, finding the soaking wet spot she'd made. Finley moved her fingers in delicate circles, bringing her higher and higher with each pass over her clit.

"Inside...go inside," Nicole gasped.

Finley pulled her hand free and spun Nicole around, backing her up against the dryer. Their lips came together in another passionate kiss as Finley worked her hand back down Nicole's pants, through her wetness, and pushing gently inside of her.

Nicole broke the kiss, teasing Finley with soft bites on her lower lip before reaching down the front of her sweatpants to the wetness she knew was awaiting her. Finley could barely concentrate on her fingers, stroking in and out of Nicole, with Nicole rubbing her swollen clit at the same time.

They traded kisses, rocking together and fighting the clothing between them as they drove each other to the edge of release. Nicole gave in first, moaning against her mouth as her body shivered with pleasure. Feeling Nicole tighten around her fingers, sent Finley spiraling into her own climax. Pulling their hands free, both women leaned against each other, nearly unable to stand.

Nicole met Finley's eyes and smiled. "You amaze me," she said softly.

Finley grinned as she gripped her hand, tugging Nicole away from the dryer as they wobbled on shaky legs down the hallway.

*

"How did it go at the DMV?" Nicole asked an hour later. She was lying in their bed next to Finley, resting her head on her arm.

"Huh?" Finley mumbled, still feeling the euphoria of their lovemaking.

Nicole grinned. "Our daughter…does she have a driver's license now?"

"Oh…yeah." Finley sat up, checking the clock. "She passed the test. I let her drive to the mall."

"What? You did?"

"Yes. She did really good. She's cautious, which is a good thing."

"It still scares me to death," Nicole sighed.

Finley pulled Nicole into her arms and ran her hand over the soft skin of her naked back.

Nicole kissed her tenderly. "Do you remember when we used to lie around in that little double bed in our first apartment?"

"Yeah." Finley grinned. "With you and that giant pregnancy pillow, I barely had any room to sleep."

"I don't recall us sleeping much."

"Me either," Finley replied, kissing her. "This bed has a lot more room. Here, let me show you," she added, rolling Nicole to her back.

*

Later that afternoon, Finley went for a jog around the neighborhood. The cold air tingled her sensitive skin as she trudged along. A light dusting of snow covered the sidewalk, and the white frost on the leafless trees made them look like giant twigs. She'd loved living in Florida, mostly because of the year round warm weather, but the beauty of winters at home were just as nice.

Nicole was in the den when she heard Finley kicking the snow off her shoes before stepping through the front door. She'd just finished doing laundry, and had literally thought about taking a nap.

"How was your run?" she asked, meeting Finley in the kitchen.

"Not bad. The corner house is for sale."

"Oh, really. Are we looking?" Nicole questioned, raising a brow.

"No." Finley shook her head. "I just happened to notice the sign. We can't buy anything. My post here will be up in less than a year."

"Did you put in for the six-month extension?"

"I did. I'm still waiting for an answer," Finley stated. Caitlin would be in the middle of her high school senior year when Finley's transfer came up. She'd put in a request to extend her post six months so that she'd still be in town. "I'm sure I'll get it," she added.

"What about your next post? Any idea where we'll be going?"

"No. I haven't thought much about it. At least not right now, anyway. You know I want to do one more stint in the field, then maybe come back here and instruct until I'm ready to retire."

"I wouldn't mind going back to Florida, or maybe the Bahamas." Nicole smiled.

Finley laughed and shook her head. "I think it really depends on where Caitlin goes to college. I'm sure we'll want to be in the same state at least."

Nicole went to say something, but stopped to answer her phone. "Speaking of the kid…" she whispered.

"I'm going to go shower. We have to be at my mom's in an hour for dinner, so tell her we're coming to get her."

Chapter 7

Jordy stared at the blank computer screen. She wasn't much of a writer, doing the basics to get out of high school and into college. "What does being a Rescue Swimmer mean to me?" she said allowed. "Everything. It means everything. How the hell do I turn that into 500 words?" she mumbled.

"Maybe by starting with how you got to this point," Rich said from the doorway.

"I thought I was alone."

"Nope. You don't mind do you? When everyone did this earlier, I waited so I wasn't rushed. With only six computers in here, I figured it would be a free for all after muster this morning."

"No problem. I did the same thing," she replied, going back to the blinking insertion mark on the screen. *Alright, Senior Chief. You want to know why I'm here...why I chose one of the hardest jobs to obtain in the military? Here goes,*" she thought as she began typing: *Helicopter Rescue Swimmers are the last lifeline for those in distress. When someone is on the verge of death, it is a Helicopter Rescue Swimmer who plucks him or her from the clutches of the devil known as the sea. They are fearless, weaponless, true-blue, blood, sweat, and tears: heroes. They wear the badge of honor on their chest and the patch of courage on their shoulder. Being a Helicopter Rescue Swimmer is something you earn. It's not given to you.*

Those who are lucky enough to wear the badge, aren't the lucky ones at all. It's the people they save who are fortunate, because someone put their own life on the line without hesitation to save them...a complete stranger that they will more than likely never see again.

Jordy sat back and reread what she'd typed, before moving on to complete the assignment. When she'd finished, she turned her focus to: TEAM. She thought about the different school teams she'd been on over the years. Nothing stood out enough for her to write a paper about it, so she switched gears and wrote about trust and how if you don't trust someone you can't completely work together. One of you is always working against the other. She circled that back around to team, and how as a team, you must trust each other fully, especially in the Coast Guard, because your life depended on it.

After typing the 507th word, she'd completed the second assignment and glanced at the clock on the wall. She'd been there for three hours. The click, click, click sound of Rich typing away, was the only sound in the room. She pushed the button to print her papers and slid her chair back from the table to go retrieve them from the printer at the back of the room.

"What do you think she's going to do with these?" Rich asked as he clicked the print button.

"Use them to light her fireplace, I hope." She grinned.

"We're about to play Texas Hold 'Em. Are you in? Ericka is playing."

Jordy shrugged. She loved a little harmless competition, and the stubborn blonde was proving to be her biggest competitor. "Absolutely," she replied.

Jordy held the king of hearts and jack of diamonds in her hand. The king of spades, jack of spades, nine of spades, nine of clubs, ace of hearts, and three of diamonds, were lying on the floor as the flop, the turn, and the river. The bet coming at her was twenty-five dollars. She didn't need to check her hand again. She had two high pairs. She met the bet and raised it a few more chips, increasing it to nearly a hundred dollars.

Ericka glanced at her cards as Rich folded when the new bet rolled to him, leaving just she and Jordy in the game. She was about out of chips with a little more than enough to cover the bet, but she wasn't going to let herself lose to her, so she went all in.

"Are you sure you want to do that?" Jordy asked, thinking she was betting solely on the pair of nines in the flop.

"You're damn right I am! I don't need you looking out for me. I got in here all by myself. I'm a grown woman. I don't need or want your help! Not with training and certainly not with a simple game of cards!" she snapped. Raising an eyebrow, she added, "Now, are you in or not?"

"Whoa, tell us how you really feel," Evan said.

"I'm sick of her thinking she's so much better. Yeah, you're stronger than me, Ross, but it doesn't make you any better than me. I'll still be standing at graduation. Where the hell will you be?"

Jordy set her cards down. "You want to make this about me and you, fine. Bring it on. I never considered you competition to begin with, so this ought to be fun," she laughed as she got up and went to her bunk.

"Hey, Burney, you can join our party," Jon yelled across the room where he and a few other guys were sitting around telling tall tales. "There's room on my lap," he added with a laugh.

"Kiss my ass!" Ericka retorted.

"Oh, I'd love to, baby!" he replied with a sneering grin.

"I'll die here before I let him beat me at anything either," Ericka muttered under her breath as she too, left the game.

Rich flipped the cards over. "Girls, just so you know, Ericka would've won with a flush."

Jordy shook her head and Ericka ignored all of them as she jammed her iPod headphones into her ears.

*

Sunday went by slightly smoother. Jordy spent the first part of the day in the pool, swimming lap after lap. A couple of other cadets had joined early on, but none stayed as long as she had. In the afternoon, she opened her old copy of *The Old Man and the Sea* by Ernest Hemingway. The pages were dog-eared, and the cover was tattered, but it was the only thing she had to remind her of her grandmother, the only person in her life to actually say, 'follow your dreams.' Her grandmother had given it to her just before she passed away, and Jordy cherished it like the Bible. She'd read it so many times in the past year, she had it memorized.

Reading the story helped her pass the time, but it also helped clear her mind. Her focus was on the next seventeen weeks ahead of her, not the previous week and what could've been done differently. She tried not to listen as a number of cadets went over their past week's mistakes, beating them like a dead horse. Ericka was one of them, and Jordy wondered why that bothered her. The young blonde was clearly on a mission to prove she was better than her.

"What is this?" Rich asked, pulling the book from her hands as he sat on the edge of her bunk.

"Something you've probably never read," Jordy replied.

*

Ericka tried not to pay attention, but Jordy was in the bunk next to hers, and Rich was above her. She was somehow always in their conversations. She watched as Jordy nonchalantly tucked a loose piece of dark hair behind her ear that had fallen out of the tight bun she'd kept it in. Turning her head away, she went back to the letter she was writing. So far, she'd started three of them, but hadn't finished a single one. Somehow, she couldn't describe her daily life at the swimmer school. No one would understand. Whoever said you leave your blood, sweat, and tears behind when you leave the ASTC, wasn't kidding. She thought about her family. *Mom would tell me to give up and come home. Dad would tell me to toughen up, but then again, he's been a firefighter for over twenty years, so he knows what hard work and dedication are. I'll never quit because of him and the values he instilled in me.* She looked down at the name on the paper. *Toni...I've failed you in so many ways,* she thought. *When you've dated someone long enough to live together, and build a life, but keep finding reasons not to...* she trailed off in her head.

Unable to write a complete sentence, she balled the paper and got up to toss it in trash can.

"Hey, Ericka, have you ever read this?" Rich asked, handing her the book.

"Yes," she replied, glancing at the cover, slightly surprised that Jordy was also a fan of the story about an old fisherman with bad luck, who never gives up. "It's a classic. I actually wrote a paper on it in English Lit back in high school."

Rich nodded and handed the book back to Jordy, who simply stared at Ericka. She couldn't figure her out, and the more she tried, the more confusing she became.

"What do you think this week is going to be like?" Evan asked, walking up to their bunk area.

"Hell times two for those who can't keep up," Jordy mumbled, shoving the book under her pillow.

"I'm looking forward to it," Ericka added, looking in her direction.

Chapter 8

On Monday morning, Finley dressed in the dark-blue shorts and t-shirt that she wore in the pool room. Then, she pulled her gray sweat suit on over it. She thought about dinner at her mother's house the night before. Jackie Morris had been ecstatic to find out that she and Nicole were finally getting married. Albeit, she wasn't too thrilled when they'd told her it was going to be small, and without a lot of hoopla. They'd wanted a simple ceremony in front of family and a few friends, and that was it. She smiled, remembering the tears in her mother's eyes.

After sliding on her sneakers, she headed down the stairs. Caitlin was at the dining table, eating a bowl of oatmeal with granola and a side of scrambled egg-whites, when she walked through to the kitchen.

"Do you think I could drive us today, Mom?"

Finley pursed her lips. "I don't see why not," she replied, throwing together the ingredients for her own breakfast as she pushed the button on the one-cup coffee maker.

"Can I stay after school today for the basketball game?" Caitlin asked as Finley sat down next to her with a cup of black coffee and two toasted, whole-wheat tortillas, smothered in peanut butter, topped with banana slices, and rolled up like burritos.

Finley raised a brow. "Since when are you interested in basketball?"

"My friend Will and a few others play on the team."

"Don't you have swimming after school?" Finley questioned between bites.

"Yes, but the game is after that."

"I'm not the one who picks you up after school, so you should be asking Mom."

"I know, but she's asleep. Besides, if you say yes, then I can go."

"What makes you think she'll say no? And she's not asleep. She was getting into the shower when I came downstairs."

Caitlin rolled her eyes. "She'll probably say I need to come home and do my homework."

"Well, it is a Monday night. Do they have any other games? Maybe I'll go with you."

"Why can't I go alone?"

"I never said you couldn't, Caitlin. I merely thought it would be nice to spend some time together." Finley finished her breakfast and washed the plate off. "I'll talk to Mom about it before I leave."

"Mom..." Caitlin said, walking up behind her. "I'm sorry. I want to spend time with you, too. I guess I take for granted that we're all a family now, and I get to see you every day."

"It's okay. I also know what it's like to be a teenager and want to hang out with your friends. If Grammy had tagged along with your mother and I, well..." She trailed off and thought for a second. "You're not having sex are you?"

"No. Oh, gross, Mom! It's just a basketball game."

"What's going on?" Nicole asked, walking into the kitchen with an odd look on her face.

"Caitlin wants to stay after swimming today to go to a basketball game," Finley answered.

Nicole nodded. "That's fine. I have a meeting this afternoon, so I'll push it back a little bit."

"Also, she doesn't want us at the game. Apparently, we are uncool," Finley added, wigging her eyebrows and laughing.

Nicole chuckled.

"I have to get to the base. I love you both," Finley said, hugging them. She was barely inside her SUV when she got a text message.

Is there a boy I need to be worried about?

No, she replied, adding: *I'm pretty sure they are just friends. She freaked out when I asked her if they were having sex.*

OMG, I'd kill her myself!

Finley looked at the last text and laughed as she backed out of the driveway. "I'd kill him," she whispered as she turned up the radio.

*

"Welcome to week two," Finley said, standing in front of the cadets, who were wearing their swimming gear, and lined up in a row with their backs to the pool. "About face," she called. Everyone spun around to face the water. "Starting with the first person on the left side of the line, every other person look to your right, and so on down the line. This will be your teammate for the day's training exercises. I suggest you learn to work together quickly."

"Damn it," Ericka whispered, looking at Jordy, who grinned at her.

"At the bottom of the other end of the pool, you will find a 40lb cinderblock between your lanes. On my whistle, you'll jump in and pop up, swimming as fast as you can to the other end. Then, you'll swim down, retrieving your team's block together. Bring it to the surface and swim back across the pool with each of you holding one side of the block so that it is up and out of the water. If the block touches the water, you must swim it all the way to the bottom together, and back up, before continuing down the lane with it up in the air. When you get back to this end, you'll swim it to the bottom and back up, before heading back in the opposite direction with the block in the air. You'll keep going back and forth with the brick up and out of the water, swimming it to the bottom and back up at each end of the pool, until you hear my whistle again."

"Can you keep up?" Jordy muttered.

"We'll see who drops it first," Ericka sneered.

Finley pushed the start button on her watch and blew the whistle.

Jordy jumped into the pool, wasting no time popping up and freestyle swimming as fast as she could. Ericka arrived at the brick at about the same time. It was nearly weightless under the water as they hefted it to the surface. Both women pushed the brick up and out of the water as they headed back across the pool.

Two teams made it halfway before having to swim down to the bottom and back up because their brick touched the water. Jordy and Ericka made it easily to the other side, where they took deep breaths and swam the block to the bottom.

Five minutes into the exercise, multiple teams started touching the water with their blocks.

"Come on!" Jordy yelled when Ericka's arm started dropping.

"My arm's cramping!" Ericka shouted at her as she let the brick go.

"Son of a bitch!" Jordy growled before flipping over and swimming down to the bottom. She and Ericka grabbed the brick and swam back up. They completed four more passes back and forth, having to go down to the bottom at least once on each pass, before the whistle was blown.

"Take your bricks to the bottom and come back up without them," Finley instructed. She and Neil watched everyone swim to the bottom, then pop back up. "Anyone ready to quit?"

"No, Senior Chief," the class said in unison.

"Great! Now, go back down and push your bricks across the bottom to the other side. If one of you needs to come up for air, you bring the brick up with you, holding it out of the water until you're ready to go back down and continue. When you tag the wall on the opposite side, swim up without the brick, take a breath, and go back down, pushing the brick back to the other side. Go back and forth until you hear my whistle."

Jordy's body was already fatigued from the multiple swims across the pool. She took a couple of calming breaths to relax her lungs.

Ericka's body was worn slap out. Her chest burned, and her arms felt like mush. *Don't quit. You've got this,* she thought, mentally pushing herself.

Jordy and Ericka shared a sneering look before going back under at the same time and swimming down to push the brick along the bottom of the pool.

Finley and Neil watched as a number of teams began coming up with their bricks to take breaths. She paid close attention to the pairs who were struggling to work together as a team: Ross and Burney; and Parish and Gilliland.

Ericka needed to come up for air, and Jordy shook her fist at her in frustration as they heaved the brick to the surface.

"Damn it! We can't stop every ten feet! Hold your breath!" Jordy growled.

"I am holding my breath!" Ericka spat. "And it's not every ten feet!"

Finley shook her head. What the two arguing women didn't notice was, every team was coming up for air at about the same pace. If they would stop arguing and keep moving, they'd probably be ahead of the rest of the class.

Parish and Gilliland were coming up for air twice as often as everyone else. After a couple of passes back and forth, Parish refused to go up when Gilliland pointed. He shook his head no, pushing the brick forward. Gilliland tried desperately to continue, but his lungs burned. He reached over, tapping Parish on the arm, frantically pointing up. Parish ignored him and kept going.

"Do you see this?" Neil asked.

"Yeah," Finley muttered as she blew the whistle multiple times.

All of the teams rose to the surface with their bricks.

"Come back to this end of the pool. Bring your bricks with you," Neil said.

Gilliland could barely swim with the brick. He was out of breath and struggling to keep going. Rich and Evan, who were in the lane next to him, helped keep him above water as they neared the edge.

"Everyone out of the pool!" Finley yelled. "Dry off and double-time it to the mess hall for lunch chow. I want to see you back at my pool in thirty-five minutes. Everyone but Gilliland, is dismissed!"

"Aye-aye, Senior Chief," the group said before disbursing.

Finley leaned against the back wall with her arms crossed. "Daniel, you're struggling day after day, and this is only week two. The training is going to get progressively more difficult as the days and weeks go by. I have to cut you loose."

"I understand, Senior Chief."

"I wish you the best of luck with your career in the Coast Guard," she added, shaking his hand, before looking at Neil to take over. She left the room as Neil instructed him to go to the locker room to change clothes, prior to heading over to personnel to get discharged from the ASTC and reassigned to his previous unit.

*

Jordy walked through the buffet line, taking a serving of everything offered to her without looking to see what it was. She was worn down to the point of exhaustion, and all she wanted to do was eat. There could've been a grilled cardboard box, dipped in barbecue sauce on her plate for all she cared.

"This isn't all about you, you know that right?" Ericka muttered, walking past her.

Jordy rolled her eyes. "So, I've heard," she replied, going in the opposite direction to find an empty seat.

"Man, when Senior Chief blew the whistle, I thought I was going to die. There's no way I would've made another lap," Evan said.

"Yes, you would have. If she'd said get out of the pool and do a hundred burpees, you would've done it. You know why? Because you're here to be a God damn rescue swimmer. Helicopter Rescue Swimmers do not quit!" Jon yelled loud enough for the entire group to hear. "So, stop complaining about this and that hurting, you're tired, or other pansy-ass excuses you have. If you can't cut it, there is the fucking door! And that goes for you girls, too!"

"Tell us how you really feel, dickhead," Rich said.

"We're supposed to work together as a team," Evan added.

"Yeah, well none of you even know the definition of team," he snarled.

"What exactly is that definition?" Finley asked from her position in the doorway.

Everyone jumped up from their seats, knocking chairs to the floor as they popped to attention.

"I'm waiting, Petty Officer Parish. Or, should I say Specialist Parish?" Finley walked further inside. "I have a better idea, why not tell everyone why you are no longer in the National Guard?"

Jon Parish didn't say a word, but his jaw clenched tightly as she moved closer to him.

"You have twenty minutes to be in front of my pool. I suggest you not be even half a second late," she said, stepping past him to go out the side door.

*

When Finley finally dismissed the class for the day, she took a long jog around the base to clear her mind. Running always helped her work things out mentally when they were bothering her. The class was nearly halfway through Phase One. She had a few standouts, a few stragglers who probably wouldn't make it much further, and a few headstrong cadets that could easily be at the top of the class if they stopped tripping all over their egos.

"How's the new class going, Senior Chief?" Lieutenant Commander Raymond Phillips asked. He was the Operations Duty Officer for the Search and Rescue team stationed at the air base.

"Not bad. I've only lost three so far," she replied with a smile, stopping to stretch her legs.

He laughed and waved as she headed off in the opposite direction.

After another couple of miles, Finley made it back to the parking lot near where the pool, mess hall, and dorm buildings were located, completing her four mile run. She stretched her legs and walked over to her SUV to head home for the evening.

*

Ericka was beat. Her muscles ached and her body was just plain tired. However, when one of their junior instructors walked into the dorm with their mail for the week, she perked up like a little kid.

"Expecting something good, Burney?" one of the cadets asked.

"Maybe," she replied.

As the letters were dispersed, Jon grabbed an extra envelope with his. "Oh…who is Toni DiVianno?"

"Give it here, asshole!" Ericka growled, snatching the letter.

"So, you do have a boyfriend," he said.

"I never said I was single," she growled, walking back across the room as she opened the letter.

Jordy watched the exchange from her bunk. She hadn't expected any mail and hadn't received any since she'd been there. Of course, she hadn't sent any either. She had nothing to say to anyone back home. Crossing her feet at her ankles, she picked up her book and went back to reading.

Chapter 9

Four weeks later, and countless hours of physical fitness in and out of the pool, they'd reached the last day of Phase One. Finley had slowly whipped them into better shape than when they'd arrived, and along the way, she'd washed out a total of four cadets, two males and two females.

Finley walked in front of the group standing in muster formation under the flag. The morning sun slowly rose behind her, painting everything in an orange glow. "Each of these four logs behind me weighs 175 pounds. I'm going to put you in teams of four, and together, you're going to pick up one of the logs and run three miles. If you have to set your log down or drop it, everyone on the team must do ten burpees and ten jumping jacks before you pick it back up." She nodded at Neil as she stepped to the side.

He started naming off the groups. Jordy and Ericka wound up on the same team, and Evan, Rich, and Jon also wound up together. Everyone stepped up to their logs with two people on each side.

"On my whistle, lift your log and go. Chief Denny will lead the group, setting the pace, and I'll be in the back." She blew the whistle and watched as each team hefted the heavy log up onto their shoulders and took off running, one team behind the other in line. Neil led, keeping them at a steady, ten-minute mile tempo.

"What are we in?" Finley yelled, starting a marching chant.

"The United States Coast Guard," the group shouted.

"What is our job?" she asked loudly as they passed by the administration office.

"Helicopter Rescue Swimmers," the class replied.

"What do we do?" she asked as Neil turned them down one of the side streets between buildings, leading them on a previously mapped out course around the base that would come back to their starting point and equal exactly three miles.

"Save lives!" the cadets said loudly.

"Why do we do it?" she yelled.

"So others may live!" the group shouted.

The cadence carried on as they moved into mile two.

"Pick it up in the front!" Jordy said, presumably to Ericka who was first on the log.

"I've got it; you just worry about keeping pace!" Ericka growled. "Let's go!"

The team in front of them fell out of line when they started the third mile, setting their log down to catch their breath.

"Hit the deck!" Finley yelled.

The four teammates dropped down on shaking arms to do their pushups.

"Stay together. Up...down...one," Finley called out.

After finishing their jumping jacks, the team lifted their log and began running.

"Come on, pick it up!" Finley urged, jogging behind them. "If you cannot jog while carrying this log, you will never make it through Phase Two. Do not quit on me!" she yelled.

*

After lunch chow in the mess hall, the class was back in the pool, treading water for twenty minutes, followed by a couple of rounds of swimming lap after lap with their equipment on, and working in pairs to push concrete blocks along the bottom of the pool. They repeated the sequence of treading water, swimming laps, and pushing the blocks until they were utterly exhausted.

"Welcome to the end of Phase One. Congratulations. The sixteen of you have made it through to Phase Two," Finley said as they stood at attention on shaky legs. A few of them looked like they were either about to pass out or puke, maybe both. She wasn't sure. "You're being granted liberty. There are two white vans that have been issued to Class 16-20 to use this weekend. For those of you who are of age, no more than two alcoholic beverages per person, per day. Your curfew is ten p.m. tonight and Saturday night, and eight p.m. Sunday. I have eyes and ears all over this city. If you break any of my rules, you're out. This is a privilege, but being a cadet at this school is an honor. I suggest you not take that lightly, and present yourself with the upmost respect anywhere you show your face. You must also be in your Operational Duty Uniform if you leave the base."

"Aye-Aye, Senior Chief!"

"The entire class must be in formation for muster at 7 a.m. Monday morning, ready to begin Phase Two. Class 16-20, dismissed."

"How much trouble do you think they'll get in this weekend?" Neil asked, watching them stagger to the locker room.

"I'm sure half of them won't be able to lift their legs in the morning," Finley replied. "At least they've finally started working together."

*

Nicole was curled up on the couch, with a folder full of papers in one hand and a glass of red wine in the other, when Finley walked in. "Long day?" she asked as Finley bent to softly kiss her.

"Something like that," Finley replied, sitting down and kicking off her sneakers. "Is that homework?" she joked.

"It's wedding planning stuff," she said.

"Oh, who's getting married?" Finley teased, running her hand over Nicole's silky, smooth calf.

"Well, this sexy Coast Guard Rescue Swimmer asked me, but I don't know. We have a pretty hot neighbor that has been giving me the eye too," Nicole retorted, raising a brow as Finley's hand rose higher, nearing the edge of her shorts.

"Hmm...I'm assuming you mean Mrs. Henderson with the blue hair in rollers and painted on make-up. I'm sure she drives her husband wild...when he can get it up, of course." Finley moved further, sliding her hand under Nicole's shorts, teasing her panty-covered center. "Shall I go get her? I'm sure she'd love to—"

Nicole set her glass on the end table behind her head, placed the folder on the floor, and grabbed the middle of Finley's sweat shirt, pulling her on top of her. Their lips met in a sensual kiss.

"I love you," Nicole murmured against Finley's mouth.

"I never get tired of hearing that," Finley said, nuzzling her neck. She knew better than to go any further. Caitlin was lurking around upstairs. "What's with all of the brochures and stuff?" she asked, sliding to the side and pulling Nicole into her arms.

"Your mother brought it to me at the office today."

"Really?"

"Yes. I asked her if she'd help me with the details. It's not like my own mother wants to be involved."

"Have you told her yet?"

"I sent her an email that went unanswered. I guess I could post an announcement in the country club newsletter."

Finley laughed. "I'd pay money to see her face."

"She and my father think I tarnished their name and ruined their reputation when I divorced the man they forced me to marry and went back to the only person I've ever loved in my entire life, who happens to be a woman." Nicole shook her head.

"You know how I feel about both of them," Finley uttered.

"I do, but they are still my parents and Caitlin's grandparents. I can't completely write them out of my life. If they can, then that's all on them."

"So, what kind of stuff did my mother bring you?" Finley asked, changing the subject. She hated talking about the infamous Wetherby family. As far as she was concerned, they could go to hell.

"Some venue stuff and dress styles."

"You could wear a potato sack, and we could get married right here in this den with two witnesses and a notary. It doesn't matter to me as long as you become my wife."

Nicole ran her hand over Finley's cheek. "I've had the long white dress, large bridal party, and hundreds of guests. It was a fairytale, but without my knight in a wetsuit and dive mask."

"You want me to wear my rescue gear?" Finley grinned and shrugged. "It's more comfortable than my Full Dress Uniform anyway."

"Uh, no. The dress uniform will be fine," Nicole replied with a smile. "I'm just not sure what I want to do. I've already worn white, so I was thinking maybe a crème color like ivory or bone, and certainly not a long gown."

"Nicole, you're the most beautiful woman I've ever laid eyes on. I love you, and I'm sure whatever you choose will be absolutely perfect."

Nicole pulled back slightly, staring at Finley's blue eyes.

"What?"

"You never call me Nicole unless you're mad or being very serious."

Finley smiled. "Well, I am serious. The details mean nothing, as long as you and I are happy and we say 'I do'." She kissed her tenderly, lingering for an extra touch of her lips on Nicole's.

"Seriously?" Caitlin screeched, coming around the corner and seeing them together on the couch. "Do I need to start banging pots and pans together when I'm in the vicinity or something?"

Nicole laughed. "Apparently, we can't be affectionate because it grosses out our teenage daughter," she said, kissing Finley's cheek before getting up.

"What's for dinner?" Caitlin asked, ignoring them.

"I don't know. When are you going to learn to cook?" Nicole replied with a raised brow and crossed arms.

Finley sat up and stretched her back as Nicole walked into the kitchen. She patted the couch cushion next to her and nodded for Caitlin to sit. "What's going on with you? You've been a little preoccupied and snippy lately, kiddo."

"I don't know."

"Does it have anything to do with Will?"

"What? No. We're just friends."

"Okay...maybe the regional swim meet, then?"

"I'm a little nervous, I guess. If I don't win, I may not get called into the Junior National Team camp."

Finley nodded. "Train your hardest, and go out there and do your best. Leave nothing in the tank. That's all you can do, honey. If you qualify or get invited, then you go, and do it all over again. If you don't, it's unfortunate, but it's not the end of the world. You're being recruited by four top universities right now, and you're only a junior." Finley wrapped her arm around Caitlin's shoulder's in a side hug. "I hate that you're under so much pressure at such a young age," she added. "Just know Mom and I are here for you. Let us work with you, not against you. Okay?"

"Thanks, Mom," Caitlin sighed.

"How's everything else going with school?" Finley asked, removing her arm and leaning back with her head resting on the couch.

"Good. I got an A on my Chemistry test. How's the training class?" Caitlin answered, mocking her position.

"They survived Phase One," Finley stated.

Caitlin laughed. "How many washed out?"

"Four."

"Oh, you're getting soft, Mom. Wasn't it six or seven with the last class?"

Finley elbowed her. "I am not getting soft! This group is simply in better shape."

"Uh huh," Caitlin giggled, causing Finley to chuckle too.

Nicole heard the laughter and walked around the corner to check on them. Finley and Caitlin looked so much alike, and their mannerisms were nearly the same. Nicole had to remind herself sometimes that she was the one who'd given birth. She couldn't help smiling at the site of the two of them. Her life had changed so much in the last two years. She was thankful to have love and laughter around her again.

"Why don't we all go out to dinner?" Finley said. "We don't get to do that often with our schedules, and it is Friday night."

"We can't ever decide on a place. That's why we don't go out to eat," Caitlin corrected.

"Alright, fine." Finley left the room and returned a minute later. "Here, everyone write down where you want to go, fold the piece of paper, and put it in this bowl."

All three of them wrote down their choice, then wadded their small papers up and dropped them in.

"Age before beauty," Finley said to Caitlin as she reached for the bowl.

"I do believe I'm a month older than you," Nicole chided, taking a piece of paper from the bowl before Finley could get to it.

"Yes, and it shows with that gray hair you have coming in up top," Finley teased.

"Yeah right," Nicole laughed, opening the paper.

"Looks like we're going for Mexican," she added, showing them that Sombrero's was written on it.

Chapter 10

Jordy's eyebrows rose when she stepped into the bar. The training class had divided into two groups, each taking a van and going a different way. The nearest establishment was a rundown bar just outside of the base called Sully's. The sign out front read: *Award Winning Carolina Burgers.* Evan, who was driving the van, pulled into the parking lot and cut the engine. It was karaoke night, and a bald man wearing jeans and an old white t-shirt with a tattered dish towel over his shoulder, was belting out Rod Stewart's hit song, *Do Ya Think I'm Sexy?*

"Come in. Take a seat anywhere," the older, gray-haired woman behind the bar yelled as she poured a round of beers for a table. "Don't mind my husband up there. You are sexy, baby," she said with a loud catcalling whistle.

"I guess we're staying," Ericka laughed.

"They do have the best burgers in town. Their menu even says it," said one of the other cadets who had ridden in their van. "I don't know about you guys, but I'm starving. A big, greasy burger and a basket of onion rings sounds wonderful."

"Hey, Rich, isn't this your jam?" Jordy teased.

"Oh, yeah," he laughed. "If you want my body," he sang, sliding up behind her.

Jordy chuckled as she glanced over her shoulder, moving against him while they looked around for a table. About a dozen people were on the dance floor, and most of the tables were occupied by older, active-duty and retired Coasties.

Evan and Ericka pushed two empty tables together to accommodate the eight of them. Everyone was under the drinking age of 21, so they all ordered food and various non-alcohol beverages when the waitress came over.

"At least we're not the only cadets," Ericka said, noticing a table in the back with young guys and a couple of girls from the Aviation Maintenance Technician school. They had a single pitcher of beer and a couple baskets of food in front of them.

"I don't care who's here, as long as I don't see Senior Chief Morris or Chief Denny," Rich said. "I plan on having a good time."

"Cheers to that," Jordy said, holding up her glass of tea.

A few more karaoke singers serenaded the bar with various tunes from Eddie Money to Garth Brooks while the rescue swimmer cadets dined on juicy burgers, fried chicken fingers, fries, and onion rings.

"I'm not looking forward to Monday," Ericka muttered.

"Who is?" Jordy replied. "But, it's Friday, so loosen that stick that's up your butt, and have a good time!"

"Why do you have to be so…"

Jordy leaned over the table, staring directly into her eyes. "So…what?"

"Never mind," Ericka grumbled, looking away.

"Come on, let's dance," Rich interrupted, grabbing Jordy's hand.

The bartender's husband and cook, was called back to the stage. As soon as Rod Stewart's song *Maggie May* started, Jordy began singing along. He noticed and quickly pulled her up next to him, handing her the microphone, before heading back to the kitchen.

Jordy belted out the song like she'd been singing it all of her life. Her voice even sounded a little raspy like Rod's, which wasn't normal. She glanced at Ericka a few times, directing certain lyrics towards her.

Rich, Evan, and a couple more cadets, danced with the crowd on the floor, cheering along as she sang. The rest of their table also cheered and clapped. As soon as the song was over, Jordy headed back to the dance floor with Rich, while another girl was called up to sing Whitney Houston's *I Wanna Dance with Somebody.*

Ericka finally got up, joining the rest of her table mates on the dance floor. Most of the bar was up dancing by this point, including the cadets from the other table in the back. Ericka danced near Rich and Evan, but kept her eyes on Jordy, who'd moved to the opposite side of the floor.

Jordy was about to go back to their table to get a sip of her drink, when one of the female cadets from the other group stepped onto the dance floor and grabbed her hand, pulling her close. Jordy grinned. The cadet was cute with light brown hair pulled back in a bun and brown eyes.

Ericka watched Jordy dancing with the female cadet. They were close, like they knew each other, but had enough space between them to keep the dancing clean.

"Are you in A school?" the cadet asked when the next song ended.

"Yes. AST Rescue Swimmer school. You?"

"AMT school. What's your first name?" she asked, looking at the last name stitched on Jordy's uniform.

"Jordy."

"I'm Olivia, but everyone calls me Liv."

"Nice to meet you." Jordy smiled.

"Is that blonde your girlfriend?" Liv asked.

"What? Who?"

"The one from your table who is staring daggers at me."

Jordy turned in time to see Ericka spin around. "No. She hates me. Those daggers are pointed my way, trust me."

Liv looked her in the eyes. "That's good to know. Hey, are those guys with your group?"

Jordy noticed Jon and the other cadets walk in. "Unfortunately," she mumbled. "Look what the cat drug in," she said, elbowing Rich, who was nearby.

"Aw, man. I thought we were rid of his ass for the night," he sighed.

"Hello ladies," Jon stated, referring to their entire group. "Did we crash your party?" he asked, moving into the middle of the dance floor and rather close to Liv.

Everyone ignored him and kept dancing.

"Jordy, come sing with me!" Rich yelled into the microphone.

Jordy shrugged and headed up on stage as Meatloaf's *Paradise by the Dashboard Lights* started. She sang along with him, getting into the song like they were giving a concert for thousands of people. Most of the bar was cheering, clapping, and singing along. Jon didn't look too pleased, albeit his eyes were on Liv as they danced together.

As soon as the song was over, Jordy and Rich left the stage, smiling and giggling like little kids.

Liv walked away from Jon, who was still trying his moves, and met Jordy over by her table. "Are you sure she's not into you? She couldn't take her eyes off you when you were singing. I can't blame her. Your voice is very sexy."

Slightly surprised, Jordy turned to look at Ericka, before shaking her head no. "It looks like Jon's pretty into you though."

"Good for him," Liv said, rolling her eyes. "What about you?"

"Maybe." Jordy smiled.

"Good. Here's my information. Send me a letter sometime. Maybe we can 'run' into each other on the base, Petty Officer Ross," she said, stuffing a piece of paper into Jordy's upper breast pocket.

"Yeah…maybe," Jordy replied, watching her leave with her group.

"Did you get her number?" Rich teased.

"Why? Did you want it?" she countered with a raised brow and thin grin.

Ericka ignored them and sipped her water.

"Damn lesbians!" Jon growled. "Women don't belong in the military and neither do lesbians! You want to be a man, grow a dick!"

Jordy was about to say something when Jon stormed out of the bar…alone. The sound of squealing tires could be heard over the music.

"Well, it looks like we're all riding back in one van," Evan uttered, shaking his head.

*

The cadets were sound asleep when Finley and Neil walked into their dorm, banging metal garbage can lids together at four a.m. on Monday morning.

"Everyone get up! You have two minutes to be dressed in your swim gear and in the pool room for muster!" Finley yelled.

"Move your asses!" Neil added, still banging the lids.

"If they're not awake yet, they will be in a few minutes," Finley said as they walked to the pool room.

*

"Man, she means business. I have a feeling we're about to train until one of us drowns," Evan muttered.

"Hey, make sure you put your big girl panties on," Jon snickered, looking towards the other end of the dorm. "If you need help with your tampons, I'm sure the other girls can help you."

"If I washout, I'm going to punch him in the face on my way out of here," Ericka growled.

"Parish, why don't you worry about finding a sports bra for those boobs you call pecks," Rich countered.

"Everybody grow the fuck up and get moving! If we're late and have to work extra hard because you guys want to sit around and talk shit, I'm going to lose it on one of you!" Jordy snapped. "Now, let's go. We'll double time it together as a team!"

"Who the hell put you in charge, Princess Dyke?" Jon snarled.

"Fine, you want to be a dick, go for it," she spat, storming out of the dorm.

"I don't get what his problem is," Evan said, jogging next to her towards the pool building.

"He obviously has a complex. He's probably really a momma's boy," Jordy replied. She turned around to see most of the class jogging in line behind her.

*

"Welcome to Phase Two! This is where we separate the rescue swimmers from the rest of the Coast Guard. Everyone grab a dumbbell and get into the pool!" Finley yelled. "Tread water while holding up the weight with both hands. Do not drop the weight into the water. Do not touch the bottom or sides of the pool!" she demanded, sounding a lot like a drill sergeant.

Neil grabbed the fire department water hose and began spraying the line of cadets back and forth.

"If you think this is hard, you have a rude awakening coming. Being in the middle of a storm at sea with twenty-knot winds and seven-foot seas is nothing like this!" Finley barked. "It's twice as bad when you not only have to keep yourself afloat, but also hold the weight of a victim that is depending on you to save his or her life." Finley paced back and forth at the edge of the pool. "Phase One was about getting you physically fit to do this job. Phase Two is about being able to save the victim. This phase will break you down mentally and physically, pushing you well past your limits. Nearly half of you will washout before it is over."

Neil turned the pressure up higher in the hose, and continued spraying the line of cadets back and forth.

"That weight you're holding is only ten pounds. Imagine trying to hold a 150-pound person while treading water enough to keep both of your heads above the surface," Finley said loudly as she checked her watch. They'd been at this for five minutes.

*

Jordy's face stung from the spray of the hose, and she choked on the water that had gone up her nose and into her mouth. She squeezed her abs as tight as she could, kicking her legs back and forth to remain out of the water. She kept her arms in an L-shape, but they slowly began to burn as her body started to fatigue. *Focus*, she told herself.

Ericka began to struggle with the weight as she fought to tread water. The water spraying her face made it nearly impossible to concentrate. Her arms shook, but she refused to drop the weight. *I'm not quitting,* she thought.

*

"Come on, Burney! You're an open ocean lifeguard. I expect you to be able to tread water twice as long as the rest of the class. Get that weight up!" Finley yelled.

"Aye-aye, Senior Chief!" Ericka said.

"You too, Ross. You're one of the fittest cadets in this class. Don't you dare let that weight touch the water!"

"Aye-aye, Senior Chief," Jordy stated.

"Owen…if that weight hits the water, I'm adding two more minutes for the rest of the class!" Finley shouted.

"Don't you do it, Owen!" Jon growled. "Get that weight in the air!"

"Let's go. You've got this. Mind over matter," Rich said to the struggling cadet next to him.

When Owen's weight hit the water, Finley called for him to get out of the pool. Once he was out, the rest of the class had to go for two more minutes. After the time was up, everyone got out of the pool and stood at attention near the edge.

"Pansy ass," Jon sneered in Owen's direction.

Finley raised a brow, but kept silent as she and Neil jumped into the water to demonstrate how to swim with a victim. "Always approach your survivor with caution. He or she could be delusional or scared. Always assess the situation from a few yards out. Tell them who you are, and remind them that you're there to get them to safety," Finley said. "It should go like this: I'm with the United States Coast Guard and I'm here to help you," she shouted. "Feel free to tell them your name or rank and name if you want, but make sure you get the point across of who you are and what you are there for. Once you've established verbal communication and it's safe to approach, grab the survivor from behind with your arm going over one of his or her shoulder's, around the front of the neck, and underneath the opposite armpit. It should look like this," she stated, grabbing Neil from behind. "Pull the survivor towards your chest, keeping his or her head out of the water, and begin swimming using your legs and free arm. If you approach a survivor who is facedown, roll him or her over. Then, proceed with the same grab and swim technique. Always make sure your survivors head is out of the water. Once you have it down, swim with your survivor to the other end of the pool, change places and the new rescuer will swim his or her survivor back to this side of the pool. Keep going back and forth until you hear my whistle."

The class watched as Neil and Finley showed them over and over how to approach a face up and face down victim, grab him or her, and begin to swim. After a number of demonstrations, Neil and Finley got out of the pool.

"When I call your name, pair up and get into the water," Neil said. "Webber and Burney, Owen and McDonald, Parish and Ross," he stated as he continued calling the names.

"She hates me," Jordy murmured as she jumped into the water next to Jon.

"I'll go first," he said.

Jordy rolled her eyes and pretended to be a survivor, bobbing in the water.

"I'm with the Coast Guard and I'm here to save you," Jon said, grabbing a hold of Jordy roughly, and swimming with her a few feet.

When he let go, Jordy held her breath and floated face down. Jon rolled her over and grabbed her quickly, squeezing her tightly in the swim hold before she could take another breath. Jordy struggled until he let her go. She gasped and choked as she tried to get air.

"You son of a bitch!"

"What's your problem? Can't hold your breath?" he snickered.

Jordy ignored him as they switched places. Jon bobbed in the water as Jordy swam over to him. "I'm with the Coast Guard and I'm here to help you," she said. As she moved to grab him from behind, he began flailing around like a drowning lunatic. It took all of Jordy's strength to grab him and swim. Jon kept jerking around, pushing her under the water. She finally let go of him and shook her head.

Jon changed positions and floated face down. Jordy swam up, rolled him over, and commenced with the grab and swim. Once again, Jon flailed around, pushing her under water and fighting against her.

"What's wrong, Ross? Are you too weak to hold a grown man up out of the water and swim with him? I guess you can't be a rescue swimmer then," he snickered. "I told you, girls have no place here."

"Go to hell," Jordy growled under her breath. She wanted to smack him in the mouth, but thought better of it.

Finley looked at Neil, who was about to pounce on the cadet, and shook her head. The rest of the pairs were working on the grab, hold, and swim technique over and over. "Ross and Webber change places," she said, moving Rich with Jon and Jordy with Ericka. She watched as Jon once again man-handled his rescuer. Rich fought back a little more than Jordy had, but Jon still managed to push him under.

"Just like I thought, you belong with the girls. Don't forget to hide your tampon string," Jon laughed.

Jordy shook her head as she watched.

"Aren't we supposed to be working on this?" Ericka huffed, completely unpleased that they'd been paired together.

Jordy spun Ericka around and pulled the blonde against her chest, holding her perfectly as she swam across the pool. When she let go, Ericka looked stunned. "What's wrong?" she asked.

"Nothing."

"Did I hurt you?"

"No. Come on," Ericka said, moving to grab her and swim back.

*

After a few more minutes, Finley blew her whistle. "Everyone out of the pool. There will come a time when the survivor is frantic and fights you. You must know how to subdue the survivor in order to keep you both safe. You will also have to deal with multiple survivors all trying to climb on you while you save them one at a time. They will push you under, grab and claw at you, anything to get to safety. You have to know how to fend them off. Chief Denny and I will demonstrate that now," Finley said, jumping back into the water with Neil.

She flailed around while he tried to rescue her, and even jumped on his back. Neil easily maneuvered out of her grasp and grabbed her in the hold position, swimming away with ease.

"We need a volunteer," Finley said.

Jon jumped into the water before anyone else could, which caused Finley to nod at Neil.

"Parish, you'll be the rescuer and Senior Chief and I will be the survivors," Neil stated.

Jon nodded and went for Finley. Just as he grabbed a hold of her, Neil jumped on his back, shoving him under the water. Jon fought to get to the surface, but couldn't with the two of them pushing him down. He finally swam away from them and surfaced, gasping for air.

"Swimming with a survivor is the hardest thing you will do as a rescue swimmer. This is the core of what you are training for," Finley said, addressing the entire class. "Parish, you be the survivor this time."

Finley anticipated Jon trying to do to her what he'd done to Jordy. She waved Neil away and swam over to Jon. "I'm with the U.S. Coast Guard and I'm here help you," she announced, moving to grab him.

Jon floundered around, trying to push her back and pull her under. Finley dunked him one time to shock his system, then grabbed him forcefully and swam off. She let him go a few feet away. "No matter how big or small your survivor is; the same technique works on everyone. If the person is scared and acting hysterical, you have to do something to shock him or her. This will calm the person enough to grab and hold them in position. Usually a quick dunk gets their attention, but sometimes you have to get a little more physical to get the point across. Be careful not to hurt the survivor or get yourself hurt in the process." Finley climbed out. "Everyone back into the pool with your same pairs. Let's work on subduing a frantic survivor and swimming to the other side like before. Keep in mind, you will be tested on this technique multiple times during this phase. It is a pass or fail grade. If you fail, you washout."

"I think you scared him," Neil whispered, watching Jon Parish act a little calmer during this new exercise.

"Good. Serves him right," Finley replied, eyeing Jordy and Ericka. She hadn't meant to put them together, but she'd noticed a lot of tension between the two of them over the past six weeks and wanted to see how it played out with this drill.

*

Jordy played the survivor first, quickly thrashing around and pushing Ericka under water. Ericka had a difficult time breaking free. She finally got angry and shoved Jordy as hard as she could, but still couldn't get a hold of her in the grab.

"Damn it," Ericka spat. "Calm down so I can do this."

"You're supposed to be able to grab me and swim off."

"I can't with you climbing on my back and pushing me under!"

"Let's switch places," Jordy said.

Ericka played the survivor, moving around in a frenzy, so Jordy dunked her. Ericka came up, gasping for air, and Jordy grabbed her swiftly, pulling her into the hold. She swam off, holding her, before Ericka realized what had happened.

Finley took mental notes on who was struggling with the method when it was chaotic. In a calm situation, everyone was able to grab their survivor and swim fifty-meters. However, in a hectic, unstable situation, nearly half the class was having difficulty. She blew the whistle.

"We're going to work on the most important part of the survival retrieval method, which is swimming with the survivor. In your pairs, grab, hold, and swim your partner as the survivor, to the other end of the pool and back. Switch off when you return to this end. Keep going until you hear my whistle."

"Aye-aye, Senior Chief!" the class yelled.

*

Later that night, Jordy laid on the floor of the dorm between her bunk and Ericka's, performing various yoga stretches to ease her stiff, sore muscles. She thought about asking Ericka, who was sitting in her bunk, reading her latest letter from Toni, if she wanted to join her. As much as Ericka seemed to hate her, Jordy still found her attractive. The ongoing competition between the two of them, which seemed to be fueled by Ericka's loathing, had actually turned into the highlight of Jordy's days. She found the unfriendly banter slightly amusing, and wondered if on the outside, they'd actually ever be friends. Friends weren't something she'd had much of. In fact, she could count them all on one hand, and most of those she hadn't spoken to since she'd left college to pursue a career in the Coast Guard. She looked over at Rich and Evan, who were both asleep. She could possibly consider them friends, at least while they were in Rescue Swimmer school. With eleven weeks to go, there was still a lot of time. She thought about graduation, closing her eyes and picturing the day in her head. More importantly, the one singular moment, when she'd get the Rescue Swimmer Badge. It would solidify her reasoning for dropping out of college. It would pave the way for not only a rewarding career, but an exciting future. Simply put, it would mean everything to her. All of the hard work and dedication would finally pay off, and she'd be doing something she wanted to do for the first time in her life.

Hearing delicate sobs, Jordy opened her eyes in time to see Ericka storm off to the bathroom, leaving the handwritten letter behind. She contemplated reading it, but she didn't want to get involved. Instead, she got up and headed towards the women's bathroom. Ericka was leaning against the sink, splashing water on her warm, red cheeks, trying to hide the remnants from crying.

"What do you want?" Ericka spat, seeing Jordy's reflection in the mirror.

"Is everything okay?"

"Like you care," Ericka snapped, drying her face on a nearby towel.

"I'm not a heartless bitch."

Ericka stared at her for a second. Jordy's hair was down, resting on the top of her shoulders in a natural wave, after having fallen out of the loose bun she'd put it up in when she began her yoga. In the past seven weeks, Ericka had only seen her hair down when it was wet after she'd just showered, but Jordy had always put it up in a bun, or the occasional ponytail. After what seemed like a full minute, Ericka looked at her chocolate-brown eyes and simply said, "I'm fine."

Jordy arched a brow and sighed as she watched her walk away.

Chapter 11

"Can we not go straight home?" Caitlin asked when Finley picked her up from her afternoon swimming practice.

"Sure," Finley murmured. She'd spent the last three days with the class in the pool, doing the same grab and hold drill, with the cadets swimming each other back and forth as survivors, until it was embedded into their brains like second nature. A scenic drive with her daughter sounded like a great idea. "What's going on, kiddo?"

"Nothing. May I drive?" Caitlin said as they walked outside.

"I think you should tell me what's bothering you first," Finley answered as they got into the SUV. "Is everything okay with school? I thought your latest report card was all A's?"

"School is fine."

"What about swimming? Mom's been taking you to practice every morning, right?"

"Yes." Caitlin turned, looking out the window. "Have you ever failed at something?" she uttered.

Finley thought for a minute. "Sure. But failure isn't the end of the world. I've always used it as a tool to grow even better. What are you failing at?"

"Nothing. Well, nothing yet," she sighed. "If I don't win this regional, my chances of making the Junior National Team are gone."

Finley pulled the SUV into the drive-thru of the Twisty Cone, a family owned business that stayed open year round, despite the cold winter months. "What would you like?" she asked. Going for ice cream had been a staple of theirs since she was a little girl. Even when they lived hundreds of miles apart and only saw each other a couple times a year, they always went for ice cream.

"Same as you," Caitlin replied.

"Two chocolate dipped cones with Moose Tracks ice cream," Finley ordered. She pulled around to the back of the waiting line. "Caitlin, swimming has been your thing since I first taught you how when you were a little kid. If you don't want to do it anymore, all you have to do is say so. Mom and I only push you to follow your dreams. If swimming is no longer one of them, that's fine," she said, lowering her window to pay and grab the two cones.

Caitlin took her ice cream, biting a chunk from the top. "Mom, it is my dream," she mumbled as she chewed. "I want to go to the Olympics. I want it so bad, I've practically given up everything else. So, if I fail, I have nothing. It scares the he…"

Finley smiled. "That would scare the hell out of me, too." She took a bite of her own cone and pulled back into the traffic. "You're very talented, and you've put yourself under so much pressure at such a young age. Take a step back, and look around you. You're almost sixteen, and you have your whole life ahead of you. If you don't make the team this year, it's not the end of the world. There is still plenty of time."

"I guess you're right. I just don't want to work this hard and not make it."

"You'll make it. You have to trust your training, kiddo. When I was flying rescue missions every day, I relied heavily on my training, which gave me the knowledge and confidence to do what I did, and save the people whom I saved. With training, you learn the skills that give you knowledge, and grow strength that gives you confidence. These are things I teach the cadets every single day."

"Thanks, Mom." Caitlin smiled.

"You're welcome. Promise me you'll ease up on yourself a little bit, okay?"

"I will."

"Do you want to drive?" Finley asked, noticing she'd finished her cone.

"We're almost home."

"Doesn't mean we have to go there," Finley replied, pulling over on a side road.

They quickly changed places, and Caitlin pulled back onto the main road as Finley wrestled with her melting ice cream. It was still cold at the end of February, but the heater in the car kept it a balmy sixty-five degrees. "Don't say anything to Mom about this," Caitlin muttered.

"Why not?"

"She worries about me enough as it is."

Finley nodded. "It's just because she loves you."

"I know."

"We don't keep secrets from each other, but I won't bring it up."

"Thanks. By the way, we forgot to get Mom something at the Twisty Cone."

"She doesn't eat ice cream," Finley said. "Besides, she has a late meeting. She called me earlier to say we were on our own for dinner."

"I see. I was wondering how you were going to explain us getting home late and having dessert first." Caitlin grinned.

"Speaking of dinner, what did you have in mind?"

"I could go for pizza."

"You can always go for pizza," Finley laughed. "If you weren't an athlete, you'd be 300 pounds."

"Exactly. I need to refuel my body. I just swam a crap-load of laps."

"Crap-load?"

"That's not a cuss word."

"Touché. Just don't let your mother hear you use that phrase. She'll blame me."

*

Finley was sitting on the couch, watching a video on her laptop and writing notes on a legal pad. Classroom instruction was starting soon for Class 16-20, and she was deciding what videos to show, as well as the topics to discuss with each one. As the lead instructor, she had access to thousands of firsthand video taken of rescues at sea, and she put together a new set of videos for each class.

She pulled the headphones from her ears when Nicole walked into the room, running her hand over Finley's shoulder as she passed by. "How was the meeting?" she asked.

"Do you feel like having a glass of wine?"

"That bad?"

"Yes and no," Nicole sighed, wiping a tear from her eye.

"Nic?" Finley murmured, standing to pull the blonde into her arms.

"I made a huge mistake."

"Okay? Did you get fired?" Finley questioned, running her hand up and down her back.

"I wasn't at work," Nicole whispered.

Finley's back stiffened. "Where were you?" When she didn't answer her, Finley pulled back, looking into her tear-filled, hazel eyes. "Nicole?"

"I was with my mother," she finally muttered.

"What? Your mother?"

"Yes. I know I should've told you I was meeting her."

"Why didn't you?" she asked, breathing a sigh of relief, albeit she was still pissed that Nicole had kept a secret from her, especially one that involved the only person to ever come between them.

"I know how you feel about her."

"So you lie to me instead?" Finley said sternly.

"I know you would've wanted to be there with me."

"You're damn right," she huffed.

"I'm sorry," Nicole replied, brushing her hand over Finley's cheek. "I had to do this, and I had to do it alone."

"It obviously didn't go well."

"No. No, it didn't," Nicole sighed heavily. "She said if I marry you, she no longer has a daughter."

Finley held her anger in check and simply shook her head as she pulled Nicole into her arms once again. "I'm sorry. I'm sorry that you have such a vindictive, spiteful person for a mother. And I'm sorry that once again, she's caused you pain because of me." Finley kissed away the tears on her cheek. "I love you, Nicole, more than I could ever express in one lifetime. And I plan to spend all of my days showing you how much, in every way that I am able."

"That sounds like vows," Nicole said softly against her neck as Finley held her tightly.

"Maybe they are. All I know is, I'm not letting that hateful bitch hurt you anymore. She's out of our lives for good...*all* of our lives."

Nicole simply nodded. "I love you with all of my heart. I always have, and always will," she whispered.

"Hey, Mom...I'm going to go to Sir Henry's, the mini golf place, this weekend with Will and a couple of other friends. Is that okay?" Caitlin asked as she bounded down the stairs. She found her mothers' locked in what looked like a serious embrace when she stepped into the den. She raised her eyebrows at Finley, who was facing her.

Finley winked, letting her know she hadn't spilled her secret. "Sir Henry's is fine with me. I can take you on my way to the base Saturday if you want."

"I'll ride with Will."

Finley nodded.

"Goodnight. I love you both," she said, heading back up the stairs.

"Love you too," Nicole said without turning around. "You're working this weekend?" she asked, pulling back to wipe the tears she'd hidden from her daughter.

"Neil is on muster duty, but we're doing a surprise dorm inspection. We haven't done one yet, and we just began Phase Two. It should only take an hour or two. Why? Did we have plans I forgot about?"

"No." Nicole shook her head. "It will be nice to have the house to ourselves for a bit." She smiled.

"I'm sure once she has her regular license, we'll be alone a lot. She's become quite the social butterfly this year," Finley replied.

"Yeah, I noticed that too. Maybe we should talk to her about dating."

"I was kind of waiting for her to bring it up. I don't think she's interested in that, at least not right now. She's having fun with her friends, but all she talks about is swimming. She told me the major of her ROTC brigade wants to move her up to captain and have her command a company next year, but it will be her senior year. Who knows what will be going on with swimming and everything else."

"I think she'll do it."

"Why do you say that?"

"She loves swimming, and going to the Olympics is her dream, but you're her hero, Finley. She's wanted to be just like you since she could walk."

Finley smiled. "Maybe she will be Superwoman, and do it all. She's extremely talented and definitely smart enough."

Nicole nodded in agreement. "I don't know about you, but I've had a long day from hell. I want to take a hot bath and go to bed."

"Want some company?" Finley questioned, wiggling her eyebrows.

"Do I ever say no?"

Finley grinned like a Cheshire cat.

Chapter 12

"Every rescue swimmer you see has been through the exact training you're going through now. He or she shed their blood, sweat, and tears, while learning to do this job, maybe even in this same room," Finley said, pausing the rescue clip playing on her laptop. The cadets shifted their eyes from the large screen at the front of the room to the lead instructor standing in the back as she continued. "No matter what the conditions are like, we go out, and we do our best. There are days when our best isn't good enough. Each of these videos represents two solemn oaths. They weren't cited when you were sworn in. They're not posted anywhere for you to read. They are merely imbedded deep within each of us who has come through this training, experienced the darkness that lies beyond it, and witnessed the light that shines on the other side. These are the two things that go through our head every time we are called out. Number one: We never quit. Not on our team, not on ourselves, not on the survivor...not until we have given everything we have...including our lives sometimes. Number two: Strength and knowledge give you great power, but courage and determination are what see you through. We decide if we go in the water. We decide which survivor to rescue first. We decide who doesn't live..." she trailed off.

"I want each of you to look deep inside and ask yourself, 'Am I willing to go the distance to save someone else?' It's okay if you aren't. It doesn't mean you are any less of a person than whoever is sitting next to you. It simply means being a rescue swimmer isn't for you." She stopped talking, letting that thought sink in, before moving on. "In the twenty videos you watched today: one rescue swimmer died in the line of duty; five survivors didn't live, three of which were unable to be rescued; and the rest went on to see another day," Finley stated.

"How are we supposed to decide?" Evan asked.

"Every rescue swimmer is different. I either go to the one who needs the most help, or whoever is closest to me, if no one is in severe distress," she answered. "There will be times when it is literally life and death and you can't save them all, no matter how hard you try. There's nothing you can do about that. There's no special order to go by. It's a split second decision. You just do your job to the best of your ability and forgive yourself if the sea wins. People are going to die, whether in the helicopter on the way to the hospital or at sea before you can reach them, but this small amount of loss doesn't compare to the vast number of people whom you will save throughout your career, people who will go on to live their lives…thanks to you."

"How many have you saved?" Ericka asked.

"In over fifteen years, I'm sure the amount is in the hundreds, but I don't keep up with it." Finley shook her head. "Twelve is the number that stays in the back of my mind. Five of them were taken by the sea when their fishing trawler sunk during a storm. I went into the water, but they were all swept away in the waves before I could reach any of them. Three more were also taken by the sea during different rescue attempts in severe storms, and four others died on the way to the hospital as I sat over them, performing CPR until I was physically pulled away," she said softly.

"Eight," Neil murmured, looking over at her.

"You never forget."

He nodded in agreement.

"Class 16-20," she said, turning off the computer and stepping to the front of the room. "I will not graduate you if I think you can't handle this job. I will not put innocent lives in unwilling or untrained hands. What we do day in and day out sounds thrilling, exciting, and adventurous, but truth be told, most of it is scary, life-threatening, and exhausting. This job isn't for everyone." She gestured towards Neil as she walked out of the room.

"Be in Pool Room B for muster at 0700. Dismissed," he said.

"Aye-aye, Chief!"

*

Finley was sitting at her desk, preparing to leave for the day. She'd gone a little further than she'd expected with the classroom instruction for the day, but she wanted to drive the point home. It was better to scare the hell out of someone and make them drop out on their own, then let them get all the way through training and fail, causing the loss of a life.

"I think you woke them up today," Neil said from the open doorway.

Before she could reply, one of the cadets knocked. "Senior Chief, can I talk to you?"

"Sure," she replied.

Neil stepped out of the room, shutting the door as Airman James Whitman moved inside.

"Sit down," Finley said. "What can I do for you?"

"I…" He bit his lower lip. "I don't think I can do it."

"Do what, exactly?"

"Decide who lives and dies. I don't think I could live with myself."

Finley nodded. "Where does that leave us then?"

"I'd like to Drop On Request."

"Are you sure?"

"Yes, Senior Chief. It's taking all of the courage I have to sit here and do this. I love the Coast Guard, and I've dreamed of being a rescue swimmer, but I know I can't look at two people and decide which life is more important. I don't want that kind of responsibility. I cannot play God."

Finley's eyebrows rose and she cleared her throat. "Alright. I'll get your paperwork cleared, and you'll be on your way to your old unit tonight. If you didn't have one, you'll be assigned to a new unit."

"Thank you."

"No, thank you for being honest with yourself and having the courage to come forward. I'm sure you'll do great things wherever you go," she said, standing and shaking his hand. "Go pack your bag and meet Chief Denny in the personnel building."

Neil walked back into the office after Airman Whitman left.

"DOR," Finley said.

"Really? He was a pretty strong cadet in and out of the water."

"He doesn't want to have to decide who to save if and when the time comes." She shrugged. "At least he figured that out now and not in the middle of a rescue."

"Yeah, no kidding."

Finley filled in the boxes on the computer screen to release Whitman.

"Have you ever had that happen? A swimmer freak out on you?" Neil asked.

"This is the first cadet to DOR because of his faith or religion. As far as in the field, no. I've never had a rookie swimmer freak out on me. But, I did have a pilot once who wasn't going to let me get in the water. We were dealing with a tropical storm and a boat was taking water. The winds were crazy, too high for us to be out by the time we'd reached the vessel. The seas were holding around eight or nine feet and the helo was all over the place. I watched the boat capsize from the open cabin door. The pilot was sure the captain had drowned, but I wasn't certain. I knew he had a life vest on because I'd seen him on the stern before it rolled. The pilot wanted to go back to base and had begun radioing our plan to return. I kept watching the waves crash over the hull of the boat. Then, I caught site of the orange vest as the captain crawled on top of the overturned boat. The Flight Mech checked the line and down I went. I wound up saving the guy's life. If I had let the pilot chicken out and return, he would've died."

"Wow. I've never been stationed in Florida, but I can imagine those summer storms and tropical storms are hellacious though."

"Hurricanes are the worst. We are generally grounded, but we've gone out a few times." Finley shook her head. "Those were the only times I've ever been white-knuckled in the air and fearing for my life as I went into the water."

Neil smiled. "Yeah, boats don't tend to sink on clear, calm days."

Finley shook her head. "In Florida they do. Especially when you have inexperienced boaters who go off shore. They get swept up in a freak afternoon thunderstorm and start taking on water. By the time we get the call and reach their location, the boat has capsized, sunk, or is about to, and the sky is perfectly blue with flat seas."

"That's crazy. It sounds like the Bermuda Triangle."

"I have some friends who were stationed in Miami and the Bahamas. They've seen boats floating or motoring along with no one on board on completely calm days. The majority of their calls are sinking boats that are nowhere to be found when they arrive on scene. No survivors, no remnants of the vessel, nothing. At first, you think they are hoax mayday calls, but the people on board are never seen or heard from again, so they had to be lost at sea."

"Maybe I need to change districts," he chuckled.

"You're from District 1, right?"

"Yeah. I've been stationed in the Southern New England area for my entire ten-year career. The Bahamas sounds sunny and wonderful."

Finley laughed and handed him the printed paperwork. "He should be waiting for you in personnel. It looks like he will be going back to Texas, unless he opts to go to Yorktown and become a Boatswains Mate." She paused. "Sector Corpus Christi can deal with that. It's not my problem. Go ahead and get him processed out."

*

Jordy walked into the new pool room with the rest of the class the next morning. The first thing she noticed was the tall tower extending out over the opposite side of the pool.

"Has anyone seen Whitman?" one of the cadets asked. "He never came back from dinner chow in the mess hall."

"That's because he wasn't there," another cadet answered.

She ignored their banter as she fell in line for muster. Ericka, who was next to her, asked Evan to change places with him. Jordy rolled her eyes and shook her head.

"Straighten up!" Neil yelled when Finley walked into the room.

She set her clipboard down and stepped in front of the class. "Airman Whitman Dropped On Request yesterday," she said, crossing her arms. "Each of you had all night to think about the oaths asked of you. Are you willing to give your life so that others may live? More importantly, can you decide in a split second who lives if you can't get them all?"

"Yes, Senior Chief!" the class shouted together.

"Airman Whitman couldn't..." Finley trailed off.

"What a puss," Jon whispered.

"What was that, Petty Officer Parish?" Finley asked. When he didn't answer, she moved in front of him. "I believe you called Airman Whitman a puss...correct? Let me tell you something," she said loudly, addressing the whole class. "When you're up there in the air, getting tossed around in heavy wind with stinging rain pelting your face as you sit on the edge of the cabin door, looking down at a nearly submerged boat that has three people hanging onto the rail, none of whom have on life preservers, you have the time that it takes to free fall or ride down on the hook, to figure out who you're going to first. Petty Officer Parish, do you know how long that is?"

Jon shook his head no.

"Come with me," she snapped.

He followed as they walked around to the tower on the opposite side. She motioned for him to climb up as she stood back. He looked down at the water that seemed like a mile away when he walked out onto the platform at the top.

"You're twelve feet above the water. Rescue swimmers can safely freefall up to twenty feet because they're properly trained, but most freefalls are anywhere from ten to fifteen feet," she stated to the class. "Sit on the edge with your legs dangling over," she instructed.

Jon did as he was told.

Finley nodded to Neil, who had left the group and was now on the opposite side of the tower. He quickly flipped the switches, turning on the wave pool, hurricane fan, and pelting rain. The cadets backed away from the pool before the wind pushed them in. Jon grabbed the side of the platform, holding on for dear life as the wind rocked the tower and the rain blasted his skin. Finley threw a small yellow float and a small white one into the ripping waves.

"Which one are you going to get?" she yelled up at him.

"I..."

"Now! Decide now!" she shouted. "They're drowning!"

"I don't know!" he screamed in a panic. "Orange!"

Finley watched him gripping the tower as it rocked like a moving helicopter, hovering in position. She gave Neil the kill sign, and he turned everything off.

"Get down here!" she yelled at Jon.

He quickly climbed down the ladder, careful not to slip. Everything in the room was soaking wet, including the cadets who were on the other side of the pool.

"Why did you say orange?"

"I don't know," he said, standing at attention in front of her. "I panicked."

"Exactly!" Finley shook her head. "You freaked out and yelled a color without assessing the situation."

"I didn't have time to see what colors they were," he replied.

"You didn't have time..." Finley shook her head. "You had more time just now, than you will ever have in a life or death situation." She crossed her arms. "And you panicked. Who's the puss now?"

Jon's jaw tightened and his back stiffened.

"Get your ass back in my formation line, and don't ever let me here you speak negatively about another cadet!" she spat. "Airman Whitman made a decision yesterday that will save lives, including his own," she added as he hurried back to the other cadets. "If you can't trust your instincts and your own judgment, I can't trust you to do this job."

The class watched her walk back over to their side of the pool.

"Anyone else think they know everything? Anyone else think they're better than me or Chief Denny? Anyone else think Whitman is a puss?" she yelled.

"No, Senior Chief!" the group shouted.

"Good! Now, we can move on. When you freefall from a helo, you push off into a seated position with your knees slightly bent. You keep one hand on your mask and the other crossing your chest."

Neil climbed up the tower as she spoke. He pulled his mask down into position and waited for her to give him the jump signal.

"Your heels should enter the water first, followed by your butt. As soon as you enter the water, kick up to clear the surface, and give the hand signal that you are all right, which is a raised arm with an open palm facing forward. Chief, give the 'I'm Alright' signal!"

Neil held his arm up straight over his head with his open palm facing the class.

"No matter how you go into the water, whether it is a freefall or you are hoisted down, you always give the same signal, indicating that you are alright. After that, you swim off towards the survivors. As we move further into Phase Two, you'll learn the signals to have the sling, basket, and litter deployed down to you, as well as how to use each one, and have it retrieved. As I told you last week, this phase is all about the survivor. You will be tested in multiple areas relating to strength, mentality, and exhaustion." She looked up at the tower. "Chief, ready on my whistle. Everyone watch as he demonstrates how to freefall, surface, and give the 'I'm Alright' signal."

*

Jordy watched as Neil pushed off the platform, moved slightly into a seated position, and entered the water perfectly. He popped up quickly with his arm above his head, giving the proper signal. Her heart raced with a mixture of nerves and excitement as she got in line next to the tower with the rest of the cadets, awaiting her turn.

Each person freefell on Finley's whistle. As soon as they exited the water, she either told them to go to her left side or her right side. Ericka had gone ahead of Jordy and was told to go to the left side, along with four other cadets.

On her turn, Jordy took a deep breath to calm herself, then launched off the platform, closing her eyes as she held one hand over her chest and the other on her mask. Her heels broke the water first, followed by her butt. She immediately surfaced with her arm raised and her palm facing the tower. Finley told her to go to the right side, where the majority of the cadets were placed.

After the last cadet went, Finley said, "If you're on my right, you performed a correct freefall. If you're on my left, you made a mistake." She added marks next to those who had messed up. "Everyone back in line. We're going to do this until everyone gets it right."

*

The class spent the next hour freefalling into the pool from the platform, as well as using various hand signals to have the apparatuses deployed. Each time someone didn't do it correctly, the entire group had to do it all over again. Once they had it down enough to move on, Finley broke them off into pairs, using one as the swimmer and one as the survivor.

"Survivors, I want you to tread water on this side of the pool. Swimmers, you will freefall into the water, swim to your survivor, assess him or her, swim the person back towards the tower and give the signal for a piece of equipment. I'll call out what I want you to use each time. Again, we will do this until everyone gets it right."

Ericka looked at Jordy and shook her head. "I'll be the swimmer first."

"Fine with me," she replied. Ericka hadn't said two words to her since Jordy had found her in the bathroom, washing away her tears. Jordy hadn't bothered saying anything either.

They were the third pair in line to go. Ericka climbed the tower and Jordy jumped into the water, taking up her position.

"Ross, go face down like you're unconscious. Burney, you'll be calling for the litter. Here we go!" She blew the whistle and watched the scene unfold.

Ericka freefell into the water, quickly giving the 'I'm Alright' signal. Then, she swam over to Jordy, rolling her over. Jordy quickly began to sink down. Ericka struggled to pull her up, getting her head above water and maneuvering her into position to swim with her.

"Coast guard rescue swimming is nothing like lifeguarding on the beach. In the middle of the night, when the waves are ten feet high, with 20 knot winds, we are dropped into water that is thousands of feet deep. Lifeguards go into fifteen-foot deep water with two foot waves and an undertow, while pulling a floatie behind them. Lifeguards sit in a chair and work on their tan. Is that what you are, Burney? A bikini babe with a floatie and a tan?" Finley yelled.

"No, Senior Chief. I am a Coast Guard Rescue Swimmer!" Ericka replied, struggling to get Jordy into position to swim with her. She finally made it back to the platform and quickly threw up the signal for the basket instead of the litter.

"Wrong signal," Jordy hissed.

Finley blew the whistle and had them stand on the left side of her as the rest of the class went through the drill.

"Damn it!" Jordy growled.

"You could've helped me instead of acting like a wet sack of potatoes!"

"She told me to act unconscious!"

"Whatever!"

"Ladies, you're a team. If one fails the exercise, you both fail," Finley muttered, overhearing them as she watched Rich and Evan perform a slightly different variation.

"Bikini babe with a floatie and a tan?" Neil murmured with a raised brow, stepping over to her as the two female cadets got back in line to go again.

"I was on a roll." Finley shrugged and smiled.

Chapter 13

The next day, the class found themselves in the same pool, doing the same drill as the day before. Finley had made them keep the same partners as well, which had only added fuel to the fire.

Each time Jordy was the swimmer, she got everything correct. However, Ericka struggled here and there, forgetting a step or simply struggling to perform the movement.

"I tried to tell you what to do," Jordy growled after another mistake.

"Stop telling me what to do. I didn't ask for your help, and I don't want it, or you!" Ericka huffed before stomping back over to the tower to go again.

"Huh?" Jordy mumbled, trying to make sense of what she'd just said.

Finley watched the interaction for an extra minute, before moving on. "Chief Denny and I are going to demonstrate how to get someone into the sling, the basket, and the litter. Then, we're going to allow each pair to get in the water and do it, before moving to the tower. Remember, if the survivor is alert and uninjured, the sling is the first choice. If the survivor is alert, but fatigued, slightly injured, or simply unable to go up in the sling, use the basket. Finally, if the survivor is unconscious, on the verge of being unconscious, seriously injured, or DOA, you use the litter. We will get further into alert statuses and so forth in the coming weeks. Until then, you should be able to tell which piece of equipment to use based on how you assess the survivor. Chief, let's start with the sling."

Finley, playing the swimmer, quickly grabbed Neil and swam him towards the sling. Then, she put it over his head and under his arms. After that, they moved to the basket, and finally the litter, before climbing back out of the pool.

"Everyone get into the water and hold onto the edge. When I call your names, swim out to the middle and perform the maneuver. Climb out when you are finished."

Over the next hour, Jordy and Ericka fought with each apparatus as they learned how to get each other in and out of them. By the time they'd moved on to freefalling from the tower, swimming to the survivor, signaling for the equipment, and getting the survivor loaded inside, they'd stopped talking altogether.

Every pair of cadets struggled at some point or another during the drill with improper assessment of the survivor, thus using the wrong hand signal, or incorrect form when preparing a survivor for retrieval. They also battled fatigue as the day went on, which had only made the training that much more difficult.

"Everyone out of the pool," Finley called. "Now!" she yelled.

The cadets hurried out of the pool and stood at attention, facing forward.

"There's a change to your schedule. Instead of a classroom session tomorrow, we'll be back here at the pool, reviewing how to freefall, swim to a survivor, assess the survivor, and prepare the survivor for retrieval, as well as all of the proper hand signals for communication. These five skills are the fundamentals of being a rescue swimmer, and they must be second nature to you. We will do these drills until they are so ingrained in you, you are doing them in your sleep!" she growled like a drill sergeant.

"During Phase Two, you will be tested on these maneuvers. This will be a pass or fail test, meaning if you fail, you washout. There will be no second chances." She stepped away from the group, pausing next to Neil on her way out of the room. "Send Burney and Ross to my office," she said.

"Get some chow, get some bunk time, and be at muster at 0700 for morning PT. Dismissed," Neil said sternly. "Burney and Ross, get into dry uniforms and report to the senior chief's office."

"It's about time they kicked the two of you out of here," Jon sneered as they walked past him in the hallway after drying off and changing clothes.

Jordy ignored him as she kept walking. A hundred scenarios were racing through her head. Sure, they'd struggled as a pair, but she knew the maneuvers and hand signals and had only made a few mistakes. "I better not be washing out because you won't listen and can't seem to figure out what the hell to do," she muttered harshly.

"Oh, please, don't blame me. You screwed up too, and if you hadn't been so busy trying to tell me what the hell to do, I probably wouldn't have had so much trouble. I think you did it on purpose."

"You think I sabotaged you?" Jordy's face scrunched with surprise.

"Sure." Ericka shrugged. "You want to be the only female to graduate, and I'm standing in the way."

"Are you kidding me? I don't give a shit if you washout or graduate. I don't care. I'm here for me and only me."

"Whatever," Ericka spat.

Jordy nodded towards the closed door. The nameplate above it read: SCPO Finley Morris.

*

Finley sat at her desk, making notes in her computer about the schedule change for the next day. She looked at the white dry-erase board to her right, where all of the candidates' names and ranks were written in black. The six that had washed out had red lines drawn through them.

A loud knock on the door grabbed her attention. "Come in," she said, closing the window on the screen as Jordy and Ericka walked inside, standing at attention in front of her.

"Have either of you ever seen the movie: The Black Swan?" Finley asked.

Jordy scrunched her brow in thought. She wasn't much of a movie buff.

"No, Senior Chief," they said simultaneously.

"It's a psychological thriller about two female ballet dancers, both very different, both vying for the same role as the lead in a production of Swan Lake. One of them is so hell bent on being perfect, that she loses control, unraveling and sabotaging herself, all the while, blaming the other for everything that is happening to her. The movie is more of a metaphor about achieving perfection, and the lengths at which the mind will go to attain it."

Jordy glanced at Ericka.

"Anyway," Finley continued. "Over the past seven weeks, I've watched the two of you slowly slip into these roles, forming an unhealthy competition that one of you is willing to risk everything to win." She put her elbows on the desk, raising her hands up to form a triangle in front of her mouth as she stared at the two of them. "A little over fifteen years ago, I stood right where you are now, fighting the same battle, only I played both roles. You see, I was in competition with myself, being pulled in so many directions, I didn't know which one was the correct path anymore. This place breaks you down to nearly nothing, allowing your mind to twist around until you're lost. Rescue Swimmer school is as much a mental game as it physical. If you forget why *you* are here, you'll be lost, circling to find your way until you washout," she sighed. "Coast Guard Rescue Swimmer school is one of the hardest training schools in the military. Our attrition rate is higher than the Navy Seals. No one ever said it would be easy. No one expects it to be easy. But, if you're fighting against yourself the entire time, you're only going to make it that much more difficult. What's tough for men here, is twice as hard for women. The number of graduating cadets who are female is less than one percent. The odds are stacked against you before you even arrive," she said, crossing her arms over her chest as she leaned back in her chair.

"I thought this rivalry between the two of you would fade away once you became the remaining female cadets. But, it looks as though it's only gotten worse. The two of you should look at the rest of the class like they are your competition. If you beat them, you beat the odds. You are stronger together, as a team, than you are individually, especially when you're against each other at every turn. Everyone has strengths that help them prevail and weaknesses that they must overcome if they want to succeed here. Don't be each other's weakness. If you fail and wash out of here, let it be because you gave everything, leaving your blood, sweat, and tears behind. Don't let it be because you got lost in yourself and couldn't find your way. You might as well quit."

Finley pushed her chair back and stood. "Talk to each other. I bet you don't even know where the other is from or why she's even here. What's her story, her motivation? What's yours? I don't care if you leave this base and never speak to each other again, but I'm telling you right now, if you don't learn to communicate, you'll both washout. The animosity between the two of you will see to that," she finished with a sigh. "Dismissed."

*

Jordy walked out of the office and stopped midway down the hall. She leaned back against the wall, staring up at the ceiling. There was no way she was going to let this hothead drag her down. The senior chief had hit the nail on the head. Whatever it was causing the rift between them needed to be dealt with. She glanced to her left, but Ericka was already gone from the building. She bounced off the wall and headed towards the dorm.

"Get your bathing suit and meet me in pool room B," Jordy said, jogging past her.

"Why would I do that?" Ericka replied.

"Did you not hear anything she just said to us?" Jordy growled, stopping and turning to face her. "I'm not going to washout because you're too pigheaded to listen to me. We're going to go in there and learn to work together. You need my help, and whether you ask for it or not, I'm going to give it to you."

"Why?" Ericka stared at her. "Why would you help me?"

"Because I'm not the asshole you think I am!" Jordy shook her head.

Ericka ignored her as she went into the dorm to get a clean, dry bathing suit.

*

"Come on. Do it again," Jordy said, playing the survivor as Ericka swam to her, did the assessment, and signaled for the equipment.

"I know what hand signals to use," Ericka huffed.

"Then, use them!"

"Don't yell at me!"

Jordy tightened her jaw to keep from saying anything she'd regret. They'd been at it for nearly an hour, freefalling from the tower, swimming to the survivor, and giving hand signals. "Let's move on. I'll be the survivor. I may be alert, unconscious, or injured. You decide what method of retrieval to use and swim me to that piece of equipment," she said, placing the sling, basket, and litter in various sections of the pool. Then, she swam out to the middle. "You don't have to go off the tower. Just swim from the edge of the pool."

"Fine," Ericka said, pushing off the wall. She reached Jordy, who was alert and uninjured. She turned her around and pulled her close, assuming the grab position as she began to swim her towards the sling. She helped Jordy get inside, before backing away and giving the 'all clear' signal to lift her up.

"Run it again," Jordy said as she swam back to the middle.

Ericka sighed as she swam back out to her. Finding Jordy injured, she gave the signal for the basket, then she swam her over to it. "You have to help," she growled, pushing Jordy's solid frame up inside with assistance from her. She backed away, giving the all clear once Jordy was secure. Then, she swam back to the edge to start all over again.

Jordy took a deep breath and floated facedown. Ericka swam over quickly, rolling Jordy to her back. She held her head out of the water as she pulled Jordy's body against her. Forgetting to tread water for a second as their bodies touched, they both went under. Jordy popped up quickly, spitting water out.

"What the hell!"

"Sorry," Ericka mumbled, grabbing her again.

When she reached the litter, Ericka struggled with Jordy's body, but she managed to get her inside and give the signal. She hastily swam away, leaving Jordy on her own to get back out.

"What's wrong with you?" Jordy questioned harshly.

"Nothing. Are we doing it again, or what?" she huffed, holding onto the side wall.

They went through the scenarios again with Ericka still struggling to get her into the basket and the litter.

"If I'm an unconscious survivor, you can't expect me to get into the litter, and if I'm injured, I'll need help with the basket." Jordy swam closer. "You can't be scared to touch me."

Ericka stared at her brown eyes and turned away, climbing up out of the pool. "We're done for the day," she uttered, grabbing her towel and walking away.

Jordy shrugged and got out as well.

Chapter 14

Finley walked into the house, kicking her shoes off at the door and pulling her USCG Helicopter Rescue Swimmer Instructor sweatshirt over her head. The reflection she saw staring back at her from the glass in the nearby picture frame, looked tired.

"What's wrong, babe?" Nicole asked softly, sliding up behind Finley, wrapping her arms around her waist.

"Nothing now," Finley murmured, smiling as she breathed in the clean vanilla scent of Nicole's shampoo mixed with the light lavender of her perfume. She spun around, picking Nicole up easily with one hand behind her legs and the other at her back. She moved over to the floral couch in the formal living room, a sofa they'd both hated, but since their rental house had come furnished, they'd simply ignored it. She sat down with Nicole in her lap.

Nicole threaded her arms around Finley's neck and stretched her legs out along the cushions.

"Do you know how much I love you?" Finley said. "You're the first thing on my mind when I wake up. Whether I see you or not, your beautiful eyes and adorable smile are there. You're also my last thought as I fall asleep at night with the comfort of your warm body against mine."

"Wow," Nicole whispered, taken aback. "Where did that come from?"

"I don't know. I guess I'm feeling a little nostalgic today. A lot of old memories came flooding back from my time at AST Rescue Swimmer training, and the years we spent apart. They're like day and night. When I was in swimmer school, I was fighting myself because I wanted it all, to be the best, but I also wanted to be with you, protecting you, loving you...so much so, that I almost threw away my career before it ever began. The time we were separated was just as tortuous. I no longer had you in my life. I buried that anger and resentment so deep that it ate away at me a little at a time, causing me to stop feeling. I kept my own daughter at a distance because it hurt so much to be with her and have to let her go, back to you and your new life. It was like losing you both all over again. I eventually learned to move on and enjoy my life, relishing in the honors and accolades I'd received, and cherishing the time I got to spend with Caitlin."

Nicole had tears running down her cheeks when Finley looked up at her.

"What's wrong?" she asked.

"I'm sorry that I caused you so much pain."

"It wasn't you. That's not what I'm saying. I did it to myself, like self-sabotage. I've been so happy these last two years, that I'd forgotten about those darker days."

"What brought all of that up?" Nicole asked, wiping away her own tears.

"These two female cadets in my class. Ironically, each reminds me of one of those times. They are both so...I don't know even how to put it. I actually referenced the movie The Black Swan while lecturing the two of them today." She shook her head.

"What do you think is causing it? Are they about to washout?"

"Yes and no. They have this loathing between them that is unlike anything I've ever seen. Instead of working against the class, they're completely against each other. I think it's much deeper than what I'm seeing on the surface though."

Nicole raised a questioning brow.

"I think they need to either fuck or fist fight… hell, maybe both."

"Oh, my God," Nicole laughed.

"I'm serious, Nic. You can cut the tension with a knife. If they don't get this under control, they're both going to washout. One is so hell-bent on beating the other, that she's just plain lost. The other is fighting herself day in and day out, pushing herself to the limit, like anything but first isn't good enough, but she's letting this competiveness control her. She's good and she knows it, so she's condescending when she tries to help, which only succeeds in pissing off the other one because she doesn't want the criticism, whether it is constructive or not." Finley let out a deep breath. "They're making me crazy."

"I can see that, honey," Nicole grinned, kissing her softly. "The best thing you can do is let them work it out."

"I know. I honestly don't want to see either of them fail. They're both strong-willed women and would be great rescue swimmers."

"You said you spoke to them, right? How'd that go?"

"I don't know. They looked like deer in the headlights when they walked out of my office."

"Give it some time and see what happens. Maybe you lit a spark or hit a nerve. Either way, they'll figure it out."

"I hope they do before it's too late," she murmured, burying her face in Nicole's neck, under her shoulder-length, blonde tresses.

"Hey, on a lighter note, I have some wedding news," Nicole said.

"Oh, really?"

"I know you're not into a big wedding, and honestly, I don't want another one of those either. I've looked at venues, but what do you think about Waterfront Park, down by the river?"

"It's beautiful there. You know that is my favorite place in this city."

"Mine too. Why don't we just do a small service there with a few friends and family? Then, have a party somewhere."

Finley nodded. "That sounds good to me. What about the officiant?"

"Gladys, in my office, is a notary. She said she'd be honored to marry us."

"Wonderful. That's two things down." Finley smiled.

"That leaves us with the date."

"I'd like to do it after the class graduates. Maybe that same weekend even. I get liberty for a week. Maybe we can go on a honeymoon."

Nicole smiled brightly. "Now, that sounds like a plan. Somewhere warm!"

"Agreed," Finley said, kissing her.

Nicole ran her fingers into Finley's short, dark curls.

"Oh, my God. Do you two have to do it all over the house?" Caitlin growled, spotting them as she walked through the front door.

Finley rolled her eyes. "Where were you?"

"At the movies with my friends."

"What about swimming practice?" Nicole asked, sliding off Finley's lap.

"We went after that."

"Was Will there?"

"Yes," Caitlin mumbled over her shoulder as she headed up the stairs.

"Do you think she's dating this boy, Will?" Nicole said.

"I don't know, but it's time we had a little talk with her about dating, and boys in general," Finley replied, standing up.

"Now?"

"Why not?" Finley shrugged, heading up the stairs.

Nicole hurried after her. "I was thinking of doing this after the regional swim meet."

"It's next weekend."

"I know that. I don't want to upset her and throw off her routine or anything. She's nervous as it is."

Finley laughed. "Talking to her about dating Will, and more importantly, not having sex with him, isn't going to have an effect, adverse or otherwise, on her swimming."

"I hope not," Nicole whispered as she knocked on the closed door. "Can we come in and talk to you for a minute?"

"What's up?" Caitlin asked, opening the door. "I'm doing my homework."

Finley noticed the large, opened textbook on her desk with a notepad next to it. "Have a seat," she said.

Caitlin sat back down at her desk while her mothers sat on the bed adjacent to her.

"You'll be sixteen in a few months, and you've been spending a lot more time with your friends, which we are fine with, but we need to lay down some ground rules about dating," Nicole stated.

"Seriously?" Caitlin questioned, looking at Finley.

"Hanging out with friends and going on dates with boys are two very different things. Teenage hormones are racing and things happen."

"Look, it's okay to have a boyfriend, but it's not okay to be having sex at your age. In fact, you shouldn't do anything intimate until you are with someone you want to spend the rest of your life with. Sex isn't something to do to look cool, or fit in with a crowd. You have your whole life ahead of you."

"I'm not having sex!" Caitlin squeaked.

"Great!" Finley exclaimed. "But, that doesn't mean some boy isn't going to try to get you to do it. We just want you to know the consequences of your actions, and having sex when you're under eighteen, still in high school, and more importantly, still a kid, is not the right action to take."

"Mom, I know. I'm not going to do anything stupid."

"We know you like Will, and that's great. But, school and swimming come before boys and dating. If you want to go on real dates, without your friends around, we want to meet him first. We'd also like to meet his parents," Nicole said.

"We're not dating. We're just friends that like each other and hangout a lot."

"Okay, well if it gets to that point, we want to know about it. You might be growing up, but you're still our little girl. It's our responsibility as parents to keep you safe, and make sure you know how to keep yourself safe and what to do if you get into trouble," Finley stated.

"You remember your karate lessons, right?" Nicole asked. Both Finley and Caitlin giggled. "What?" she asked.

"Mom, I was like seven or eight."

"So, something like that should stick with you."

"I'll be fine."

The doorbell rang, causing Finley to leave the conversation. She shuffled down the stairs and pulled the door open. A girl who looked about Caitlin's age, with light brown hair pulled back in a ponytail and big brown eyes, was standing on the doorstep.

"Uh, hi. Caitlin left this in my car, and I'm pretty sure she'll need it in the morning," the girl said, handing Caitlin's swim bag to Finley.

"Thanks. Would you like to come in?"

"Oh, no. I need to get home."

Finley nodded. She couldn't remember seeing the girl before, and was sure she wasn't on the school swim team. "What's your name?"

"Willa, but everyone calls me Will," she said with a smile.

Finley's jaw dropped. She stood in the open doorway stunned as the girl walked down the driveway and got into her small, dark-blue car.

Nicole walked down the last couple of stairs as Finley closed the front door. "What's that?"

"Caitlin's swim bag."

"Where did you get that?" Nicole questioned.

"Will just dropped it off."

"Oh, really? Why didn't you invite him in? What does he look like?"

"Sit down," Finley mumbled.

*

Jordy stood at the sink brushing her teeth. Ericka's eyes lingered over her in a deep stare for a split second as she prepared to get into the shower. Jordy tried ignoring her, but Ericka's naked body was clearly visible through the slightly open side of the shower curtain. Jordy leaned against the sink, watching her rinse the conditioner from her hair and begin to lather her silky smooth skin. Without hesitation, she crossed the room, pulling the shower curtain all the way open.

"What the hell!" Ericka shrieked.

"Why do you hate me so much?" Jordy inquired.

"What?" Ericka mumbled, looking at the brown eyes staring back at her. "I..." she swallowed the lump in her throat as Jordy moved closer.

"Answer me."

"Because."

"Because why?" Jordy questioned, running her eyes over Ericka's wet, naked body.

"Damn it!" Ericka growled, barely able to form a sentence. "I...hate you...because,"

Jordy raised her eyes to Ericka's.

"Because I want you," Ericka sighed. "I want you so damn bad," she whispered.

Jordy stepped into the shower, pushing her back against the tiled wall as the hot spray soaked her clothing. Their lips met in a frenzied kiss that left them both breathless.

Ericka reached up, tugging her dark hair loose from the bun it was in as she traced the outline of Jordy's thin lips with her tongue. At the same time, Jordy ran her hands down Ericka's wet body, caressing her breasts and flicking her nipples with her thumbs. Ericka moaned into her mouth. Jordy kissed her hard, before replacing her thumbs with her mouth, suckling one nipple while pinching the other one in a mixture of pleasure and pain that drove Ericka wild. She pushed her small breasts together, allowing Jordy to lick and suck them back and forth.

The spray of the shower felt hotter on her back as Jordy ran her hand down Ericka's slick thigh to the warm, wetness awaiting her. After a couple of lazy strokes and circles, Jordy pushed two fingers deep inside of her. Ericka sighed audibly and lifted her leg with her foot pressed against the side wall to give Jordy more access.

Jordy moved from suckling Ericka's breasts to kissing her passionately, matching the rhythm of her thrusts. Ericka hissed and gasped as she began to tremble. She wrapped her arms around Jordy's shoulders, gripping her wet t-shirt as she rode the waves of pleasure.

"I've got you," Jordy whispered in her ear as Ericka slowly lowered her leg to the shower floor.

They shared another passionate kiss, lingering against each other's lips before Ericka reached down to Jordy's pajama sweatpants. Despite being soaking wet, she was able to peel them down far enough to get to what she wanted. Jordy watched Ericka move to her knees and take her into her mouth.

Ericka could tell it wouldn't be long. Jordy was nearly gone just from touching her. She swirled her tongue around the warm, wet folds and sucked her center, before pushing her tongue inside. Jordy put one hand on the back of Ericka's head and the other on the wall of the shower as Ericka repeated the same licking and sucking pattern over and over.

Her legs quivered, barely able to hold her up as Jordy's body let go. She let out a guttural sigh before pulling Ericka to her feet. They fell into each other's tired arms as the water began to cool. Ericka reached back, turning it off while Jordy pulled her pants over her feet and tossed them into the sink across from them. She stepped out of the shower, removing her soaked t-shirt, flinging it into the sink on top of the pants.

Ericka stood on wobbly legs as she grabbed her towel and began to dry off. Jordy was a few feet away, wrapped in a towel, ringing the water out of her shoulder-length, chocolate-brown hair. Ericka's eyes turned shyly towards her, surprised to see Jordy looking back.

"We should get back to our bunks," Ericka muttered, as she began putting on her pajamas.

"I need dry clothes," Jordy stated. "I guess I could parade around in a towel. It's not like I give a shit what any of those guys think of me anyway." She shrugged, moving to walk out of the bathroom.

Ericka grabbed her arm. "Give me a minute," she sighed, tossing her wet towel into the laundry chute before leaving the room.

Jordy leaned against the sink, waiting for her to return. She hadn't intended on having sex with Ericka. In fact, that was the last thing on her mind. She honestly thought if anything physical happened between them, it would be a cat fight. Still, she couldn't resist temptation, especially when it was staring her right in the face. She'd been attracted to Ericka since the moment she first saw her, but the hostility she'd faced from her only succeeded in pushing Jordy to counterattack her with the same negative behavior.

Jordy shook her head. She'd been intimate with a few women, but had never been in a serious relationship, or in love for that matter. She was used to playing the game, giving and taking just like everyone else, but the situation with Ericka felt different.

"Here," Ericka said, handing Jordy a fresh t-shirt and pair of sweatpants. "I wasn't sure if you wanted anything to go under them, but since this was all you had on before…"

"It's fine." Jordy grinned.

"Okay," Ericka mumbled, walking back out of the room.

A lot had transpired, so Jordy wasn't expecting her to be very conversational, and maybe now wasn't the time, but they still needed to talk at some point.

*

"Are you serious?" Nicole exclaimed.

"Ssshhh!" Finley said.

"Why wouldn't she tell us Will was a girl?"

"I don't know."

"Is she gay?"

"I don't know. I didn't ask her!" Finley squawked.

"Not her! Caitlin!"

"I don't know!"

"Be quiet," Nicole hissed.

The two of them stared at each other for a second.

"What if she is gay?" Nicole whispered.

"Well, we're gay, so…"

"I know that. I mean…Hell, I don't know what I mean," she sighed, placing her hand on her forehead. "She should trust us enough to talk to us about it."

"Maybe she's confused, or even scared. I remember what life was like at her age."

"Yeah, me too. Maybe we should talk to her about it. What if she's not gay, but thinks she's supposed to be because we are?"

"Nic, you're reading way too much into this. If she's gay, she'll come to us when she's ready to tell us. For all we know, she could simply be testing the water."

"Oh, and that's better?" Nicole huffed, raising a brow.

"Well, no." Finley stared at her. "Do you want to go up there and point blank ask her if she's gay? What would you have done if your parents had done that to you?"

"I see your point. I guess…I guess I'm just surprised. The idea of her being gay never occurred to me," Nicole said, shaking her head in disbelief.

"Honestly, I wondered about it when she came down to stay with me that summer, but I figured I was merely seeing traits of myself in her, and that didn't mean she was gay."

"Why didn't you say anything to me?"

"Really?" Finley crossed her arms, giving her a stern expression.

"I know…we weren't exactly communicating back then," Nicole muttered, thinking back to that time in her life and all of the mistakes she'd made leading up to it. "I don't know about you, but I need a drink."

"After the day I've had…absolutely!"

They got up and walked to the kitchen together. Nicole poured herself a glass of wine, and Finley made a double whiskey on the rocks.

"Cheers to one of the weirdest days of my life!" Nicole laughed, clinking their glasses together.

"Amen!" Finley chuckled before taking a long swallow, feeling the slow burn as the alcohol made its way down to her stomach.

Chapter 15

Jordy and Ericka were in the pool yet again the next day, going through survivor retrieval drills with the rest of the class. This time, they were working with the hoist, learning the hand signals and procedures for being lowered and retrieved on the hook themselves first. Then, they moved on, adding the retrieval of a survivor to the mix, which put them back into pairs. Finley had paired Jordy and Ericka once more.

"Come on, ladies! Get it right. Burney, you have to be able to get Ross into the basket first. You cannot give the retrieval signal if your survivor is not secured!" Finley yelled.

Jordy was beginning to wonder if somehow Senior Chief knew what had transpired between her and Ericka. She seemed to be coming down on them twice as hard for the same simple mistakes other teams were making. Then again, maybe it was all in her head, and that's what was causing the mundane mistakes to begin with.

Finley watched Jordy and Ericka, and shook her head. They were still barely communicating, even after her lecture. "If the two of you don't communicate, you're going to bring each other down! Ross, get up on the tower. You're the swimmer now. We're changing things up."

Jordy sighed as she climbed out of the pool and headed up the ladder to the hoist unit. She sat down, waiting for Neil, who was acting as the Flight Mechanic, to connect her harness to the hook. She gave the ready signal and he raised the hoist to check the weight. Jordy gave him a thumbs up and he began lowering her down to the water. She unhooked the hoist and gave the 'all clear' signal, before swimming towards Ericka who was on the opposite end of the pool, floating on her back.

Finley motioned for Rich to get into the water quietly while Jordy swam out. He was told to play a second survivor who was panicking.

"I'm a Coast Guard Rescue Swimmer and I'm going to save you," Jordy said, from a few feet away. "Are you hurt?"

"No. I'm just very tired," Ericka responded. "Get me out of here."

"Turn around. I'm going to do the swimming for both of us," Jordy said.

Finley nodded for Rich to join in. He quickly swam up, grabbing Jordy from behind, dragging both her and Ericka underwater. Jordy let go of Ericka, pushing her back up as she fought to get Rich off of her.

"What the fuck!" she choked, gasping for air at the surface.

"Always check your surroundings. You need to know how many survivors there are, and whether or not any of them are in panic mode. Continue!" Finley stated.

Jordy swore under breath and turned back towards Ericka, who looked just as pissed. "I'm going to swim her to safety first. I'll be right back for you," she said to Rich. Then, grabbing Ericka once more, she pulled her close and swam over to the tower, giving the signal for the basket.

Neil lowered the equipment on the hoist. Jordy helped Ericka get inside and secure herself, before swimming away and giving the signal to retrieve her.

141

Ericka was lifted back up to the tower as Jordy swam back to Rich.

"Come on, you ass," she muttered, grabbing a hold of him.

"Hey, Senior Chief made me do it," he replied as she swam them back across the pool.

"Oh, I'm sure she did. She hates me and Ericka."

"Really? Why?"

"No idea," she said. "What's wrong with you, anyway? Are you good to go up in the sling, or are you dying and shit?"

Rich laughed.

"What's so funny over there?" Finley growled. "Is this a game to you?"

"No, Senior Chief!" they said simultaneously.

"Do a double pickup," Finley yelled.

"Damn it, I forgot the signal," Jordy whispered.

"There's no specific sign. Just signal for pickup, like you would for yourself," he whispered back.

Jordy connected the locking hooks from her harness onto the lifting ring of Rich's harness and threw up the signal to be retrieved. She waited for the hook to touch the water, so it didn't shock her, then she connected the hoist hook to her lifting ring and signaled that they were ready to be picked up. As soon as she was out of the water, Jordy wrapped her arms and legs around Rich to keep him still. When they reached the tower, she made sure he went into the makeshift helicopter cabin first. Once she was inside and the survivor was secure, she released the hoist hook from her harness.

"Get down off my tower!" Finley yelled.

When everyone was back on the ground, standing at attention, she paced the floor in front of them. "Mistakes are still being made. Simple, ignorant, mistakes! Chief Denny, what happens when you make a mistake with a survivor in six foot waves, over a hundred miles off shore?"

"Someone dies, Senior Chief!"

"Exactly! Someone dies." Finley shook her head. She stopped pacing, coming to a halt in front of Jordy and Ericka. "If you cannot communicate with your survivor or with your crew, you are deaf and blind in the water. That is the absolute last place you want to be. Pay attention! Know your surroundings! Use the correct hand signals! If you want to laugh and play games, there is the door. Go pack your bag, and I'll have you on the first plane or bus out of here!"

The class remained quiet and perfectly still as she began pacing again.

"You are here for two things. The first, is to see if you are physically capable of becoming a Helicopter Rescue Swimmer. The second, is to see if you are mentally able to handle the rigorous work that comes with the job. If you cannot get these maneuvers and hand signals down in a ten-foot deep swimming pool, you will never be able to handle them in the ocean waves and rotor wash!" She put them in groups of three, keeping Ericka, Jordy, and Rich together. "Now, we're going to rerun the same scenario until every team of three has a successful double retrieval. If we have to stay in here all night, then so be it! Get back in line for the tower!" she shouted. "You want to play God damn games in my pool, we'll play them!" she spat angrily.

"Man, Ross, you really pissed her off," Evan mumbled.

"Me? I don't even know what I did."

"Be quiet down there!" Neil yelled to the cadets standing in line.

*

It was after dark when the cadets had finally succeeded in getting through the drill without missing steps, using the wrong hand signal, or handling the situation incorrectly. As soon as they were dismissed, they changed into dry clothes and raced over to the mess hall for dinner chow as fast as their tired bodies would allow.

"That woman is itching to see me quit," Jordy huffed.

"She has a hard-on for all of us because you girls keep screwing up," Jon growled.

"Oh, please. We all made mistakes! If anyone is to blame, it's the entire class," Evan said. "We are one unit, remember? Rise together, fall together."

"Get your lips off Senior Chief's ass," Jon spat. "I'm here for me. I'm not failing and washing out because a bunch of pansy-asses can't figure out how to give a hand signal and shove someone into a God damn metal basket!"

"Look, jackass, we all had problems, including you and your team, so don't act like you were exemplary. Everyone overcame their issues and got through the drill. Move the fuck on...Okay? It's over with," Jordy said, shaking her head.

"No, you look, bitch!" Jon shouted, jumping out of his seat. He lunged towards her with his fist out, but Rich blocked him, connecting his own fist with the side of Jon's jaw, splitting his lip.

The two men tussled, rolling around on the ground. Evan, Jordy, and a few of the other guys finally got them apart just before Finley and Neil arrived, after being called by the mess hall staff.

"What the hell has gotten into all of you?" Finley yelled as they stood at attention in front of her, along the front wall of the mess hall. "I've been here almost three years, and I've never seen a more immature group of cadets come through this school. Each one of you is still here because you've made it this far, but it doesn't mean you all deserve to be here. Being a Helicopter Rescue Swimmer is an honor! A privilege to less than one percent of the United States Coast Guard! The next time any of you shames another, plays games, or just plain fucks up...you are out of here! I will not let you shame the honor that we carry. Do you hear me?"

"Yes, Senior Chief," they said together.

"Now, sit down, eat your chow, and get your asses back to the dorm! Webber and Parish, I'll deal with you two in the morning. Be at my office at six a.m.," she growled before walking away.

"You guys are almost halfway through this," Neil said. "Why jeopardize it? When you lie in your bunk tonight, look back on how far you've come. A third of your class has washed out because they couldn't cut it, and here you are fighting with each other because you're a bunch of hotheads who know nothing about accountability. What a disgrace to the uniform you are wearing," he finished, shaking his head, before yelling, "Dismissed!"

*

Finley avoided going back to her office. She was already mentally drained from the long, frustrating day of training in the pool room. The debacle in the mess hall had been the final straw. She simply needed to go home before she failed the entire class. The dark, cloudless sky was full of stars. The steady hum of a C-130 flying low in the distance, preparing to land, was the only sound she heard as she crossed the parking lot.

As soon as she was inside of her SUV, Finley tossed her uniform ball cap into the passenger seat and started the engine. Aerosmith's song *Dude (Looks Like a Lady)* was playing on the radio. She cranked the volume and sang along at the top of her lungs as she drove down the road.

By the time Finley arrived at home, her aggravation had subsided. She pulled into the driveway and climbed out with a smile on her face, thinking back to when she and Nicole once sang that song at a karaoke bar when they snuck in as teenagers. As soon as she was out of the truck, a small blue car pulled into the driveway behind her. She turned around, trying to see inside, but it was too dark. The passenger door swung open and Caitlin stepped out.

"You're getting home a little late," Finley muttered.

Caitlin shrieked, nearly jumping out of her skin. "We were studying and lost track of time," she said.

Finley nodded, noticing the Starbucks cup in her hand. "Since when do you drink coffee?"

"It's green tea."

"Is that the stuff your mom drinks?"

Caitlin nodded. "She said it's better for you than coffee."

Finley rolled her eyes. "Come on," she said, gesturing towards the passenger side of her SUV.

"Where are we going?" Caitlin questioned as she slid into the passenger seat.

"All of this talk about coffee makes me want some," Finley replied, starting the car. Foreigner's song *Hot Blooded* began blaring on the radio.

"What the…" Caitlin reached for the volume.

146

"Don't you dare change my music!" Finley chided, singing along. "This is much better than that trunk-thumping crap you listen to." She shook her head. "I'll have you know; this band was my first concert!"

Caitlin laughed, noticing the Sirius XM station was Classic Rock. "And I don't listen to rap, which is what you're referring to. I like pop music, you know: Pink, Rihanna, Taylor Swift, Beyonce—"

"Uh huh. Does Will listen to that same music?"

"No. Country," Caitlin sighed. "But, I'm trying to change that."

Finley pulled into Dunkin Donuts. "Come on. We'll sneak a doughnut. Mom will never know."

Caitlin chuckled as she got out.

*

"You know she always knows when you try to hide something from her," Caitlin chided as they placed their order.

"That's because I tell her. We don't keep any secrets from each other. It's damn near impossible anyway. You'll figure that out one day when you are in a relationship with someone you love," Finley said, sitting down in the booth across from her daughter. She had a small regular coffee in front of her, and they both had a marble, frosted doughnut.

"Yeah…" Caitlin mumbled. She stared out the window for a minute, then turned back to Finley. "Mom…when did you know?"

"Know what?" Finley asked, sending Nicole a text message that she had Caitlin and would be home in a bit.

Caitlin waited for her to look up, at which time she cocked her head to the side and said, "You know…"

Finley furrowed her brow as she ate her doughnut. Then, like a bolt of lightning, it hit her, causing her to choke. She took a sip of her coffee to wash the food down and calm her nerves. *Is this it? Are we seriously about to have this talk in the middle of Dunkin Donuts?* she thought. "Well…" she croaked, clearing her voice. "I probably knew for a long time, but I guess I was around your age when I figured it out."

"I…I don't know if I can handle it. There's so much pressure. I mean, I'm not even sixteen yet."

"Caitlin, you're absolutely right. You're still so young. You have your whole life ahead of you, and who knows, you may decide to date both guys and girls. You don't have to narrow it to one or the other right now, and no one should be pressuring you to do so. Just because you have two moms, doesn't necessarily mean you're gay, too."

"What!" Caitlin shrieked.

"You asked—"

"I didn't mean that! I meant with being really good at swimming and having Olympic potential. Coach said there is a possibility I could be scouted for the regular national team, not the juniors," she said, shaking her head. "I thought he talked to you."

Finley shook her head no.

"And by the way, I'm not dating Will or anyone else. I have too much going on right now with swimming to think about any of that," she added, eating her doughnut.

"Okay," Finley uttered, finishing her coffee and doughnut. "With the regional meet this weekend, Coach Whitehall should've gone over the scouting with Mom and I, especially if that's true."

"I figured he did."

"No. At least not with me. It was chaotic today at the base with my class, so I haven't even talked to your mother. Anyway, don't worry about it. You go and swim your races the same way you always do, no matter who is watching. If your coach is pressuring you, then that's something he and I need to have a discussion about."

"He's a great coach. I think he just wants to see me succeed. He tells me all the time that I have the potential to be at the top. He said this weekend is my time to shine and prove that I belong there."

"Caitlin, you have so much ahead of you. It doesn't have to be right this minute. You can try to make the national team, or even Olympic team, ten years from now, if you want to. You know that, right? Most competitive swimmers peak in their twenties anyway. Win or lose, no matter what, I'm extremely proud of you, and I always will be. If you told me you never want to swim again, I'd say okay without questioning you."

"I know, Mom. I love you for that."

Finley stood up and hugged her daughter. "Let's head home. I'm sure your mom has dinner waiting for us."

*

After dinner, Caitlin went up to her room to work on her homework before getting ready for bed. Finley poured a tumbler glass of whiskey on ice and sat down on the couch in the den.

"Rough day?" Nicole asked, rubbing her hand over Finley's shoulders as she passed by, moving to sit next to her.

"Something like that," she sighed. "My cadets got a little out of hand today, which led to our drill going some three hours longer than normal. They were aggravated, tired, hungry, you name it. Anyway, two of them squared off in the mess hall. Neil and I had to break it up."

"Wow," Nicole exclaimed in shock.

"Yeah. Needless to say, they're probably all going to hate me after tomorrow."

"I bet," Nicole laughed. "I know how hard-nosed and unrelenting you can be."

Finley furrowed her brow in disagreement.

"Don't look at me like that. I've been on the receiving end of your angry side a few times. It's not fun."

Finley's blue eyes softened, remembering how difficult things had gotten between them when they were apart.

"I'm only saying, I feel a little bad for the cadets." She smiled as she leaned in, kissing Finley's soft lips.

"They should be tossed out of the school," Finley uttered.

"Yes." Nicole agreed. "Instead, you're going to give them a Senior Chief Finley Morris wake-up call. Am I right?"

"You know me too well," Finley chuckled.

Nicole raised a brow and gave her a sly grin.

"Hey, speaking of hard-asses, have you spoken to Coach Whitehall lately?"

"Not since I booked our trip to Atlanta for the regional swim meet, which was about a month ago. Why?"

"Just something Caitlin said to me tonight. I think he's putting her under too much pressure."

"What was it?"

"He told her national team scouts were coming to watch her swim."

"Well, they are."

"No, not the junior team. He said they are looking at her for the regular national team."

"Seriously? Why haven't we heard anything about this? She's not even sixteen years old."

"I don't know. She thought he'd talked to one of us."

"It wasn't me," Nicole huffed. "If she fails, this is going to crush her."

"We had a long talk, after I embarrassed both of us, of course."

"What happened?"

"I thought she was coming out to me."

"What? You mean like…"

"Yes!"

"What made you think that? Weren't you at the doughnut place?"

"Yes!" Finley shook her head. "She asked me when I knew."

"Knew? About what?"

"Exactly," Finley stated with a stern expression. "I thought she was asking me if I knew when I was gay, so I told her. Then, I went into how she doesn't have to decide right now, blah, blah, blah."

"Oh, my God," Nicole laughed. "I bet she wanted to crawl under the table."

"I think we both did," Finley chuckled.

"It sounds like you were on completely different pages."

"Hell, we were in different books!"

Nicole giggled. "Do I even want to know how it all ended?"

"She freaked out at first, but then she told me about Coach Whitehall talking about the national team. She did tell me she wasn't dating Will or anyone else and didn't plan on it. She's really put herself under a lot of pressure." Nicole shook her head.

"I told her she could stop at any time, and we would be fine with that, but it's her dream. She wants to be an Olympian."

"She's so much like you," Nicole muttered. "I remember when swimming for the University of South Carolina was all you talked about. Then, becoming a rescue swimmer took over your life. You give everything you have when you set your mind on something. It's a true passion. Most people will go their entire lives without ever having that kind of drive and determination." She squeezed Finley's hand. "I even see it now, with you instructing at the school. You give everything to each class that comes through there, making sure those who are lucky enough to graduate, are worthy enough of the honor they're receiving."

"Thank you," Finley murmured, wrapping her arm around Nicole.

*

The next day, which was Friday, class 16-20 was huddled together, shivering in a small, three-and-a-half-foot deep inflatable training pool.

"We usually do this at the end of Phase Two, but after recent events, I decided the entire class needed to cool off," Finley said as she began explaining the effects of hypothermia while Neil tossed more ice inside the cold water. She kept the time on a stopwatch as she observed the temperature, slowly moving lower.

"Whether you work in Florida or Alaska, you need to know what this is like; how your body reacts to it; and most importantly, how to save someone who is suffering from it."

Jordy's teeth chattered and her body trembled. She'd never been so cold in her life. Her feet and legs had begun to go numb, making it difficult for her to stand. The water was only waist deep, but the cold temperature of her lower extremities had worked its way throughout her entire body. This same effect had happened to the entire class, showing them what it was physically like when hypothermia began to set in. She looked over at Ericka who was about five feet away, also quivering from the cold. They'd barely said two words to each other since the shower incident three days earlier. Jordy figured she needed time and that's why she hadn't spoken to her, other than class related conversation while working together in the pool.

"The longer you stay in there, the more the cold will spread, slowly shutting down your circulatory system until your heart finally stops," Finley stated. "Now, since you all like games, let's play one. Parish and Webber, get out of the water."

Both men looked at her oddly, but quickly climbed out of the pool.

"Alright. Hit the ground and give me ten pushups. When you're finished, you will both add more ice, and then get back in the water. I'll call on one of you to pick one of your classmates to get out and warm up. After that, you'll do it all over again. We're going to keep going until you either get everyone out of the water and save them from the nasty effects of full-blown hypothermia, or one of you quits and washes out right here."

Jon and Rich stared at her with wide eyes.

"Hit the deck!" she yelled.

The rest of the class counted each pushup and the guys moved up and down. When they finished, they added more ice and climbed back into the frigid water.

"Jon, you go first," Finley said.

His teeth chattered as he called a name. The cadet slowly got out, grabbing the towel that Neil held for him. Then, he headed towards a heated pool on the opposite side of the room that was being used to bring their temperature back up.

"Back out of the water, gentlemen!" Finley yelled.

Both men shivered through their pushups, added more ice to the pool, and climbed back in. The two men had to wait in the freezing cold pool until the cadet they called was all the way across the room and into the other pool, before Finley told them to get out again.

"Rich, pick a classmate."

He quickly said Jordy's name, knowing Jon would leave her for last. She waded over to the side, climbing out with no assistance as she quivered.

"Senior Chief," she said through rattling teeth. "Can I join them?"

Finley looked at her with a raised brow. "You want to do pushups and get back into the cold water, instead of getting warm?"

"Yes, Senior Chief. We're a team. No man left behind."

"Alright. Webber and Parish, get out. All three of you, hit the deck!"

Jordy closed her eyes and used everything she had to concentrate on the pushups. She couldn't simply watch Rich go through all of that knowing he'd fought with Jon because he was lunging for her. As soon as they were back into the pool, she felt her heart rate sky-rocket. Finley called her name to choose a cadet. Knowing Ericka was so cold her lips were turning blue, she quickly said her name. Ericka could barely climb out of the cold pool, and needed Neil's help to get over to the warm one. It took two more rounds for each of them, but together, they got the rest of the cadets out of the cold pool and into the warmer water. Then, they joined the group.

"After you've spent fifteen minutes in the warming pool, you can head to the locker room for a hot shower before dinner chow," Finley said, prior to leaving Neil in charge, as she headed out for the day, a little early.

*

"Thank you," Ericka muttered as Jordy stepped out of the shower stall next to the one she'd just exited.

"No problem," Jordy said, looking into her eyes. "I couldn't let you stay in there, freezing to death." She quickly dried her body with a towel.

Ericka moved to walk away.

"Wait. Can we talk?" Jordy said, grabbing her hand.

"I don't know what to say."

"How about we start with, I'm glad we got that hate thing cleared up?" She shrugged.

"It's a little more complicated than that," Ericka replied.

"I'm all ears," Jordy stated, letting go of her. "I'd say we have all night, but I'm done with being cold." She smiled.

Ericka wrapped her towel tightly around her midsection, tucking the corner at the top between her breasts. Jordy did the same.

"Seven weeks ago, I was in a relationship that had lasted over two years, and I was starting an incredible journey towards the next chapter of my life," Ericka said. "Then, I saw this girl walk by, taking my breath away with her beautiful brown eyes and adorable smile as she passed. I tried to calm my racing thoughts, remembering my life back home and the reason I was here," she continued. "Something shifted. That exciting, incredible day turned ugly in a split second. A stupid, sexist comment was made and I just stood there, taking it. That girl, the one who had my head spinning in the wrong direction, countered the attack, standing up for me. I had never felt so small in my life. I was embarrassed for a multitude of reasons. Here I was ogling a complete stranger, something that had never happened before, all the while in a committed relationship, so I felt guilty as hell. Then, I looked helpless after she stood up for me because I was too distraught with my own thoughts to do it myself." Ericka stopped and looked up at Jordy.

"So, you see, you've been in my head, bouncing around like a pinball for the past seven weeks. I hated the fact that you were there. I hated myself for putting you there. I hated that I looked weak in front of you. But...I never hated you, Jordy. None of this was your fault," she began to cry.

"Hey..." Jordy said, stepping closer.

"You think I'm crazy. Don't you?" she sniffled, wiping her tears.

"No." Jordy shook her head.

"I've gotten so lost in my own head, trying to be better than you and causing fights between us, all because I have feelings for you, and I made you think I was weak," Ericka sighed.

"I never thought you were weak, Ericka. I honestly had no idea why you acted like you hated me, but it only fueled me more, driving me to focus on competing against you." She grabbed Ericka's hands. "I thought you were beautiful when I saw you the very first day. Even when you acted like an ass, I still found you cute, and that drove me crazy." She smiled. "If we'd only communicated with each other, these past seven weeks would've been a lot different."

"I was in a relationship," Ericka said.

"I'm assuming that's over."

"Yes, or I never would've done what we did."

Jordy nodded.

"What about you? There's no one waiting back home?"

"There is no home," Jordy muttered.

"What?"

"That's a story for another time, but no, I've never been serious with anyone."

"Where does this leave us?" Ericka said, brushing her fingers over Jordy's cheek.

"Right here, for the next twelve weeks at least." Jordy grinned.

"I don't think there's anywhere I'd rather be, and this place is like hell with a water slide."

Jordy laughed. "Let's make a deal to get through it together."

"There's no one I want standing next to me, more than you, at graduation," Ericka replied, kissing her softly.

"Are you sure? Jon could be available," Jordy teased. "He did have a hard-on for you at one time."

"I'd rather run my fingers through a food processor than have sex with him," Ericka grimaced.

Jordy laughed, pulling her into hug. "I'm kind of fond of those fingers of yours, so I'll make sure Jon keeps a safe distance," she teased.

Chapter 16

Nicole and Caitlin had flown down to Atlanta for the regional swim meet earlier in the day so that Caitlin could get acclimated to her setting and quell some of her nerves, leaving Finley to fly alone after work on Friday. She'd tried to catch a cargo transport headed in that direction, but the next flight out would put her arrival literally two hours after the meet was set to begin Saturday morning. Therefore, she settled on a Delta flight that would get her there just after dinner.

Tossing her small overnight bag into the overhead compartment, Finley squeezed herself into the middle row seat in the coach section. She didn't have a lot of room to stretch her legs, especially after a large man with a handlebar mustache and a bald head, squished himself into the aisle seat. She nodded politely and glanced at the empty window seat beside her, hoping whoever had purchased that one was the size of a midget, or they were going to have one hell of an uncomfortable flight.

After a few more minutes passed and boarding seemed to have ceased, Finley stretched more into the empty seat and buckled her safety belt. The planes twin turbine engines were humming steadily, and the flight attendants were moving quickly down the aisle, closing all of the overhead bins.

All of a sudden, a last minute passenger appeared, shuffling her way towards Finley, with her large, round bosom flopping from side to side under the floral printed top she was wearing. The gargantuan purple hat she was carrying smacked people in the face as she pushed passed them, and her reading glasses swung around on their chain, bouncing on her full bust.

"Oh, shit," Finley whispered, watching the woman read the row numbers.

Sure enough, the older woman stopped next to the man beside Finley.

"I think that's my seat," she said. "Is this 29C?"

Finley sighed and unbuckled her belt as the man got up. She too, got out of her seat so that the woman could get to the window.

"This is my first time flying," she said excitedly. "The security people had to go through my bags. Apparently, you can't bring hair spray on a plane," she added, shaking her head. "Oh, well. When your kids get you a trip to the Bahamas for your sixtieth birthday, you go, right?"

Finley nodded as the plane pushed back from the gate and headed out towards the runway, bouncing lightly across the asphalt.

"My name's Betty. And you are?"

"Finley," she said, trying not to disappear between the two people on either side of her as the plane lifted off the ground, rising into the clouds.

"That's a unique name. Anyway, it's nice to meet you. Where are you headed?"

"Atlanta," she muttered, wishing she'd brought her headphones and iPod.

"That's a short ride for you then. I'm headed all the way down to Grand Bahama Island. My daughter and her husband live out in Texas where he is stationed in the

National Guard. Anyway, they booked this week long trip for all of us for my birthday. It was a huge surprise," she rambled. "So, what's in Atlanta? Is that where you're from?" she asked, eyeing Finley's jeans and gray, cable-knit sweater.

"I'm from Charleston. My daughter has a swim meet down there this weekend," she replied, wondering why she was still talking to this woman. She snuck a peek at the man next to her. He'd been smart enough to bring headphones and was watching a movie on his phone. *Remember now why you don't fly commercial...ever?* She mentally chided herself.

"My daughter tried swimming once, but that didn't pan out," Betty went on. "However, she went on to discover dancing. That took her all the way through college with aspirations of dancing in a ballet company. Oh, she danced beautifully," she beamed. "Anyway, she met her husband, and well, now she's a military wife, following him all over the globe," she sighed.

Finley raised a brow. She wasn't exactly sure what to say. She knew that scenario all too well. It's part of what drove the wedge between her and Nicole the first time around, and here they were, headed in the same direction. Life certainly wasn't easy for the spouse of someone in the military, especially those who traveled frequently and were often stationed overseas. The woman's comment made her stop and think about Nicole. They'd only briefly discussed her next post. What were Nicole's true thoughts and feelings about it? The first time around they'd simply packed up and moved every three years. Nicole had gone along, no questions asked. Maybe this time, Finley needed to start asking questions. She'd do anything to keep from losing Nicole again…possibly even retire early. That thought scared the hell out of her.

The plane touching down on the runway in Atlanta, jolted her back to reality. She couldn't believe she'd let this complete stranger send her mind off into left field. One thing was for certain, she needed to talk to Nicole. They were set to walk down the aisle in eight weeks.

*

"Hey, Mom. How was your flight?" Caitlin asked, hugging Finley when she walked into the hotel room.

"Mind-numbing. I was squished between a giant man and an older, round woman with huge boobs, who literally talked for the entire hour and twenty minutes," Finley said, wrapping her arms around her not-so-little girl. "Did you go to the aquatic center?"

"Yes. It's so cool! Did you know our meet is being held where the 1996 Summer Olympic Games were?"

"Mom mentioned it. That's pretty neat. Where is she, by the way?"

"She went to go find some bottled water. The tap water tastes like rusty pipes."

Finley gave her a stern look. "What do you think of this room?" she asked, checking out the two-bedroom suite they were in. "It's about the size of the first apartment your mom and I had together."

"That's exactly what she said." Caitlin smiled. "I'm just glad I have my own room. I need absolute quiet so that I can concentrate and get enough sleep."

Finley rolled her eyes at the overdramatic teenager and changed the channel on the TV in the small living space.

"Hey, you," Nicole said with a smile, noticing her as soon as she walked in. "How was your day?"

"There's not enough alcohol in this room," Finley mumbled, getting up to help her with the plastic bag full of bottled water. She leaned in, kissing her softly.

"There's no alcohol," Nicole laughed.

"Exactly."

"That bad?"

"The class was fine. I pretty much froze them half to death during hypothermia training. It was part punishment for the childish behavior the day before, as well as a team-building exercise. Let's just say I won this round. I doubt they'll do anything to piss me off anytime soon."

Nicole nodded as she began putting the bottles into the refrigerator. "The water is gross. Don't drink it."

"I heard it tastes like pipes," Finley stated.

"Ugh...yes. This place reminds me so much of Oak Grove Apartments."

"Me too! Lucky number 7B," Finley chuckled.

"The water there was disgusting too." Nicole smiled, reminiscing about their first place together. "Only two burners on the stove worked, and the carpet smelled like cat pee, but we were in hog heaven!"

"Hell yeah we were. No parents, no rules...just you, me, and that thing," she said, tilting her head towards the bedroom Caitlin was in as she smiled.

"I think about that time often, before she was born. It seems like a lifetime ago."

"In a way it was, for us at least."

"Are we going to dinner anytime soon? I ate a lot of carbs today, so I'm just going to have veggies for dinner, but I don't want to eat late. My first prelim is at eight a.m.," Caitlin said, stepping out of the bedroom.

Nicole shot Finley a look, as if to say 'The Diva has spoken.'

Finley suppressed a grin as she shrugged. "I think I saw an Olive Garden down the road. Will that do?"

"It was Olivia's," Nicole corrected.

"Oh. Well, I was close."

"I saw their menu when I was downstairs. It looked pretty good."

"Do they have vegetables?" Finley asked. "Michael Phelps needs her veggies," she joked.

"Funny, Mom. Ha-Ha," Caitlin chided, crossing her arms. The stern look on her face was the same one Finley had seen on Nicole a number of times.

"Come on. I'm sure they do," Nicole said, grabbing their room key and her purse.

*

The aquatic center was chaotic the next morning as parents, coaches, family members, and scouts gathered for the races. Finley and Nicole had given Caitlin a brief pep talk and one last hug, before taking their seats in the stands.

"I don't think I've ever seen this many people at one of her swim meets," Nicole said. "She's going to have a lot of competition."

"It's the southeast regional, so there are people here from multiple states," Finley replied, looking around. "She'll be fine. You worry enough for the three of us."

Nicole smiled and bumped shoulders with her.

"I've been looking all over for the two of you!" Jackie Morris said, making her way through the crowd to sit with them as the preliminaries began.

"I thought you weren't going to make it," Finley questioned, hugging her mother before she sat down beside her.

"I didn't think I was, but the plumber finally got everything fixed by ten o'clock last night. I felt bad for him, but he kept saying he wasn't leaving the job unfinished. As soon as he left, I booked the first morning flight."

"She'll be happy to see you," Nicole said with a smile. "I'm glad you got everything taken care of."

"Me too. I'm only glad the damn pipe burst before I left. Otherwise, I would've come home to a swimming pool on my first floor!"

"That's crazy," Nicole replied.

"Are you staying at the same hotel as us?"

"Yes. I only canceled last night," Jackie replied. "If he wasn't able to get it fixed, I was going to shut everything off and deal with it on Monday."

"Here we go," Finley cheered as Caitlin stepped up onto the block for her first of two preliminary races.

*

By the time the preliminaries were over, it was almost eleven a.m. Finley's butt hurt from sitting on the metal bleachers. Caitlin had easily qualified for the semifinals in both of her races, which would take place after the medley and relay semifinals.

Nicole, Finley, and Jackie spent the afternoon cheering on all of the kids with the rest of the crowd until the freestyle semifinal events started.

"I wish I could give her another hug," Nicole mumbled, watching Caitlin walk out for her race, the 50-meter freestyle.

"She knows we're here," Finley said, squeezing her hand as she studied their daughter's every move.

Caitlin removed her warm-up pants and jacket, placing them to the side with her sandals. She adjusted her swimsuit and glanced up at the crowd before pulling her goggles down over her eyes. After stretching her arms out to get the blood flowing, she climbed up onto the block and got into position.

"Swimmers...take your mark. Get set..." *Beep!* The buzzer sounded and Caitlin dove off the block into the pool. She dolphin kicked under the water for a few strides, before coming to the surface. She swam overhand, breathing in on every other stroke, kicking her legs with practiced precision as she propelled herself across the pool.

"Go, Caitlin!" Nicole cheered.

"That's my girl!" Finley yelled as Caitlin's name flashed across the large screen in first place.

"Man, that kid can swim," Jackie said with a smile and a little fist pump.

The family watched the kids from earlier, swim in the medley and relay semifinals. Then, an hour later, Caitlin's family watched and cheered as she did the same thing as before for the 200-meter freestyle, once again finishing first.

*

The final races began around 5p.m. Everyone in the crowd was on the edge of their seat, cheering wildly, as each race finished in dramatic fashion. It reminded Finley of watching the swimming part of the summer Olympics. The cheers and chants echoed in the large room, bringing her adrenaline level that much higher as she watched her daughter step up on the block one more time. The 50-meter freestyle was the fastest of all the races, followed by the 100 meter and 200 meter in the same event. They were the same three races that she'd participated in as well.

Both on their feet, Nicole grabbed Finley's arm as the buzzer beeped. For the next twenty-six seconds, they each held their breath. It felt like they were watching in slow motion as Caitlin seemed to find another gear that no one else had, pushing herself nearly half a body length ahead of the next fastest girl.

Finley began jumping up and down as Caitlin's name flashed on the screen in first place. "Yes! Yes! Yes!" she yelled and fist pumped the air with excitement written all over her face, before hugging her mother and Nicole.

Caitlin smiled and waved up at the crowd, not quite sure where her family was, but she heard them shouting her name. The mass of people kept the cheers going for the boy's 50-meter freestyle, which was next.

"How much time do we have before her next race?" Jackie asked.

"Probably an hour," Finley replied. "I'm about to starve to death. That lunch in the café was no bigger than a snack."

"I'm hungry too, but right now, I have to pee."

Nicole laughed. "I'll go with you."

*

Caitlin went on to win her second race with the same charismatic fashion as the first, drawing huge cheers from the crowd. She smiled and waved as she stood on the podium, accepting her first place medals after all of the events had finished for the day.

Once the award ceremony was over, Finley, Nicole, and Jackie rushed over to her.

"Grammy!" Caitlin squealed. "I thought your house was flooded?"

"It was, but I wouldn't miss this for the world. I love you, kid!" Jackie replied, giving her a big hug.

"I knew you could do it. You had yourself so worked up over nothing," Finley said, pulling Caitlin into a tight hug.

"It's tomorrow's race that I'm not sure about. I knew I had these two in the bag after prelims," Caitlin said with a sly grin identical to Finley's.

Finley laughed and shook her head. "We're all hungry, so what do you want for dinner? Our options are limited if you only want veggies again, Phelps."

Caitlin rolled her eyes. "No. I need to refuel on carbs. So, any kind of pasta place is good with me."

"Wonderful. There's an Italian place next door to the hotel," Nicole said.

*

After dinner, Caitlin took a shower and went straight to bed to rest up for the next day, leaving Finley and Nicole alone since Jackie was in her own room, on a different floor.

"Do you want to take a walk with me?" Finley asked, the thoughts that were provoked by the conversation with the odd woman on the plane, were still weighing on the back of her mind.

"Um...ok? Did you have a place in mind?" Nicole questioned, looking oddly at her.

"I was just thinking maybe out by the pool or something. You know, get some fresh air. I feel like my lungs are full of chlorine."

Nicole chuckled and grabbed her coat. "What if she wakes up and we're not here?"

"She's almost sixteen. I'm sure she'll see our stuff is still here and realize we haven't abandoned her," Finley said.

The air was cool and crisp, but not as cold as Charleston. Finley held Nicole's hand as they walked down the path that led around the outdoor pool, to the gazebo on the opposite side.

"What do you want to happen when my post is up?" Finley asked, sitting down on the wooden bench as Nicole sat next to her.

"What do you mean?"

"We haven't really talked about it."

"I guess we'll go wherever the Coast Guard sends you. Isn't that how it works?"

"Well, yes. But, is being a military wife what you really want? Moving every three years?"

"Finley, where is all of this coming from?" Nicole asked, looking into her deep blue eyes.

"I've never asked your opinion. I always just expected you to pack up and go with me. I think that was part of our problem the first time around. I don't want to make the same mistake twice," Finley sighed.

"Honey, my mother was our problem, not your job. Yes, moving every three years is a hindrance, but it's not going to keep us apart, not now, not ever again. I'll move to the middle of the desert, and ride a camel to work, if it means I get to have you by my side as my wife."

Finley smiled. "I love you."

"I love you, too," Nicole said, leaning in to kiss her softly.

*

Sunday's races had gone quite the same as the day before, with Caitlin winning the 100-meter freestyle, by a noticeable margin. When the competition officially ended, a man and a woman approached Nicole and Finley while they waited for Caitlin to finish taking pictures with her grandmother on the podium. The two people were dressed in jeans and polo shirts with USA Swimming stitched on the upper left chest.

"I'm Matt Dowling and this is Cynthia Regatta. We're with the USA National Swim Team," the man said, shaking their hands. "We'd like to talk to you about Caitlin's performance this weekend."

"Since she won all of her events, will she be invited to the Junior National Team tryouts for all three?" Nicole asked.

"Absolutely," he began. "However, Caitlin's times were much faster than what we are looking for at the junior level."

"Wow," Finley uttered. "I knew she was fast…" She shook her head.

"We are inviting her to come try out for the full USA National Team."

"Are you serious?" Nicole mumbled, looking wide-eyed at Finley.

"Yes, ma'am. You'll receive the official invite in the mail within the next week," Cynthia stated. "Caitlin has a lot of talent. We're looking forward to seeing what she does in our pool."

Finley and Nicole said goodbye to them, then simply stared at each other in disbelief.

*

The short plane ride home was quiet. Finley and Nicole hadn't spoken to Caitlin, other than to say she was invited for tryouts in all three of her events. She'd already put herself under so much pressure, and that was for the junior team tryouts.

"What do you think we should do?" Nicole asked, as they unloaded the luggage from Finley's SUV.

"I don't know," she sighed. "I'm sure her coach knows. He's liable to blab about it first thing in the morning when she goes to practice." She closed the door, checking her watch. "Maybe we should tell her tonight."

"I agree," Nicole replied. "Caitlin," she called, walking into the house. The teenager had already rushed up the stairs to her bedroom to clean out her suitcase, put her winning medals on the wall with her others, and get ready for school the next day.

"Yes ma'am?" she asked, trotting down the stairs.

"We want to talk to you for a second," Finley stated, motioning for her to go into the den.

"What's up?" she asked, sitting on the couch.

"You know you did really well at the swim meet," Nicole started, taking the seat next to her.

Caitlin nodded as a grin began to form on her face. "I'm going to junior national team tryouts, right?"

"No, not exactly," Finley said, leaning against the side of the couch with her arms crossed.

"What? I thought they take the top performers? I won three events!"

171

"You've been invited to try out with the full team."

"Huh?"

"As in Team USA. You know: The Olympics, World Nationals, US Open…"

"Are you serious?" Caitlin squealed. "Oh, my God!"

"Yes, but you have to understand that this is one of many opportunities. Don't get it into your head that this is your one and only shot, okay? You'll make yourself crazy for nothing. As long as you train hard, take care of your body, and keep your grades up, you'll be fine," Finley said. "I can't begin to tell you how proud I am."

"Thanks, Mom. This is unbelievable. I mean, Coach said it could happen, but…," Caitlin uttered, shaking her head. "Team USA. Like the *real deal* Team USA," she beamed.

Nicole looked up at Finley and smiled.

"When do we go?"

"We're not sure yet. We should get the papers in a couple of weeks. I'm sure you'll have to miss school. So, in the meantime, you need to talk to your teachers. Find out if you can start working ahead, or if you'll just need to take it with you and turn it in when we get back," Nicole answered.

"This is crazy," Caitlin mumbled, still trying to let it sink in.

"Yes it is, but you've worked very hard for this, and you deserve it," Nicole said. "We love you so much."

"I love you both, too." Caitlin leaned over, hugging Nicole. Then, she stood and hugged Finley. "I'm going to go call Will," she said excitedly as she rushed through the kitchen and up the stairs.

"I wish she'd talk to us about Will, and what's going on," Nicole sighed.

"She will in due time. You remember what it was like when we were her age. We hid all kinds of stuff from our mothers because we thought we were smarter than they were. Hell, I'd go to tell my mother something and she'd already know more than I did about it. Having a teacher for a mother had its ups and downs for sure."

"I try to model my parenting from your mother. She's always there with a smile, a tissue, a hug, a funny story, a stern lesson, whatever it may be, no matter what. I love her for that. She's taught me a lot."

"Me too. I've never met a stronger, more sincere, and caring person in my life. I try to be like her as much as I can."

"You are. I see a lot of your mother in you and the way you parent Caitlin."

"Thanks." Finley smiled.

Chapter 17

On Monday morning, Finley was back to the grind. The class was in the middle of Phase Two and progressively getting more difficult.

"I can't believe we're halfway," Ericka said.

"Me either," Jordy replied, brushing her teeth at the sink. She turned, locking eyes with her. "I'm not sure I want it to go by fast anymore."

"Why is that?"

"I kind of like being around you." She grinned.

Ericka smiled and rolled her eyes. "You have toothpaste running down your chin."

"Do you find that sexy? Come here," Jordy said, moving closer, while trying to kiss her.

"Um…no," Ericka giggled, backing away.

Jordy laughed and rinsed her mouth and face. "How about now? I'm minty fresh," she beamed, smiling brightly.

"I never want to stop," Ericka murmured, stepping into her arms and kissing her passionately.

*

"Stand tall!" Neil yelled as Finley stepped in front of the class, who was standing at attention in muster formation under the American flag. They were finally into March, and the temperatures were slowly beginning to rise.

174

The cadets had their bathing suits on under their sweatpants and t-shirts.

"Left face," Finley called. "Double-time jog on my pace!" She blew her whistle to start them, then stayed at the front left, running the group at about a ten-minute-mile pace. Neil brought up the rear, dealing with any stragglers who couldn't keep up.

Jordy stared straight ahead and slightly left as she jogged along, trying not to look at Ericka's ass moving under her sweatpants as she ran in front of her. She couldn't believe how close they'd gotten in only a week. She'd never met anyone with whom she'd wanted to share every minute of her life with…until now.

"Let's go, cadets! Pick it up!" Finley shouted, bringing Jordy's head out of the clouds. "We're only at mile one. We have two more to go…three if you don't pick up the pace!"

"I don't know, but I've been told," Neil began chanting loudly from the back of the group. The class repeated each line. "Rescue swim school is halfway done."

Finley led them on a course around the base. Each time they went by the American flag, the command center where the officers were located, or any officer who happened to be out and about on base, they turned their heads in that direction and held up a salute until they passed.

By the end of the third mile, a few of the cadets were huffing and puffing, and they all had a light sheen of sweat covering their arms, necks, and faces. Finley brought them to a stop outside of the building that housed all of the pools and the locker room.

"Everyone double-time it inside to Pool Room A," she said, following the group. "You should be warmed up and ready to go. Now, it's time to see what you're made of. You have one minute to get out of those shoes and sweats, into your survival gear, and in the pool." She blew her whistle and watched the seconds count down on her watch. With two seconds to spare, everyone was in the water. "Let go of the edge of my pool! If you have to hold the edge, you don't belong here, and I've failed at my job for keeping you around this long!" she yelled. "Line up for laps. Begin on my mark." She blew the whistle again.

The cadets swam to the opposite end of the Olympic-sized pool, turned and headed back towards her.

"I think we have one or two who aren't going to make it through today," Neil said.

"Then, they'll wash out, won't they?" She shrugged, counting the laps in her head. "Let's go!" she yelled. "My mother can swim faster than this!"

Ericka's legs burned, but she kept kicking harder and harder. She tried spotting Jordy, but knowing her, she was well ahead and gliding through the water like a dolphin.

"Stop!" Finley yelled, blowing the whistle again. "Pair up with the person in the lane next to you. Together, you will swim down to the concrete block at the bottom. Sit on the pool floor with each of you holding one hand on the block, and count to 60. Then, jointly, swim the brick to the surface and begin swimming towards the other end of the pool, holding the block up out of the water simultaneously. When you reach the other side, take the block back to the bottom, sit there with it and count to 45. Bring it up, swim back to this side with the block out of the water. On this end, you will go back down, sit and count to 30, come up, swim across, go down and count to 15. When you swim back this way, you'll go to the bottom once again to deposit the block, and then surface without counting." She looked at all of the cadets who were treading water and staring back at her.

Jordy lightly kicked Ericka, who was paired up with her. "We've got this," she whispered. "Just control your breathing. I'll be right beside you."

"Begin!" Finley yelled, blowing her whistle.

Jordy flipped over, diving down head first towards the block underneath her. She quickly sat down with her right hand on the block. Ericka did the same with her left hand as they began counting in their heads. Their lungs started to burn and Jordy pointed to the surface. Ericka grabbed her end of the block and they easily pulled it up with them. As soon as they surfaced, Jordy and Ericka pushed the block up out of the water and together, they began swimming across the pool.

Reaching the other side, Jordy and Ericka both took a deep breath and headed back to the bottom with their block, to sit and count. The number 45 couldn't come quick enough for Ericka. She gasped a few times once they surfaced.

"Come on, you can do this," Jordy encouraged as they began swimming the block back to the other side. This time at the bottom, she put her free hand on Ericka's hand that was holding the brick to help calm her. Then, she pointed up and they surfaced hastily. "Almost done," she uttered, catching her own breath.

Finley watched in amazement at the two women who had finally figured out how to work together as a team. She felt a smile cross her face, before moving on to the one pair who was struggling. "There's no resting period!" she yelled. "Move it!" Once the final two had finished, she continued the drill. "Now, get into the swim hold with one of you as the swimmer and one the survivor. Swimmers, you will swim your survivor to the other end, changing places when you reach the wall and head back this way. You will keep doing this until each of you has swam the other person four times. Do not hang onto my wall! You should be treading water at all times. Begin!" she yelled, blowing the whistle.

Jordy knew Ericka was running out of energy, so she let her be the survivor first. When they arrived at the opposite wall, Jordy quickly changed places with her, happy to not have to use any energy as she was taken back across.

Ericka fought hard, pushing her body to the limit as she swam with Jordy pulled tightly against her.

Finley observed one of the guys a few lanes away, struggling to swim with his survivor. After watching him go under, taking his survivor with him twice, she stepped in front of their lane. "Move your ass, Breckenridge! If you dunk him one more time, you're out!" she shouted.

"Come on, man! It's the last lap!" Rich said from the next lane over, trying to encourage him.

As soon as he reached the wall, Breckenridge let go of his survivor and sank to the bottom. The cadet who'd been paired with him, quickly grabbed his arm, pulling him to the surface as he coughed and choked.

"Out of the pool, Breckenridge," Finley stated.

He hung his head as he climbed out shakily, still gasping for air. Jordy and Ericka watched from a few lanes away, where they were trying to catch their breath after finishing.

"Airman Steven Breckenridge, you're done here. Go get dry clothes on, clean out your locker and bunk, and head up to personnel."

"Yes, Senior Chief," he said.

As soon as he walked out of the room, Finley addressed the class. "If you think you're good because you've made it this far, think again. We're only at the halfway point. You're going to bend a lot further during these last nine weeks than you ever thought possible. Those of you who are not strong enough, will break." She turned to Neil. "I'm going to get his paperwork ready, then you can meet him in personnel. Go ahead and send them for chow."

"Aye-aye, Senior Chief," he said. "Everyone out of the pool. Get dried off and double-time it to the mess hall for lunch chow. Be back here, ready to go in formation in one hour. Dismissed!"

*

Finley sat at her desk, filling out the papers to process Airman Breckenridge out of AST Helicopter Rescue Swimmer school. She hated releasing cadets, but it was as much for their own good as it was for those who would be working with them, and those counting on them to save their lives. If they couldn't make it at the school, there was no way they'd ever make it as a rescue swimmer in the real world. She remembered what it was like when she was a cadet, watching people leave every couple of weeks. She also thought about the first person who washed out with her as the lead instructor. She was heartbroken for the young guy, but she knew then that she was doing the job right. For a rescue swimmer school instructor, the numbers weren't about how many you washed out from each class, but how many go on to become as successful as they possibly can, using the knowledge you ingrained in them to get there.

Taped to the wall, next to the dry-erase board with her current class information written on it, was a small card she'd received from a cadet who'd graduated in her first class as a lead instructor. The outside only had two words: Thank You. Inside, he'd described his very first save, a survivor whose boat had sunk off the coast of Maine in the middle of a storm. The rescue swimmer thanked her for pushing him beyond his limits and for forcing him to break barriers he never knew existed.

Finley glanced at the card as she drew a line through Breckenridge's name on the board before walking out of her office.

*

"I don't even think I can eat," Ericka mumbled, moving through the food line.

"I'm starving," Jordy replied.

"You're always hungry," Ericka chuckled, shaking her head. "I'm starting to wonder where you put all of the food you eat," she added, looking her up and down.

Jordy winked and grinned at her.

"Hey, I'm just happy I can catch my breath," Evan said. "I thought she was literally trying to drown one of us."

Jordy laughed. "Too bad it wasn't Jon."

"No kidding," Rich uttered. "I would've paid money to watch him pack his bags."

After finishing the line, the four of them took their seats at a nearby table. Jordy reached over, grabbing Ericka's potato roll without asking, knowing she wouldn't eat it. Ericka said nothing as she began cutting her chicken.

Jordy put her chicken breast between the two rolls, turning it into a sandwich.

Rich and Evan watched the scene unfold, then gave each other a questioning glance.

"Even if you're not hungry, you should still eat. Your body will need the energy. Who knows what Senior Chief has planned for the rest of the day, besides trying to kill us with physical fitness, of course," Jordy said.

"I know," Ericka replied, as she began eating her pasta.

*

The class was standing at attention in front of the pool when Finley walked into the room. They'd changed back into their bathing suits and survival gear after lunch.

"We're going to start with intervals of thirty pushups, thirty burpees, thirty leg raises, followed by thirty seconds treading water in the pool. I'll count you down for each exercise and blow the whistle when time is up in the pool. Each round will lessen by five. So, round two will be twenty-five burpees, twenty-five leg raises, and twenty-five seconds treading water. We're going all the way to zero. Everyone hit the deck in pushup position. We begin on my whistle," she said loudly. *Tweet!* "Down...up, one. Down...up, two," Finley called. As they reached thirty, she instructed them to switch to burpees position. Then, she began the down, up count. "Everyone into the pool!" she yelled when they finished. "Do not touch the bottom or the sides of the pool," she added, watching the seconds tick by on her watch.

Jordy locked eyes with Ericka for a split second, trying to give her as much mental strength as she could, knowing her own legs and arms felt like jelly. She focused on the words: *So Others May Live*, which were scrolled across the wall behind Finley. Her mind drifted back to Ericka. She'd never expected to go to rescue swimmer school and make friends, but to find someone who took her breath away with a casual look or simple smile, blew her mind. Jordy had never been in love. She had no idea what a soul mate was. The only thing she knew for certain was she couldn't wait to wake up every morning and see Ericka, and she couldn't get through the day fast enough, to their few stolen moments in the bathroom before lights out. Ericka's eyes on her, made her chest tighten, and the feeling of Ericka's lips against hers, made Jordy weak in the knees. Yes, she'd come to the school with the idea of being the best, and proving to herself that she deserved to be there, but she hadn't planned on meeting someone who would literally turn her world upside down.

Staring at the words on the wall, gave Jordy the strength to keep going, round after round as her body hit the brink of exhaustion, but the occasional eye contact with Ericka, was what gave her the drive to push herself even harder. She not only wanted to succeed for herself, she wanted to make Ericka proud of her…that was a completely new sensation.

At the end of the final round, Finley blew the whistle. "On my mark, swim to the opposite side of the pool and back. Stay in your lane, and keep going until you hear the whistle again," she said, blowing the whistle once more.

Jordy's limbs were on fire and her chest burned. She clenched her jaw, forcing herself to keep going. *Don't you dare quit,"* she mentally chided.

Ericka looked at Jordy, who seemed to be gliding through the water with minor difficulty, and used that image to pull herself together and push her body. *"I can do this. I will not quit,"* she repeated over and over in her head.

After four complete laps, Finley instructed the class to get back out of the pool. A few of the cadets struggled to get up over the wall, literally falling back in multiple times. "Let's go!" Finley shouted. "You have three minutes to get out of that swim gear, into your sweats and sneakers, and outside in formation! Move!"

Jordy quickly pulled her survival gear off, tossing it to the side, before running over to the locker room. None of the lockers had locks on them because of the rapid pace at which they were in and out of them during drills. She quickly pulled her sweatpants and t-shirt on over her wet bathing suit, and fought to get her socks onto her wet feet.

Ericka was beside her, doing the same thing as the seconds ticked by on the clock. They both pulled their shoes on, tying them simultaneously.

"We have an extra couple of seconds," Jordy said, noting the time. She pulled Ericka close, kissing her tenderly. "Come on, let's get through this together."

"Together," Ericka repeated with a smile as they raced outside.

*

"Stand tall!" Neil yelled. "Right face!"

"Double-time jog. If you fall off my pace, I suggest you pick it back up!" Finley said loudly. "If you have to stop, you better be puking! If you puke, triple-time it back to the group as soon as you finish. Do not lag behind! If you cannot keep up, you will washout!" She stepped to the front left side of the group. "Move!" she shouted as she took off running, setting the pace.

As usual, Neil brought up the rear.

"What are you?" Finley yelled.

"Coast Guard Rescue Swimmers!" the group replied fiercely.

"What do you do?"

"Save lives!"

"Why do you do it?"

"So others may live!" the class shouted.

Ericka, along with one of the male cadets, fell off pace near the half mile mark.

"Pick it up!" Neil roared.

Ericka came to a stop, puking her guts out on the side of the road near the administration building. The male cadet fell to the ground a few feet away, completely out of breath, and also puking. He tried to run again, but fell to the ground, exhausted.

Ericka spit the remnants from her mouth and took off running to try and catch the pack. Her lungs burned, her sides cramped, her throat stung, her legs trembled with fatigue, but she kept going. Tears slowly rolled down her cheeks as she caught up to the back of the pack, just before Finley took them down to a walking pace to cool down.

Neil had stayed behind with the male cadet who couldn't continue, and was completely out of sight when Finley turned around.

Jordy was nearly limping, her body hurt so bad from head to toe. She looked around, but didn't see Ericka anywhere near her. She silently prayed she hadn't had to stop.

"Everyone fall into muster formation," Finley said as they rounded the corner where the American flag was flying high up on the pole. She watched them drag their exhausted bodies over, fumbling to line up on shaky legs. Counting heads, she realized one of the cadets was missing, as was Neil. She shook her head, seeing them walking together, off in the distance. "One of you didn't make it," she started. "Today was your phase Two Physical Fitness Test. Congratulations to the twelve of you who are standing in front of me right now. I know with some of you it was pure physical stamina, but with others it was all heart and determination. Either way, today was a test of endurance, which you all passed."

Everyone in the group cheered.

"Two of your classmates washed out today. If you think this was tough, the Phase Three Physical Fitness Test will break you in half," she continued. "Go take a hot shower and head over to the mess hall for dinner chow. Refuel your body and get some rest. Dismissed!"

"Aye-aye, Senior Chief!"

She watched the class limp away, before jogging to catch up with Neil and the cadet who was walking. "Cargill, you were unable to complete the final segment of the Phase Two Physical Fitness Test. You're out," she said. "Go pack up your bunk and head up to the administration building."

"Aye-aye, Senior Chief," he mumbled, walking away with his head hung low.

"What happened?" Finley asked, walking with Neil towards her office so she could complete their paperwork.

"He fell to the ground, cramping, gasping for air, you name it. He couldn't continue. Burney also stopped to puke, but she kept going."

"Yeah, she finished with the pack," Finley said, surprised that she'd fallen off pace and had been able to catch back up.

"That's two in one day," Neil stated, shaking his head.

"We're down to twelve," Finley added. "I'd rather graduate two cadets who will not fail on the job, than twenty who can't handle the physical or mental demands."

"I completely agree," he said.

*

"I wish we had a tub. I'd soak for the next twenty-four hours," Jordy sighed, standing under the hot spray of the shower.

"Me too," Ericka replied from the shower next door. They'd contemplated showering together, but they were both too tired to do anything other than stand under the spray.

"I can barely lift my arms to apply soap, much less wash my hair."

Ericka chuckled. "I'm scared to even try. I'm glad we're in the classroom for the next two days."

"If Senior Chief told me to swim a lap tomorrow, I'd washout because I'd probably push her into the pool," Jordy said, matter-of-factly, causing Ericka to laugh again.

"I have an idea," Ericka said, pulling back the curtain to Jordy's stall as she stepped inside.

"Oh, really?" Jordy grinned.

"Maybe if we wash each other, it won't be as difficult." She lathered the washcloth and began running it over Jordy's muscled, upper body.

"Great idea," Jordy mumbled, feeling Ericka's hands massage her sore body. She quickly did the same in return until both women were covered in soap. They rinsed off together, then washed each other's hair.

"Can we stay like this?" Ericka asked, standing under the hot spray with her arms wrapped around Jordy's shoulders.

"Forever," Jordy replied, tightening her hold around Ericka's waist as their lips met softly.

Ericka moved her hips against Jordy's as their lips parted, deepening the kiss, and Jordy moved her hand between them, sliding her fingers through the warm wetness.

"I don't think I can stand," Ericka murmured.

"Hold onto me," Jordy whispered, moving her fingers in slow circles.

Ericka kept one arm around Jordy's neck as she drug the fingers of her other hand down the front of Jordy's body, from her small breasts to the tight muscles of her torso, before sliding lower. Jordy spread her legs slightly, giving her enough room to go where she wanted.

Their lips met in a fierce kiss, fighting for control under the mist of hot water as their fingers moved in a slow, steady rhythm. Ericka dipped inside, causing Jordy to gasp. Her hips bucked with every stroke, taking her higher and higher. She threw her head back against the tiled wall, unfazed by the water spraying her in the face. Release hit Jordy so hard and fast, she nearly fell to the ground as her legs trembled.

Watching Jordy was an unexpected turn-on. Ericka felt herself let go with the last couple of strokes from Jordy's fingers. She held onto the strong body holding her up as they shared another passionate kiss.

"I want more of you," Jordy murmured against her lips.

"Me too, but I think my legs are done," Ericka said, kissing her again.

"Do you think anyone would notice if we climbed into the same bunk?" Jordy grinned, turning off the water.

Ericka laughed. "I'm sure they'd love it."

"Gross," Jordy grimaced.

"When we finally get out of here, the first thing I want to do is find a really big bed, and spend the next twenty-four hours naked in your arms," Ericka said, staring into Jordy's brown eyes.

"Only twenty-four?" Jordy teased, pulling Ericka back into her arms.

"Okay, how about forever?"

"Now, you have a deal," Jordy said, kissing her.

Chapter 18

Finley spent the following Saturday on the couch in front of the TV. She and Nicole only had eight weeks until their big day, and Nicole had decided to go dress shopping…without her, which was perfectly fine.

"Did you girls find what you were looking for?" she asked when Caitlin walked in and flopped down on the opposite end of the sofa.

"Huh?" Caitlin gave her an odd look.

"Weren't you dress shopping with Mom?"

"No." Caitlin wrinkled her brow. "She dropped me off at the mall so I could meet up with Will."

"Oh." Finley nodded. "Is everything okay?"

"No." Caitlin folded her arms over her chest. "We had a disagreement."

Finley stayed silent, hoping Caitlin would talk to her about what was going, and praying for Nicole to walk through the door so she didn't have to handle this on her own.

"We couldn't agree on a movie. I don't know. Things have been weird since the swim meet. I mean, I have a lot going on with swimming, plus school. I don't have time to be dati—" She tried cutting off the word, realizing where she was and who she was venting to, but it was too late.

Finley stared at her with wide eyes. "Care to continue?"

"Um…" Caitlin bit her lower lip as she looked everywhere, but directly at Finley.

"How long has this been going on?"

"Not long. I swear, we were just hanging out as friends."

Finley nodded.

"Are you going to tell Mom?"

"Caitlin, you know she and I do not keep things from each other."

"Aw man. She's going to flip out."

"Not necessarily. Are you and Will having sex?" she asked, cringing as she waited for the answer.

"No!" Caitlin squeaked. "We've just gone out a couple of times as more than friends. It's not a big deal."

"It is a big deal because this is the first time you've dated anyone. Am I right?"

"Yes."

"And Will happens to be another girl, so—"

Caitlin froze. "How do you know that?" she muttered.

"I met her when she dropped your swim bag off a while ago."

"What? She never mentioned that."

"How do you think it got here?"

"I knew she dropped it off, but I thought she just left it at the door or something."

"Nope."

"Great," she sighed. "What a cluster." Shaking her head, she continued, "Am I going to get the dating talk all over again?"

"I don't see why. You're going to date people. You may date guys or girls, or even both at some point. Your mother and I understand how confusing it must be for you to have two moms."

"I like Will…a lot. We have fun together, and we're really good friends."

"That's fine. But, you don't have to date her or be in a relationship with her…unless that's what you want."

"I don't know what I want. My mind is stuck on swimming and the national team tryouts."

"Well, focus on that for now."

"Mom, did you ever date guys?"

Finley cleared her throat. "Yeah, sure. But, I only did it to be cool and spend more time with your mom. We went on a lot of double dates," she laughed.

"Will asked me if that's what I wanted to do, date guys."

"Do you?"

"No…I don't know." She shrugged.

"I'm not going to lie to you or sugar coat it. Life sucks at your age. Your hormones are racing, and you're under a lot of stress with keeping your grades up to get into college. On top of that, you're a star athlete who trains rigorously for your sport. You barely have time to think, much less decide who to go on dates with. Plus, peer pressure can be an absolute bitch. At sixteen years old, everyone is going 120 miles per hour in different directions. It's hard to get on the same page with anyone, male or female. No one expects you to find the love of your life during your junior year of high school, and you shouldn't either." Finley slid over, wrapping her arm around Caitlin's shoulders. "I don't care if when the time is right, you fall in love with a guy, a girl, or a camel, for that matter. As long as you are happy and the person loves you as much as you love them. Right now, your grades should come first. I know how passionate you are about swimming, you've worked so hard to become a top athlete, so swimming should be your second priority. If after both of those needs are met, then why not hang out with friends and go on dates? That's part of what being a teenager is about, growing up."

"Thanks, Mom."

"I love you, kiddo." Finley smiled.

"I love you, too." Caitlin stood up. "For the record, Will pushes me harder than I push myself sometimes, with school and with swimming."

"That's good to know," Finley replied, pretty much to herself as Caitlin walked out of the room. She looked back at the TV. Having missed a good half hour of the movie she'd been watching, she decided to just turn it off. Her mind was still reeling about the conversation with Caitlin. She had no idea how to tell Nicole. Thinking a run would clear the fuzz in her brain, she headed up the stairs to change clothes. She stopped in front of Caitlin's door, knocking softly. "Hey, I'm going for a run. I'll be back in a bit," she said.

"Would you mind if I went with you? It might help me clear my head."

"Sure." Finley smiled, thinking how much they were alike in so many ways. She walked further down the hall to her bedroom and changed into her running clothes. The temperature was slowly coming up. In the middle of the day it was in the mid-sixties, so she chose to run in shorts and a long-sleeve, moisture-wicking shirt.

"Ready when you are," Caitlin called from her doorway at the opposite end of the hall.

"Tying my shoes, meet you in a minute," Finley yelled. She grabbed her phone and sent a quick text to

Nicole that they were going running, before heading down the stairs.

"How far are we going?"

"Oh, I don't know. Somewhere between five and ten probably, depending on how we feel," Finley said, punching in the code to close the garage.

"Miles!" Caitlin shrieked.

"Kilometers," Finley laughed.

"I was about to tell you to go on with your bad self if you were running ten miles!" Caitlin chuckled.

"I could do it."

"I'm sure you could, but I wouldn't be with you."

"Come on, we're burning time," Finley said, trotting down the driveway. "We'll do a slow mile to warm up, then pick up the pace."

Caitlin nodded as she fell instep next to her.

*

"Do you know how excited I am that it's the weekend?" Ericka asked. She and Jordy were in the pool room, swimming laps to get in some exercise so they wouldn't be so stiff on Monday.

"Is that because Senior Chief isn't here?" Jordy laughed.

"No, it's because we're all alone in here and I get to do this," she said, wrapping her arms around Jordy and kissing her in the middle of the pool.

"Is this some kind of twisted fantasy I don't know about?" Jordy teased.

"No," Ericka laughed. "I just can't ever kiss you in here, so it's a little exciting."

"What if we went up to the tower in the other pool room and did it? That would be exciting!"

Ericka smacked her arm. "Our luck, they have cameras in these rooms. I only wanted a quick kiss. Now, get back to your laps," she said, pushing Jordy away. "Oh, stop pouting."

"I'm not pouting!"

"Yes you are!" Ericka called as she swam off.

"I love you," Jordy whispered. "And I have no idea how to tell you."

Ericka tagged the wall on the opposite side of the pool. "Are you going to swim or tread water?" she yelled.

"Both," Jordy yelled back.

Ericka shook her head and smiled. She couldn't remember a time where she was this happy, simply by being with someone and spending time together. She'd loved Toni, but the more she thought about it, the more she realized she loved her because of their friendship. It was difficult to compare two years to less than a handful of weeks, but right away she could see a huge difference. Part of her wondered what was going to happen when their training was over. Would they try to make a long-distance relationship work? She knew one thing, she wanted Jordy Ross in her life.

"Now, who's the slacker," Jordy taunted, splashing her as she swam by.

*

"Do you think you can go another mile?" Finley asked, checking her watch. They'd completed three miles in less than thirty minutes.

"Sure," Caitlin replied. She had the cardio stamina to keep up, but she wasn't much of a runner. All of her exercise was done in the pool.

"If you're winded, we can head back."

"No, I'm fine. Keep going."

Finley nodded and turned the next corner, slowing their pace slightly to give her daughter the break she knew she needed, but wouldn't ask for. She was just as tenacious as Finley, and slightly more stubborn.

The early afternoon sun felt warm on Finley's face as she crossed the next block and turned into their neighborhood. A couple, who was pretty much being walked by their two large dogs, waved as the mother and daughter passed. Finley smiled and nodded her head.

"Why haven't we ever had a dog?" Caitlin asked.

"My schedule has always been too hectic for a pet, especially a dog that depends on you being home to feed it twice a day and let it outside."

"Yeah, but there are three of us in the house."

"So, you want a dog for your birthday instead of a car?"

"What?" Caitlin squeaked. "No! You get a dog. I want a car."

Finley laughed. "I don't want a dog. You're the one who brought it up."

"I was just asking why we never had one over the years. That's all."

"Your Mom and I almost got one when you were about a year old. He was some kind of terrier mix, but he was cute and feisty. A lady was trying to find him a home for her friend that couldn't take care of him."

"Why didn't you get him?"

"We went home to think about it and when we called her the next day, she'd given him away already. We figured it was for the best. We had you, and that was more than enough responsibility," Finley said as they turned down their road. "Come on, I'll race you home!"

"Wait, no fair!" Caitlin chided as Finley took off at a full sprint. She quickly chased after her.

Neither of them noticed the dark car they blew past at breakneck speed, until it pulled into the driveway behind them a few seconds after they'd arrived home.

"I thought you two were swimmers, not track stars," Nicole said, rolling the window down as she drove into the garage.

"I had you!" Caitlin yelled, laughing. "You had to cheat to beat me!"

"Uh huh." Finley nodded. "Keep telling yourself that."

"You two are a mess," Nicole said, getting out of her car. She opened the back door and pulled a garment bag out.

"Did you get a dress?" Finley asked, moving closer.

"Maybe," Nicole answered with a sly grin, closing the door and heading into the house.

"Well, come on. Let's see it," Finley urged, grabbing the bag as she walked in behind her. Caitlin had already gone inside, and from the sound of the running water, headed straight for her bathroom.

"No. That's bad luck." Nicole frowned, pulling the bag away from Finley's grasp.

"Oh, please. That's a myth."

"Well, the last sixteen years haven't exactly gone in our favor, so I'm not taking any chances. You'll see it soon enough."

"But, you already know what I'm wearing. Where's the fun in that?"

Nicole shrugged.

Stepping closer, Finley reached out and pushed Nicole's blonde hair back over her shoulder, exposing the soft skin of her neck. As she bent to place a tender kiss in the spot she knew would win her over, Nicole backed away.

"Don't look so surprised. I know what you're up to, and it's not working. Besides, you're covered in sweat and you smell," Nicole chided before turning and heading up the stairs with her bag. "I'll know if you've been in here, so don't even think about sneaking a peek," she added, nodding towards the bag.

Reluctantly, Finley headed up the stairs behind her. Despite being curious about the dress, she needed to have a discussion with Nicole about Caitlin. She still wasn't sure what to even say. She thought the run would help her sort it all out, but having Caitlin with her was both welcomed because they were spending time together, and a hindrance because she couldn't rehash the conversation.

"Are you that adamant about knowing what a simple white dress looks like?" Nicole questioned as Finley followed her into their bedroom and shut the door.

"You could wear a white garbage bag and look sexy," Finley said. "I love you and you are marrying me. That's what is important. However," she sighed, sitting on the footrest of the bed to untie her shoes. "We need to talk about Caitlin."

"What about?" Nicole asked, walking into the closet to hang up the bag. "What's wrong?" she said, noticing the seriousness on Finley's face.

"She sort of came out to me earlier."

"What do you mean…sort of?" Nicole sat on the edge of the bed with her arms crossed over her chest.

"She and Will are dating."

"What? Are you serious? She actually said that?"

"Yes. They had a disagreement at the movies earlier, and she told me about it when she came home. Apparently, it's been going on for a little bit."

"So, she's gay?"

"I don't know!"

"Well, what did she say, exactly?"

"Nic." Finley shook her head. "School and swimming are her priorities. She and Will were friends, and I guess they like each other a little more than friends. I have a feeling this is new to her, dating in general."

"Was she upset?"

"No. She's just a kid, and she has so much on her plate right now with swimming, and school on top of that. I think dating someone, anyone, for the first time, has been a little more stressful than she anticipated. She'll figure things out."

"I wonder if it's just a phase, you know. Close friends sometimes share a little too much, especially at that age. Maybe that's what it is and she's confused by it all."

"At least she's not having sex."

"How do you know?"

"I asked," Finley stated.

"Oh, God," Nicole laughed, shaking her head.

"If it's any consolation, Will is a swimming and good school grades advocate."

"We should invite her over for dinner."

"You're on your own with Caitlin on that one."

"Why?"

"Seriously? I've been through the coming out thing twice now. It's your turn to go down that road with her, especially if you want her to bring her girlfriend home for dinner."

"That sounds so…"

"Weird?"

"Yeah." Nicole nodded.

"I honestly don't care who she dates, as long as she's not out having sex, parading around school like a whore, or neglecting swimming and her grades."

"Well, me either, but I…I guess I just wanted her to be our little girl for a little longer."

"Me too," Finley replied, wrapping her arm around Nicole's shoulders.

"I love you with all of my heart, but you still stink," Nicole muttered, kissing Finley's cheek before she stood up.

Finley rolled her eyes. "I'm about to shower. Are you going to talk to her?"

"I'm going to pretend like you didn't say anything and simply see how the movie went. Then, I'll casually tell her to invite Will for dinner tonight."

"You'll be busted."

"Why? They've been spending a lot of time hanging out together. It makes sense to get to know her friends."

"Yep, but we haven't invited her over before now, and she literally just told me all of this less than two hours ago."

"Fine. How would you do it, almighty, Senior Chief?"

Finley laughed.

"Can I come in?" Caitlin called as she knocked on the door.

Finley held her hand out towards the door and bowed as if to say, here you go.

"Yes," Nicole answered.

Caitlin stepped inside. "So, I'm sure Mom told you about our conversation," she started nervously, talking like she had only a few seconds to recite an entire paragraph.

Nicole nodded.

"Do you think it would be okay if Will came over for dinner? I don't know if we'll keep dating or not, but she's my best friend anyway. I think you both would like her. She doesn't know that you know or anything."

Finley went to say something, and Nicole stepped in front of her. "I think that's a great idea," she said. "Do you want me to cook here, or would you like to go out to a restaurant?"

Finley leaned around Nicole, who was purposely blocking her, and mouthed the word: Out, while sticking her thumb to the side.

Caitlin raised an eyebrow and chuckled.

Nicole turned around, giving Finley a stern look.

"I'm going to take a shower," Finley said, removing herself from the conversation and the room.

*

Gusto's, a quaint little Sicilian restaurant that Finley and Nicole usually went to on special occasions, luckily had a table open for the evening without a reservation. Will had driven over to their house, then rode with Caitlin and her parents.

The small booth had a basket of breadsticks in the center, with four glasses of ice water, and four bread plates, one in front of each of them.

Finley knew the menu by heart, but she pretended to read it anyhow, wondering who was more nervous, Caitlin, Will, or Nicole. She'd gotten over her nerves quickly when she realized how polite and docile Will was. She sort of reminded Finley of Nicole, and since Caitlin was so much like Finley, it made perfect sense that they'd formed a friendship to begin with.

"So, Will. Is that short for something?" Nicole asked, sipping her water as she eyed the teenager. Will's straight, light-brown hair was pulled back in a loose bun with a few tendrils hanging down. Her big brown eyes darted nervously.

"Yes, ma'am. My first name is Willa. My family sort of shortened it when I was a baby and it's been that way ever since."

"Are you a swimmer too?"

"No, ma'am. I play basketball."

"You girls go to the movies a lot. What's your favorite thing to see?" Finley asked.

"I like books, so I'm a big fan of adaptations, but generally anything with a good plotline. Caitlin likes the scary ones or action-packed adventures. So, we usually see one that I like and next time one that she likes."

"That's actually what our quarrel was about today," Caitlin said. "Will wanted to see that new sappy movie about the guy who has an accident and is in a coma for years. His wife moves on with her life and he wakes up."

"You didn't want to see it?" Finley asked.

"No. It look too sad for my taste, but we talked earlier and decided to go tomorrow and see something else," Caitlin answered.

"Well, that's good then."

As their entrees came, the conversation continued towards school, college, and Caitlin going to the USA National Team camp for tryouts. By the time they'd finished with dinner, they'd learned more about Will's parents, who were divorced, and her older sister who was away at college.

Back at the house, Will shook hands with Finley and Nicole, then hugged Caitlin, before getting into her car and driving away.

"She's pretty cool, huh?" Caitlin said.

"Yeah." Finley nodded. "I like her."

"Me too. She's very sweet," Nicole added.

"Good. See, we're not having sex or doing drugs, or anything else. We go to the movies, go out for smoothies, and occasionally peruse the stores in the mall. We're a little more than friends, but I have no idea where it will go, if it even goes anywhere. Can we please move on and concentrate on the swim tryouts? That's my main focus right now."

"Okay," Finley muttered, slightly surprised.

Nicole simply nodded as Caitlin walked into the house. "Did that just happen?" she mumbled.

"I think we got put in our place...politely," Finley laughed.

"She's so grown up," Nicole sighed, shaking her head.

"Well, at least we know what's going on. She's not hiding anything from us."

"No, and they don't look that serious to begin with, so maybe it is just a phase," Nicole added, grabbing Finley's hand as they headed up the walkway together.

Chapter 19

With the final week of Phase Two fast approaching, Finley and Neil set up the equipment simulators in Pool Room C in preparation for the Rescue Simulation Test, which was a pass or fail style drill. Each cadet would have three peers to rescue from a sinking boat. One would be in the water, one would be hurt, and the other would be trapped down below as the boat turned over, all while heavy wind and rain wreaked havoc on the scene. It was a situation every rescue swimmer has been through in the field multiple times and certainly one that would be experienced by those who graduate.

Outside of the room, Jordy pulled Ericka aside in the hallway.

"We're going to be late for muster," Ericka hissed.

"No we won't." Jordy grinned, holding both of Ericka's hands. "I love you," she whispered, finally finding the courage to say those words for the first time in her life, more so because she truly meant it. Somewhere in the last eleven weeks, she fell in love. It was both frightening and exhilarating.

Ericka stared at the brown eyes looking back at her. "I love you, too," she murmured, kissing Jordy softly. "I can't wait until we graduate and don't have to sneak around to be together."

"Me too!"

"Come on. I don't want to swim laps or do burpees because we we're late," Ericka said, rushing towards the door.

"Stand tall!" Neil yelled, walking inside the room just as Ericka and Jordy took their positions in the muster formation. The class quickly straightened to attention.

"Welcome to Sim Day," Finley announced, proceeding to explain the process as she moved in front of the group. All eyes were on her as she went over the specifics of what each cadet was supposed to do. "You've been here for eleven weeks. We've drilled this scenario a hundred times. Will you be nervous? Sure. Will you make a mistake? More than likely. We're not here to score you on a scale of one to ten, taking off points for this or that. We're here to make sure you can do three things: handle the extreme conditions; use the signals, swim holds, and apparatuses correctly; and actually rescue all three survivors, getting them into the helo safely, as well as yourself. There will be high seas, heavy wind and rain, as well as rotor wash. This simulator is as real life as it gets. Chief Denny and I will be on the side of the pool, ready in case of emergency, and yes, there have been emergencies. However, we will not be able to say anything to you until the drill has ended, or you quit." She nodded for Neil to head over to the simulator control box. "There are only twelve of you left, and since this drill involves four people, I'm going to split you into three groups, A-B-C. One person will go from group A, then B, and so on, until everyone has gone." She looked down at her clipboard, calling out the names for each group.

Jordy had been paired with Rich and two others in group A, while Ericka had been paired with Evan, Jon, and one cadet in group B. The rest of the class made up group

C. Everyone stood side by side near the edge of the pool, wearing their swimsuit and survival gear.

"Group A, let's go. Ross, you will be our first swimmer, so head up to the helo. The rest of you, get into your positions. One in the water, one hurt in the boat, the other in the interior compartment. We will begin on my whistle," Finley said, signaling for Neil to start the machines.

Jordy climbed into the makeshift helo and prepared to deploy from the open cabin door. The wave pool began sloshing three foot waves in the direction of the fake fishing trawler in the middle. Industrial fans created ten to twelve knot winds, which made the waves more inconsistent, and heavy raindrops pelted her in the face as they poured down. Her heart pounded in her chest. She took a few deep breaths and closed her eyes, trying to calm her nerves.

The sound of Finley's whistle was like getting hit in the face with a baseball bat. She opened her eyes, slightly disoriented. She blinked a few times, bringing everything into focus. Fifty yards away, she saw the sinking boat, as well as the bright orange vest of the survivor in the water, ten feet away from it.

Jordy gave the signal and jumped out of the fake helo. As soon as she popped up, the hours of training kicked in. She gave the 'I'm okay' signal and began swimming over the waves, towards the survivor who was in the water.

"I'm with the US Coast Guard. I'm here to help you. Are you injured?" she yelled.

The cadet swam over, grabbing a hold of her.

"Calm down, sir!" she shouted, shoving him off her. "I will help you, but you have to let me do my job!" She swam behind him. "I'm going to grab you. All you have to do is be still," she said, placing him in a swim hold. He obliged as she pulled him across the pool and into the rotor wash. She quickly gave the signal for the sling, and helped him inside as soon as it was lowered to her.

When he was secure, she gave the 'all clear' signal and backed away as he was retrieved. Then, she spun around and headed back to the boat, climbing up inside once she reached it. A survivor was hunched in the corner of the deck, trapped under a heavy piece of rigging and clutching his leg.

"Sir, I'm with the Coast Guard. Are you hurt?"

"Yes. My leg is broken," he replied.

Jordy slid across the listing boat and assessed the equipment that was pinning him. "Okay, I need you to trust me. I'm going to help you get out from under this and into the water."

"I can't swim!"

"Sir, I understand that. I'm going to swim for the both of us. Are you ready?"

He nodded.

Jordy used all of her strength to raise the rigging section up enough to pull him to the side. She helped him up, leaning him against the side of the boat on his good leg. Then, she practically lifted him over the side. "Hold onto the boat," she said as he went into the water. She quickly jumped in behind him, pulling him back against her chest, before swimming away.

Inside the rotor wash, she signaled for the basket. As soon as it hit the water, she pushed the survivor up inside of it, and gave the 'all clear' signal. After the basket was lifted out of the water, she swam back towards the boat, climbing into it once again.

She tried the cabin door handle, but couldn't get it to budge. Taking a step back, she kicked it, sending the door swinging open. She grabbed the light that was attached to her survival harness and shined it around inside. As soon as she spotted the survivor, the boat rolled over, immediately filling it nearly to the top with water. She swam down, grabbing the survivor. The water level stopped about a foot from what was once the floor of the boat, giving them an air pocket to breath.

"I'm going to get you out of here," Jordy said. She held onto him as she shined her light around, trying to get her bearings. "We have to go underwater to get back through the cabin door," she added, seeing the opening she'd come through.

"Okay," he said.

"Are you hurt?"

"No."

"On the count of three, hold your breath. I'm going to swim down and pull you with me."

"Alright."

One…two…three!" Jordy sucked in a deep breath and dropped below the water, yanking the survivor with her as she passed through the open cabin door and out under the deck. She held him close to her as she maneuvered around the side and up, breaking the surface as rain stung her face and a wave washed over.

Adjusting her hold for a better grip, Jordy began swimming him towards the helo's rotor wash. She quickly signaled for the sling, and helped him inside once it was lowered. She backed away, giving the 'all clear' signal.

Once the final survivor was secure she gave the signal to be retrieved, and attached the hook to the D-ring on her harness. With one final signal, she was lifted up out of the water and pulled into the makeshift helo.

Finley blew the whistle, indicating her test was complete.

Jordy climbed down, feeling utterly exhausted as she rejoined the cadets who were watching and waiting in line along the edge of the pool.

"Is it really as hard as it looks?" Evan asked as she walked towards her group at the end of the line.

Jordy simply nodded. She gave Ericka a wink and thin smile as she passed by her.

*

Ericka played one of the survivors when her group performed their first drill. After they'd finished, everyone watched in disbelief as one of the cadets from group C, who was the swimmer, panicked when the boat rolled over.

Finley and Neil had another assistant instructor in the water, wearing a dive tank and mask, and watching through the side window of the simulator boat as a safety precaution. As soon as the cadet began to freak out, he surfaced with a thumbs down sign. Neil quickly pressed the button to roll the simulator back over, bringing it above the surface to the start position. The cadet rushed out, too frantic to even swim to the edge of the pool. His own teammate had to help him.

Finley shook her head and made a note on her clipboard, before blowing the whistle for group A to go once again. Rich went next performing the drill as thoroughly as Jordy had done.

"That was no joke," he said, breathless as they watched group B get ready for their turn.

"No kidding," Jordy muttered, watching Ericka head to the tower for her turn to be the swimmer.

*

Ericka took a deep breath and tried using a Yoga technique to mentally focus as she waited for the ear-piercing tweet of the whistle. She forced herself not to look out at the cadets on the opposite side of the pool, in fear that seeing Jordy would make her lose concentration.

At the sound of the whistle, Ericka gave the signal and jumped out of the makeshift helo cabin with her body positioned perfectly. She popped up, gave the 'I'm okay' sign, and swam towards the simulator boat.

"I'm with the Coast Guard, and I'm here to help you," she said to the survivor bobbing in the waves. He quickly latched onto her, dragging Ericka under the waves. She fought to get to the surface as he pulled her down once more. She put her feet against him while underwater and was able to shove him away.

The survivor popped back up a few away from where she surfaced. "You're going to drown us both! Let me help you!" she yelled. "Just relax. I'm going to hold onto you and swim us towards the helicopter," she added as she finally got him into a swim hold.

Moving through the extreme conditions proved to be much more difficult than in a stationary pool. Ericka fought the waves as she finally made it into the rotor wash with the survivor. She gave the signal for the sling, and helped him into it once it was lowered. She backed away, giving the signal for him to be retrieved, before she headed back through the tumultuous water.

Waves crashed against the side of the boat, pounding her as she struggled to climb inside. Once she was over the ledge, she found the second survivor under a large outrigger. "I'm going to help you," she said. "Are you hurt anywhere?"

"My leg is broken," he replied.

Ericka nodded. "I'm going to lift this up. Do you think you can scoot out from under it?"

"I don't think so," he said.

Ericka looked at Jon Parish, who was playing the survivor. *Asshole,* she thought, gritting her teeth as she got into position, using all of her leg strength to push the rigging up. "Come on! Slide over!"

"I can't!"

"Yes, you can!" she yelled, holding the contraption up as long as she could. He didn't budge, so she had no other choice, but to set it back down. "You have to work with me at least a little bit. I can't pick this thing up and pull you out," she explained.

Jordy stood on the edge of the pool, looking ready to pounce. Her jaw was set and her back was ramrod straight. "Don't you cause her to fail you son of a bitch," she hissed through her clenched teeth.

"She'll figure it out," Rich whispered.

Finley observed the situation, making minor notes. In all actuality, Jon was doing what he'd been instructed to do. All of the stage one survivors were told to latch on for dear life. Stage two was told to not move, and let the swimmer do all of the work, and stage three was instructed to simply go with the disorientation that would ultimately occur when the boat rolled over, and let the swimmer control the situation.

Taking a second to gather some additional energy, Ericka changed positions, using her back this time to lift the rigging, giving her room to grab the survivor's legs. She tugged as hard as she could, but Jon had a good fifty pounds of muscle and height on her. He moved a little, but would still be trapped if she lowered the rigging. "Damn it," she growled, pulling him with all of her might as the contraption crashed to the deck of the boat, narrowly missing Jon's upper body.

Completely fatigued from all of the lifting, Ericka helped him up to one leg, as she herself, wobbled around on the listing, wet deck. "You have to go into the water. Hold onto the side of the boat, and I'll go in behind you," she said, helping him over the gunwale, before jumping in behind him. She quickly maneuvered him into a swim hold, and began heading back through the waves, towards the helo.

Jon's heavy body weighed Ericka down, causing her to go under a couple of times as wave after wave washed over them. She held on, swimming with everything she had. When she reached the rotor wash, she signaled for the sling, knowing there was no way she'd be able to get him into the basket or litter. As soon as the sling hit the water, she got him strapped inside, and gave the signal for him to be retrieved as she backed away and headed for the boat one last time.

Finley made a few more notes as she watched Ericka struggle to get back into the boat.

Once inside, Ericka kicked the cabin door three times, before it finally popped open. She pulled the flashlight from her survival harness and began searching for the final survivor. She spotted him huddled in the corner as the boat rolled over, sending both of them underwater.

Ericka quickly swam up until her head broke the surface. She looked around, but didn't see the survivor. After a couple of deep breaths, she went under with her light, shining it all around until she found him. Her lungs burned as she grabbed the survivor, swimming back up with him until their heads were out of the water. There was only a small, foot-wide space between the surface of the water and the bottom of the boat above them. She shined her light around once more, looking for a way out. She was completely mixed-up with the boat upside down.

"Are you hurt?" she asked, holding onto him.

"No."

"Okay. I'm going to get us out of here. It looks like we have to go back down and find the door. I'm going to pull you along with me. Take a deep breath," she said, before going under water, towing the survivor along with her as she shined the light in the direction she thought the door was in. Together, they passed through the opening and wound up under the rear deck of the boat. Ericka slowly let air out of her lungs, trying to prolong her held breath as she struggled to get herself and the survivor up to the surface.

As soon as her head popped up out of the water, Ericka gasped for air. The survivor came up next to her. She moved behind him quickly, placing her arm over one of his shoulders, in front of his neck and under the other arm in the swim hold. After a couple of deep breaths, she started towards the rotor wash on the opposite end of the pool.

This survivor was much lighter than Jon, but Ericka was completely exhausted. She had to stop multiple times to catch her breath as she fought to keep both of their heads up in the pounding waves. She gave the signal for the sling when they reached the helo, and helped the survivor get settled, before signaling for the pickup.

Ericka went under the surface three different times as she struggled to tread water in the frenzied waves, with heavy rain blasting her face, while waiting to be retrieved. After what felt like hours to her tired, worn-down body, Ericka attached the hook to her harness and rose up out of the water. At the top of the tower, she lay flat on her back, gasping for air. One of the cadets waved for Finley and Neil, who both ran over quickly.

"I'm okay," Ericka said, coughing and spitting out water that she'd swallowed. 'I'm just out of breath."

Finley removed her harness to give her lungs and diaphragm room to fully inflate. "Take a couple of deep breaths and slowly let them out."

Ericka did as she was told as her body began to gradually relax.

Jordy watched in horror, not knowing what was going on at the top of the tower. She shook her head and stepped back, out of formation.

"If you go up there, you'll get in trouble. She'll be okay," Rich said, grabbing her arm.

*

"How are you feeling?" Finley asked.

"I'm good," Ericka said.

"Will you be able to continue the drills? Your team still has two more cadets to go."

"Yes, Senior Chief," she replied, standing up.

The class clapped as Ericka got to her feet up on the tower. Finley went down first, with Ericka coming behind her in case she had any difficulty. Neil was the last one off the tower after the other cadets.

Group B headed over to the other side of the pool together and got back into formation as Finley called group C up next.

It took two and a half hours for the rest of the cadets to finish their drills, which were all completed with very few mishaps. Everyone was exhausted in the end. Their muscles felt like jelly and their lungs were sore from choking on swallowed water.

"Class 16-20, the drill you did today was only a fraction of what it's really like out in the middle of the open ocean," Finley stated, stepping in front of the group. "Get some chow, get some rest, and we'll go over the results in the morning. Dismissed!"

Chapter 20

Nicole got out of the shower and toweled off her shoulder-length blonde hair. She cocked her head to the side when she saw a glimpse of blue pass by the mirror. Wrapping the towel around her mid-section, she stepped into the bedroom, looking around. She heard Finley's voice in the hallway just before she walked back inside the room.

"I'll take her to the pool this morning," Finley said, nodding towards Caitlin's room down the hall.

Nicole gave her an odd stare.

"What?" Finley asked, rushing to the mirror. She was wearing her Tropical Blue Uniform, consisting of a light blue, short-sleeved, button-down shirt that was adorned with ribbons and the gold rescue swimmer emblem; dark blue slacks; and shiny, black oxford shoes.

"Why are you in full uniform?" Nicole questioned, moving closer. Finley usually wore her dark-blue, Operational Dress Uniform or sweats. The full uniform was a rarity that she enjoyed seeing.

"I'm meeting with Command Master Chief Wright and Commander Hill this morning. Plus, I have my annual flight screening this afternoon," Finley replied, checking the placement of the decorations on her shirt on last time. She grinned, feeling Nicole's hands slide up her back and across her shoulders.

"Is it a good meeting or a bad meeting?" Nicole asked, kissing the back of her neck at the hairline above her collar.

"It's about the birds pooping all over my SUV during the day. We're probably going to shoot them all down with assault weapons," Finley stated seriously.

"Okay. I hope everything goes well," Nicole muttered, running her hands around Finley's abdomen, grazing the top of her belt.

Finley's brow creased. Grabbing Nicole's hands, before they loosened her belt, making her very late for her meeting, she spun around. "Did you hear anything I just said, or does this uniform make your ears wet too?"

Nicole laughed. "Of course I heard you. Just because I find you sexy in your uniform, doesn't mean I crumble like a horny teenager."

"Uh huh," Finley murmured, kissing her. She pulled the edge of the towel, working it open.

"Oh, I don't think so," Nicole chided, retightening her towel. "That's a two player game."

Finley bit her lower lip. "Rain check?"

"Maybe," Nicole teased.

"Mom? I'm ready when you are!" Caitlin yelled. The sound of her running down the stairs echoed in the old house.

"Saved by the kid," Finley said, kissing her again. "Maybe I'll wear this to bed tonight."

"Really?" Nicole uttered.

"Nope," Finley called over her shoulder.

"Now, who's being the tease?" she scolded with a sly grin as she smacked Finley's rock hard butt.

*

Caitlin was standing by the SUV when Finley walked outside. She was taken aback at seeing her daughter in her ROTC uniform. She only wore it once a week for inspection and on special occasions within the school. She'd almost given up commanding the color guard unit because she was spending so much time swimming.

"I thought you had inspection on Thursdays?" Finley asked.

"We do, but we have to present the colors today. The chief of police is speaking about safety at an assembly."

"Oh." Finley nodded, looking over her uniform. "You get any more decorations and I may have to start saluting you." She grinned.

"Well, technically, I do outrank you...so—"

"Do you want to ride the bus to school?" Finley asked, giving her a stern look.

Caitlin popped to attention. "No, ma'am, Senior Chief."

"You're a mess," Finley chuckled, shaking her head. "Get in the car."

*

Finley walked into the command master chief's office a few minutes before their scheduled meeting time.

"Morris, come in and have a seat," CMC Wright said with a smile. "Would you like a cup of coffee?"

"No, thanks," she replied, sitting in the wooden chair in front of his desk.

"I went over the file you gave me last night. Although we don't normally do this, I'm in agreement with what you're asking."

Finley nodded.

"I trust your judgment, as does Commander Hill, which is why he signed off on it this morning."

"That's—"

"Great, wonderful, surprising?" Cmdr. Hill asked from the doorway. Finley hadn't heard the door open behind her.

"Actually, sir, I was going to say outstanding," she replied.

"Does this mean you'll give us three more years?" He smiled.

"That I can't be sure of."

"I know. I'm only yanking your chain," he laughed, patting her shoulder. "You're well respected and do a damn good job, no matter what you're doing. You're also a damn fine rescue swimmer, so I can't fault you for wanting to go back into the field. Just remember, you will always have a post here."

"Thank you, sir."

"Now, back to this cadet. Command Master Chief Wright spoke with Senior Chief Gillespie, the lead instructor for the Aviation Maintenance Technician school. Anyway, I'll let him go over everything with you."

As soon as he left, Finley turned her attention back to CMC Wright.

"As he said, I spoke with Senior Chief Gillespie. His newest class is only a few weeks behind yours, so the cadet will have a lot of catching up to do. The flight mechanic portion of training will be a breeze for the cadet, but the hands-on mechanical aspect of the training could be a problem."

Finley nodded.

"It's pass or fail, just like with all of your drills. I know that's cutthroat, but we have to do it."

"I understand."

"Great. Since the paperwork is completed and signed, go ahead and send the cadet up to personnel. We'll take it from there."

"Okay," she said, standing up and shaking his hand. As soon as she was out of his office, she pulled her cell phone from her pocket and scrolled through the contacts. She pushed the green button next to the one she was looking for. The line rang four times before an operated voicemail service picked up.

"Hey, this is Finley Morris. Give me a call when you get this. I have a huge favor to ask of you."

*

The class stood in muster formation under the flag, patiently awaiting Finley's arrival. Neil stepped up in front of them. "Airman Burney and Petty Officer Crawford, report to Senior Chief's office, double-time. Dismissed," he said.

Jordy's heart sank. She shook her head no as a lone tear rolled down her cheek. She recalled the conversation she and Ericka had shared that morning while getting ready for the day.

"I know I didn't make it, and that's okay," Ericka said.

"What? There's no way she'd wash you out. You passed. Crawford, on the other hand, needed assistance to

get out of the simulator after he freaked out. You just need to get a little stronger."

"Jordy, I've been here almost twelve weeks. If I'm not strong enough now, I never will be."

"Where's your fighting spirit? You used to challenge me until you couldn't move your muscles."

"I'm still fighting, twice as hard to be here as the rest of you! I don't want to go. This was my dream as much as it is anyone else's that is here. Do you think I want this? To be standing here saying goodbye to you?"

"What? This isn't goodbye. You're not washing out."

Ericka stared at her. "I gave everything I had yesterday, I guess we'll see if it was good enough," she sighed.

"It was. I know it was. You deserve to be here as much as anyone else. If I ever get my hands on Jon Parish outside of this base, I'm liable to kill him," she growled.

"Jordy, it wasn't his fault. He did what he was told to do. Yes, he exaggerated a bit, but it wouldn't have mattered."

"We should get going."

"Come here," Ericka said, pulling Jordy into a hug. "I love you."

"I love you, too," Jordy murmured, closing her eyes as she let her body enjoy the feeling of Ericka in her arms.

"Class 16-20, double-time to the classroom. Move!" Neil yelled, bringing Jordy back to reality. She took off in a jog behind the rest of the group.

*

Finley met with Petty Officer Chris Crawford first. It only took her two minutes to tell him he'd washed out, and needed to pack his bunk and report to personnel. Ericka waited in the hallway, anticipating the inevitable, nevertheless it still stung. She'd been an open ocean lifeguard at the beach for a little over a year when she saw the Coast Guard Search and Rescue Helicopter practicing drills out in the distance off shore. She watched through binoculars in awe as the rescue swimmer went into the water, retrieved the pretend survivor, and started the process all over again using different scenarios and equipment each time. She knew in that moment that she wanted to do what they did. Now, standing outside of the Senior Chief's office, that moment felt like a lifetime ago. She wondered what she'd do now. Would they make her go to a boat unit and go to school to be a boatswain? Would she get an administration post, or would she be pushed out altogether? She had no idea what happened to those who had washed out.

"Burney," Finley called.

Ericka looked up to see the senior chief standing in her open doorway with an odd expression on her face. She was dressed in her Tropical Blue Uniform, something Ericka had only seen her in once, the very first day of Rescue Swimmer school. The large rack of ribbons and gold rank insignia were intimidating, but it was the gold helicopter rescue swimmer badge that caught her attention.

"I'm sorry," she said. "I didn't hear you."

"Come in," Finley replied, holding the door open for her. "Have a seat." She closed the door and walked back behind her desk. "Do you know why you're here Airman Burney?"

Ericka nodded.

"You completed the simulation test yesterday, which is a feat in and of itself. So, I commend you. That took courage, and an insurmountable amount of strength and determination." Finley placed her elbows on the desk and clasped her hands together. "Although you finished, it was without a doubt, extremely difficult for you. Whether Petty Officer Parish played more of an interference or not, doesn't matter." Finley shook her head. The conversation had turned out to be harder than she thought it was going to be. "You're one of the smartest cadets to ever come through here. Do you know that?"

Ericka shook her head.

"Your entrance exam and ASVAB scores are tremendous. Above that, you exude an amount of fortitude that I've never seen before. You have struggled from day one, yet you keep pushing harder and harder. I wish every cadet that stepped foot on this base had half of your guts." She paused. "You'd make one hell of a rescue swimmer, but you simply aren't strong enough," Finley sighed. "Seeing what I saw yesterday, you'd never make it in a real life scenario."

"I understand," Ericka said, holding her head high.

"You never once quit on me, or this class. Ericka, I see something in you…a light that shines brightly. I saw it on the very first day. Maybe it reminded me a little of myself back when I was a cadet here. Maybe it reminds me a little of my daughter, whom will stop at nothing to be the best that she can possibly be in her sport. Anyhow, I'm not going to quit on you either. You may not be physically strong enough to be a rescue swimmer, but you can still be a part of search and rescue, if that's something you want to do."

"Yes. Absolutely," Ericka said.

"When a cadet washes out, we usually send them back to their previous unit, where they either continue in the job they had before attempting to change over to AST; are reassigned to another school waiting list; or they're simply out of the Coast Guard altogether. I didn't want to see someone with your skills fall through the cracks, so I pulled some strings with Commander Hill this morning. How do you feel about becoming an Aviation Maintenance Technician?"

"Like a mechanic?"

Finley nodded. "You'd be a mechanic, but you can take that much further and become a Flight Mechanic on a helicopter, which as you know works directly with the rescue swimmer, or even go as far as a flight engineer on a C-130."

"I've never really thought about that. All I wanted to do was swim and save people," Ericka said. "How much time do I have to decide?"

"Right now," Finley replied. "This is extremely rare, but if you want to change over to AMT, their current class is a little behind ours, so you'd graduate about a month later. However, you'd have a lot of catching up to do. As I said, I won't quit on you. A good friend of mine is a Flight Mechanic. I've asked her to tutor you and help get you up to speed. She lives down in Florida, but she's willing to devote as much time as possible into helping you. She, like myself, wants to see women succeed in our jobs. She actually worked with me for a few years as my Flight Mech. She's very good at what she does. I think you'd get along great."

"Wow," Ericka mumbled, surprised that the senior chief would go that far for her, which was well above and beyond anything she'd ever done for a cadet. "I…" Ericka cleared her throat. "I want to do it. If I can still be in a helo, helping save lives, then that's what I want to do."

Finley smiled. "All of the paperwork has been completed. You'll need to clean out your bunk and head up to personnel. They'll change everything over, then you'll report to the AMT school, which is on the other side of the base. I'm sure you've seen it on our runs."

"Yes," Ericka replied.

"You won't be going far. You know where my office is. I'm available if you need anything at all, and I mean that. I have high hopes for you, Airman Burney." She smiled, extending her hand.

Ericka shook her hand. "Thank you, Senior Chief."

"You're welcome," Finley said. "You're also dismissed."

Ericka stood and headed for the door. She paused, turning back around.

"Yes?" Finley questioned.

"Jordy Ross—"

"She'll be fine," Finley said. "Absence makes the heart grow fonder…trust me, I know."

Ericka nodded and walked out of the room.

*

Later, after another meeting with the command master chief, and a brief lunch, Finley caught up with the class. They were in the middle of a classroom lesson, watching different rescue scenarios and answering questions on each one.

"Stand tall!" Neil yelled as Finley entered the room.

Jordy bit her tongue, forcing herself not to lash out. Everyone knew Ericka was gone. Neither she nor Crawford had returned after being summoned away that morning.

"Congratulations," Finley said, moving to the front of the room. "Those of you who are standing in front of me passed the simulator test and therefore, will be moving onto Phase Three, which begins on Monday. We still have the rest of today and tomorrow to tie up Phase Two with the remainder of these bookwork lessons." She turned to Neil. "Chief Denny, if you'll join me in the hall. I will see all of you bright and early at muster tomorrow morning," she added before leaving the room once again.

Neil followed her out.

"I got Burney transferred to AMT. She should be over there by now."

"Wow. That's great."

"Let me know if you have any issues with Ross. I suspect she hates my guts at the moment, but I don't blame her. I'd hate me, too."

"Is that going to be a problem?" he asked.

"No. If it becomes one, I will deal with it."

Neil nodded.

"I need to head over to clinic. I'm due for my annual flight screening. Leave me a voicemail as to where you leave off, and we'll pick it up in the morning. I'm hoping we can finish by lunch chow and get them back into the pool in the afternoon."

"Sounds good."

Finley turned around and headed down the hallway as he walked back inside the classroom. She wasn't thrilled about the exam, but in order to remain flight ready, she had to have the annual testing. The doctor did a basic physical, measuring her height and weight, checking her blood pressure, listening to her lungs, looking in her ears, nose, and throat, and performing a vision screening. The only thing he didn't do was poke and prod her lady bits. She had a completely different doctor with that annual privilege.

*

Finley sat in the den later that evening, writing a few notes for her class, when Caitlin burst through the front door, cheering wildly.

"It's here! It's here!" Caitlin yelled. "Mom!"

Nicole nearly fell down the stairs, thinking her daughter was injured or something had happened. She'd just been dropped off by Will, who had accompanied her to swim practice.

"What's going on?" Finley questioned as the three of them met up in the kitchen.

"I got the papers from the USA National Swim Team!" Caitlin squealed, handing Finley the envelope, which she'd already opened. "I go in two weeks!"

"I must have forgotten to check the mail," Finley muttered as she unfolded the four-page letter.

To: Caitlin Morris
C/O: Finley Morris and Nicole Wetherby

Caitlin,

You are hereby cordially invited to attend the spring tryouts for USA National Swimming. This is a ten day, in-house camp at the Olympic training center in Boulder, Colorado. During this time, you will learn about nutrition: how to fuel and recover your body; and mental strength:

how to relax your mind and focus using meditation; as well as over one hundred hours with our coaching staff in the pool, which includes a lot of one on one training.

You must have one parent/guardian accompany you and remain during the duration of the camp. You will be provided a two-bedroom style apartment in the dorm for you and your family member. Also, all meals will be provided to you during the training hours. There is a restaurant on site for your family member, as well as off-site dining, shopping, and entertainment within a five-mile radius.

Please have your parent/guardian fill out the enclosed forms. You will also need an up to date physical from your doctor. This must be within the last six months. We look forward to seeing you soon. Arrive with a positive attitude and be ready to work hard!

Sincerely,

USA Swimming

Finley looked over the last three pages. One of them was a release form for a minor to participate in the camp, and the next page was in regards to medical insurance and emergency contact information. The last page listed everything Caitlin needed to bring with her, the location, arrival day and time, and the departure day and time. Plus, it also had a syllabus on the back, breaking down the ten days of camp.

Finley handed the papers to Nicole. "There's no way I can take off ten days."

"I know. I've already cleared it with Mr. Steffen. He understands and is excited for us. This will burn a hole in my vacation time though."

"You're going to take your school work with you and complete your assignments every day," Finley stated, looking at Caitlin.

"I will."

"I'll go book the flight," Nicole said, walking out of the room.

"Yes!" Caitlin fist-pumped the air.

"I'm extremely proud of you," Finley said, hugging her. "I wish I could be there."

"I know. Me too. Mom will take video and pictures, I'm sure, and we can Skype every night."

"That sounds like a plan." Finley smiled.

"I'll go into the school on Monday and speak with the principal, as well as her teachers. That way, they can go ahead and get her assignments together. They should have plenty of notice," Nicole said, as she waited for her laptop to come on in the nearby dining room.

"I'm going to go call Will. She's going to be so excited," Caitlin exclaimed, rushing up the stairs.

Finley glanced at Nicole, but she was busy messing with the computer. She hated not being able to go, but with the class starting Phase Three, there was no way she could take any time off. These last six weeks were going to be brutal on both her and the cadets.

"How was your meeting?" Nicole asked, walking into the den after she'd finished booking the flights.

"Good, actually. I never give it much thought when a cadet washes out, but do you remember me telling you about the two females who were in competition with each other?"

Nicole nodded.

"They've come a long way in the last six weeks. One of them washed out yesterday," she sighed. "She's extremely smart, and more determined than anyone I've ever seen."

"Didn't you say she reminded you of yourself?"

"Honestly, they both do, but in different ways."

"How did she wash out?" Nicole asked.

"She's simply not strong enough. The job is very demanding. I washed her out purposely. It was a very hard decision, but when it comes down to it, I'd rather see her doing something else than hear about her getting injured or worse, while on duty because she wasn't physically able to do the job."

"I see."

Finley explained the meeting and what she'd done for Ericka. "I couldn't just let her hang out to dry. She's a good kid and deserves better than that."

"I love you," Nicole said. "You're the most considerate and genuine person I've ever met."

"Maybe becoming a mother made me softer." Finley smiled. "I guess it could be the uniform."

"Speaking of..." Nicole slid closer on the couch.

"It's up in the closet, where it is staying," Finley laughed.

Chapter 21

A sheen of misty rain filled the air as Finley stood in front of the class. They were in muster formation near the American flag pole across from their dorm.

"Congratulations, you made it to the final day of Phase Two," Finley said. "You are two-thirds of the way through Helicopter Rescue Swimmer training."

Jordy's jaw tightened as she locked eyes with the senior chief. She'd spent the past two days avoiding her classmates at all costs. When they went to the mess hall, she found herself lying in Ericka's bed, trying to remember what it felt like to hold her. The coconut scent of her shampoo had faded away quickly, leaving Jordy with nothing but cold, scratchy sheets and a flat pillow. Staring back at Finley, she tried to portray all of her hatred.

When the class was told to double-time it to the pool room, she fell back, practically walking.

"Pick it up, Ross!" Neil yelled, running behind the group.

Jordy rolled her eyes and increased her speed to a jog, but still stayed a few steps behind the pack.

Finley sighed as she watched her. While the class went into the pool building, Finley headed down the opposite hallway to her office to check her voicemail. The call she was waiting for had finally come in.

"Hey, Finley! It's good to hear from you. How is the family? Sorry I didn't get back to you yesterday. Lillian and

I were on a much needed liberty day and my phone went for a swim. I guess water resistant doesn't mean take it into the ocean with you!" she laughed. "Anyway, I'm good for whatever favor you need. You know I will always have your back, Senior Chief! Give me a call. I'm on days this week. Talk to you soon...Tracey."

Finley smiled as she tucked the phone back into her desk drawer. Tracey was the best female Flight Mechanic that she knew, and Finley had a feeling she'd make a great mentor to Ericka as well. She locked her office door and headed down the hallway to the location of the pool rooms.

The class was in the water, swimming warm up laps when Finley walked in. Neil was about to get them out of the pool and standing at attention, but Finley waved him off. "How far have they gone?" she asked.

"A couple hundred meters."

"Great. We're warmed up and ready to go," she said. "Everyone out of the pool. Pair off for today's drills."

Rich and Evan were standing side by side, so they paired up. The rest of the cadets did the same, leaving Jordy and Jon to work together. Jordy was tired from barely sleeping, and she had no desire to be swimming drills, much less working with the person that got Ericka kicked out. Looking at the simulator boat at the other end of the pool only made her angrier.

"One of you will be the survivor and the other the swimmer. As with our test last week, the survivor will be in the boat and the swimmer will be deploying from the helo. Today, we'll be hoisting you down to the water. The waves will be twice as high as they were during the Simulator Test, with heavier wind and rain. Your object in the first round is to get the uninjured survivor out of the boat and swim him or her to the helo, where you will both be retrieved using the tandem lift to save time. Each round will get increasingly more difficult, and the elements will get more extreme."

"Great," Jordy mumbled under breath.

"Don't fuck up like your girlfriend," Jon hissed.

"I'd rather watch you drown than swim your fat ass across this pool," she retorted quietly as the first pair began their exercise.

"Oh, please. You wish you were built like me. Then, you'd have to have a dick to back it up. Wait, maybe you already do."

"Your little antics don't work on me. When it's our turn, don't try the same shit you did with Ericka, or I'll knock you the fuck out and really have to save you."

"That whore got what she deserved. You don't belong here either. I guarantee you won't be graduating, especially now that your little bitch is gone. You might as well quit."

"You don't scare me," she said, stepping closer. "I'll kick your ass right here."

Jon pushed her back just enough for her to fall into the pool.

"You asshole!" she yelled, climbing out and lunging for him.

Finley had caught onto what was happening and was already headed in that direction. She quickly grabbed a hold of Jordy.

"Calm down, Ross!"

"Why should I? You'll only take his side. It's your fault, too. You quit on her!" Jordy yelled. "You said you wouldn't quit on us, but you did. You quit!"

Neil stopped the drill and rushed around the pool. Finley shook her head at him. "Petty Officer Ross, step into the hallway. Now!" Finley shouted.

Jordy gave Jon a dirty look and huffed in frustration as she walked away.

"Keep the drill going," Finley said to Neil. "I'll deal with her. I knew this was coming."

*

Jordy paced back and forth in the hallway, still dripping wet from being pushed into the pool. She'd let the anger stew for the last forty-eight hours, and it had finally boiled over. She was sure she would've punched Jon Parish in the face if he hadn't shoved her back. The fact that she didn't care, hadn't bothered her one bit. After having the only person she'd ever loved in her life, ripped away without so much as a goodbye, she felt nothing but numbness.

Finley stepped into the hallway. "Stand tall!" she growled.

Jordy snapped to attention.

"First of all, I am your superior. I don't care how mad you are at me or anyone else for that matter. I am a senior chief, and I deserve the respect for everything I went through to earn that rank." Finley moved closer. "You will not speak to me in that manner ever again. Are we clear?"

Jordy nodded.

"I know you are angry, hurt, maybe even heartbroken, but taking it out on me or your classmates isn't the way to go. This training is damn near the hardest thing to go through in the military. People wash out. That's the nature of the beast. But, they don't get to that point because another cadet puts them there. Petty Officer Parish may have played his part a little more thoroughly than he needed to, but Airman Burney washed out on her own."

"You told us to ban together. You said you would never quit on us," Jordy said.

Finley looked her in the eyes. "I didn't quit on you or Airman Burney."

"Then why is she gone? She finished the test."

"She wasn't physically strong enough. She knew it, and I think you did, too. It was just a matter of time. I let her go as far as I could, hoping she'd get stronger along the way, which she did, but it simply wasn't enough. She's better off washing out than failing on the job or losing her own life."

Jordy turned her head as a tear fell.

"I know you two had gotten close, and for what it's worth, I'm sorry. I would've done the same to you if the roles had been reversed."

Jordy nodded once more.

"If you act insubordinate again, you're out of here. Are we clear?"

"Yes, Senior Chief."

"Good. Get back in there and prepare to complete your drills."

Jordy rushed back inside, taking her same place in the formation at the edge of the pool.

"Petty Officer Parish," Finley called from the doorway.

Jon looked up and jogged over to her. Finley waved for him to step out into the hallway.

"You're physically fit. You saw combat in the Army. A lot of this training has come easy to you, I get it.

Nevertheless, none of those are reasons to treat your fellow classmates like they are beneath you."

He began to speak and she cut him off.

"Stand tall when you address me!" she said sternly.

He straightened to attention.

"I don't have blinders on, Petty Officer Parish. I see and hear everything that concerns the rescue swimmer cadets within the training center, as well as on and off this base. If I ever see or hear of you putting your hands on another cadet, you'll be out of here so fast, your head will spin. Now, get back in there and finish your drills!"

"Yes, Senior Chief!" Jon said before scurrying back inside.

Finley took over the rest of the drills when she rejoined the group. After an hour, which let her see Jon and Jordy work together three separate times with no issues, she dismissed them for lunch.

"Parish," Neil called, waving him over as the cadets left the room. "I know what you're up to. Let me tell you something, before you go mouthing off about females in the service again, why don't you look up a few names," he said, listing women who've had outstanding military careers, super exceeding men in the same field. "And while you're at it, Google Senior Chief's name as well. It might surprise you."

Jon nodded.

"Go get some chow," Neil sighed.

"What was that about?" Finley asked. She'd been on the opposite side of the room, reprogramming the simulator machines for the drills after lunch.

"Probably the same thing you called him out on."

"I saw him shove Ross into the pool. That's why she went after him."

"He has a big problem with women. He doesn't think they belong in the military."

"Oh, I knew that from the first week. I was hoping his thinking would change as the weeks went by."

"I doubt it ever will," Neil replied.

"He's on thin ice, and his skates are sharp," she said seriously.

*

Jordy spent the entire weekend with her headphones on and her nose in a book. Most of the time, she wasn't even looking at the words, and the iPod wasn't turned on. But, it had given her classmates the idea that she was unapproachable, and that's all she'd wanted. She missed Ericka more than she thought possible. Being in the dorm, the mess hall, or on the base in general, simply wasn't the same. Thinking back to the day they first met, made her laugh. Remembering the last time they'd hugged, made her cry. She dried her tears on her pillow at night. As soon as she'd found what she never knew she was looking for, it was taken away, shattering her. The fact that she had no way of contacting Ericka, drove her absolutely mad. They'd never exchanged mailing addresses or even phone numbers, for that matter. Graduation felt like it was years away. Even if she waited until then, she wondered if she'd be able to find her. The thought of never seeing Ericka again, weighed heavily on her mind as she ignored the conversations, card games, and other antics going on around her.

*

Over the past two weeks, Will had started to actually come inside when she was picking up or dropping off Caitlin. She was always polite, but quiet. Finley figured she was probably shy.

As soon as the teenagers left for the movies on Sunday afternoon, Finley went into the den where Nicole was finishing some work she'd brought home on Friday. She sat down on the adjacent love seat.

Nicole looked up with a furrowed brow.

"We're alone," Finley said.

"Is that so?"

"Uh huh."

"I take it you have an idea," Nicole replied, waiting for a response.

A sly grin spread across Finley's face.

"A hot bath," Nicole uttered at the same time that Finley said, "do it."

They looked at each other and laughed.

"Okay, clearly we're not on the same page," Finley mumbled.

"Oh, yes we are. The hot bath is for afterwards," Nicole murmured, setting her papers on the table as she stood up and walked over, straddling Finley's lap. Their lips met in a passionate kiss.

"I like the way you think," Finley whispered, pulling Nicole's shirt over her head, along with her bra. She kissed her again before turning to the side and laying Nicole on her back. Finley took her time, kissing her way down her neck and across the soft skin of her chest to her breasts.

The rest of their clothing was slowly removed piece by piece while they traded teasing kisses and tender touches. Finley leisurely slid her hand up Nicole's thigh as Nicole did the same to her. Nicole set the pace, exploring

Finley's wetness, rubbing delicate circles around her clit, edging closer to her entrance with each pass. She fought off the beginning of her own climax, concentrating on the increased beating of Finley's heart and her labored breathing.

"Come with me," Finley breathed as she kissed her.

Nicole let go when Finley's tongue touched hers. She gasped, rocking her hips back and forth as Finley's body trembled against her. They pulled their hands away from each other at the same time, both breathless and sated.

"I'm getting too old for this," Nicole mumbled as she tried to stretch out on the small loveseat they were squished in.

Finley raised a questioning brow.

"Not this-this," Nicole laughed. "We have a perfectly good, comfortable, king-sized bed upstairs. How is it we never make it that far?"

Finley shrugged. "You started it."

"True, but you finished it."

"On the contrary. I believe we did that together." Finley grinned.

Nicole smiled. "I love you," she said, kissing Finley's lips tenderly. "But, I have to get off this couch," she added, struggling to regain the blood flow to her cramped body.

"Wasn't a hot bath mentioned?" Finley questioned as she too, stood up stretching her sore muscles.

"Absolutely," Nicole sighed happily as she picked up part of their clothing pile.

Finley bent down, grabbing the rest before heading up the stairs behind her. "We still need to go car shopping," she said.

"Have we decided what we're doing?" Nicole asked, depositing the clothes into the basket in the closet.

"The Explorer is paid off. The miles aren't too high. I think we should just give her that," she replied, referring to Caitlin, who was turning sixteen in a week. "I'll buy something new."

"I still want to trade in the Mercedes," Nicole said, starting the water in the tub.

"I know you do. Trust me, I want the last reminder of your marriage gone, too. I'm glad you went back to your maiden name after the divorce."

"Me too. I never wanted to change it in the first place, but my mother insisted." Nicole shook her head. "When Caitlin was a baby, I thought about changing my name," she uttered as they slid down into the hot, bubble bath.

"Really?" Finley questioned, pulling Nicole back against her.

"Yes. Caitlin is a Morris, and so are you. I wanted to share the name of the two people I loved most."

"What about now?"

"More than anything," she answered. "We are a family and this will finally make us complete."

Finley nodded.

"Back to the car situation," Nicole said, changing the subject. "If you want to give her your SUV, I think that's a good idea."

"Alright. We should probably go looking. We only have a week."

"What are you thinking of getting?"

"I have no idea," Finley replied with a shrug.

"Me either," Nicole laughed.

Chapter 22

"Welcome to Phase Three," Finley said the following Monday morning. "During the next six weeks, the ten of you will be taken to the extreme limits of your mental and physical capacity. Whoever is left standing in the end, will graduate and become Helicopter Rescue Swimmers. It's that simple." She made eye contact with each cadet except Jordy as she walked in front of the group.

Jordy's mind was on Ericka as she stood in muster formation, wondering where she was and what she was doing, but the wandering made her lose concentration, almost causing her to miss the command to double-time to the classroom. She hurried along with her classmates, leaving her stray thoughts behind.

Finley shook her head as she watched her go. *Don't quit on me, kid.*

*

Class 16-20 spent the majority of the day familiarizing themselves with the helo radio commands, as well as how to vector a helo into position, something they would be responsible for if the Flight Mechanic was preoccupied.

"Once you get used to the terms, using the radio will come naturally," Finley said. "Always remember the tail number for the helo you're in. This is your helo's call sign, just as sector and the name of the base is the call sign for that air station. Your call sign is simply, rescue swimmer."

Jordy tried not to let her mind drift away as she took notes along with the rest of her class. She'd never used a two-way radio before, but figured it had to be fairly easy to do. The sound of Neil's deeper voice brought her back to the lecture.

"You will have a waterproof radio on you, but there are many times that the radio will not work, will get knocked off you, or you won't be able to hear it. This is why the hand signals are ingrained into your brain. If all else fails, you will still be able to communicate."

"We've also gone over how to do a medical assessment of the survivor based on the distress scale, however, you need to know how to relay that information back to the pilot of the helo," Finley continued. "It's very simple. You radio the pilot with the injury and alert status numbers from the scale, along with a very brief description." She grabbed one of the two way radios from the table in front of her. Neil had already taken another one to the back of the classroom. "We're going to demonstrate how to go through a call. Then, we're going to split off and go through calls with you individually with us as the sector and you as the swimmer." She waved at Neil as she keyed the radio.

"1620...Rescue Swimmer. Survivor one is alert: seven; injury: two, has a small laceration above the right orbital. Over," she said.

"Rescue Swimmer...1620. Copy."

"1620...Rescue Swimmer. Send the basket," she radioed.

"Rescue Swimmer...1620. Deploying basket. Status on survivor two. Over?"

"Survivor two is DOA. Alert: zero; injury: ten. Will need litter. Over."

"Rescue Swimmer...1620. Copy."

"You see," Finley began, addressing the class. "We are short and to the point. You have one second, maybe two if you're lucky, to get your message back to the helo. The pilot is communicating with you and reporting to the operations center at the same time, so you must be quick, but informative."

"This half of the class, you're with me. The rest of you are with Senior Chief," Neil said, splitting the ten of them up.

One at a time, each of the five cadets working with Finley, played the swimmer as they relayed messages back and forth on the radio. She made a note on the ones who struggled with remembering the details, one of which was Jordy, whom she knew was smarter than that. Jordy Ross had the potential to be at the top of the class, if she'd only get out of her own head.

"Stand tall!" Finley said loudly.

The class jumped to their feet, standing at attention.

"Double-time it to the mess hall for lunch chow. Be back here in exactly thirty-five minutes. Dismissed!"

"That went better than expected," Neil muttered.

"Yeah." She nodded, still thinking about Petty Officer Ross.

*

The next day, the class stood on the tarmac in their full wetsuits, boots, and survival harnesses, listening to Finley go over the Rescue Swimmer preflight checklist. A white and red HH60-Jayhawk helicopter sat ten feet away with the pilot, co-pilot, and flight mechanic all going over their own checklists.

"Once you finish your list, you sign the bottom and hand it to the pilot. He or she will add it to their log book, then you're ready to board. Always make sure you have your flight bag with you, which contains your mask, snorkel, and fins. You never know if you'll get a call out on a routine training mission, so wear your shorty wetsuit under your flight suit. Your survival harness will be on the outside of the flight suit, but in a pinch, the flight mechanic will help you get the harness off and back on in the tight space, so you can remove the flight suit and be ready to go into the water. However, the majority of the time, you'll be training in the water, so you won't be in a flight suit at all, just your wetsuit, boots, and survival harness," she explained. "When you board, get into the rescue swimmer jump seat, buckle your safety belt, and pull on your helmet. Don't forget to fasten the chin strap. The pilot will do a radio check, plus one final ready check before lifting off."

Jordy stared at the helo behind Finley as she spoke. She'd dreamed of this moment since the day she decided to drop out of college to become a rescue swimmer. The idea of jumping out of a helicopter to rescue people was thrilling, despite the fact that she'd never been in one.

As the cadets walked over and began boarding, Jordy felt a shutter of nervousness pass through her. She wished Ericka was there by her side. Anger rose in her at the thought of doing this without her. They'd talked a few times about what it would be like when they finally got to go up in a helicopter for their training.

"Petty Officer Ross, is everything okay?" Finley asked.

Realizing the other cadets had boarded and were waiting on her, she hurried inside. Finding an open jump seat, she quickly buckled her safety belt and pulled on the helmet hanging above her as the twin turbine engines began to power up.

*

Finley took a second to gather her thoughts as the whine of the engines and rancid smell of turbine fuel brought back memories. She missed being on the front lines, going on call outs at all hours of the day and night. The adrenaline rush of hurrying to potentially save someone's life, was unmatched. Sure, she enjoyed being an instructor, teaching the generation that would follow in her footsteps, but she craved the excitement and adventure that came with being a rescue swimmer.

Climbing in last, Finley sat next to the Flight Mechanic and put her helmet on.

"Great day for a flight, you think, Senior Chief," he said.

"Roger," she replied, looking out at the cloudless, blue sky.

"Sector Charleston...Search and Rescue 6027. We are ready to commence with training mission 1620. Over," the pilot radioed as all of the cadets listened in. "6027 crew, ready for wheels up?" he asked.

"Roger for wheels up," the flight mechanic replied.

Finley did the same.

"6027...Sector. You are cleared for takeoff," the operations dispatcher radioed.

Jordy felt the helo shutter for a split second as it began to rise off the ground. She held her breath, looking through the window as they climbed high and higher, before heading off to the left. Flying in a helicopter was nothing like flying in a plane. Turbulence shook the helo like a rag doll, and the turns were much more sudden and jolting than the slow banking of a plane. She thought she'd be sick at first, but the knot in her stomach finally unraveled.

"Senior Chief, we're fifteen miles out," the pilot radioed.

"Roger," she replied. "Listen up, class 16-20. We're going to go down in a ten-foot hover, at which time you will freefall one at a time. I'll go first, so I'll be in the water with you. Chief Denny will remain in the helo to help you prepare for the jump. Once we're all in the water, we'll practice a few radio calls, then one by one, get hoisted back up."

"Senior Chief, we are in position. Prepare to deploy. Flight Mech, open cabin door. Over."

"Roger," the flight mechanic said. He connected the gunner belt to his harness and slid the door open.

Finley thought she'd be more nervous as she sat down, dangling her legs over the edge, but she only felt the slight rise of adrenaline that she usually got right before she went into the water. She gave the hand signal that she was ready.

"Swimmer is ready," the flight mechanic radioed.

"Roger. Deploy swimmer."

The flight mechanic tapped Finley once on the upper chest, then once on the shoulder, signaling she was cleared to jump. She pushed off, maneuvering into the seated position with one arm over her head and the other over her chest. Her feet entered the water first, followed by her butt. The cool water felt like an awakening as it stung her face, and the taste of the saltwater on her lips was like a long lost lover. She quickly popped up, giving the 'all clear' signal.

Neil connect the gunner belt to his harness and worked next to the flight mechanic, helping each cadet get deployed.

Jordy closed her eyes and took a deep breath when it was her turn to go. She swung her legs over the edge, dangling them above the water. She peered over the side. The water looked much further away than ten feet. Finley and some of the cadets were treading water outside of the rotor wash. She gave the ready signal as excitement mixed with nerves. The flight mechanic tapped her chest. She gave him a thumbs up. Then, he tapped her shoulder. Jordy took a deep breath and shoved off. In the air, she quickly got into the same position as Finley, which was what they'd drilled over and over for weeks during Phase Two. Cold water washed over her face as she splashed down, startling her for a split second. She hurried to the surface, giving the 'all clear' sign, before swimming over to meet her classmates. Three more cadets followed her into the water.

Once the entire class was treading water, Finley told them to give the signal to be retrieved, one at a time. She watched as the hook slowly lowered towards the first cadet. He clipped it to his harness and gave the ready signal.

Jordy watched as he was gradually lifted out of the water and pulled back into the helo. She swam back behind Finley, hoping to be the last to go up. She wanted to revel in the experience of her first time just a little bit longer.

Finley looked around for Jordy once all of the other cadets had been retrieved. "It's surreal, isn't it?" she said, treading water next to her.

"Kind of like losing your virginity," Jordy muttered.

Finley laughed. "I don't think I've ever heard anyone put it that way, but yeah…I guess. Maybe a little. I can tell you, it never gets old. Nothing about this job ever becomes monotonous, no matter how many times you go out on a call or into the water."

"Ericka should be here right now," Jordy mumbled.

Finley felt her heart break a little for the young woman. "Come on, we need to go back up," she said. "Let's do a double pickup," she radioed.

"Roger," the pilot replied.

Jordy swam into the rotor wash with her as the hook deployed over them. Finley connected the hook to Jordy's harness, then connected her own harness to the D rings on Jordy's.

"Up we go," she said. "Give the signal."

Jordy did as she was told and together, they slowly rose out of the water.

*

Finley walked into the house that evening, dressed in her flight suit and boots. She was tired from spending the day jumping, as well as hoisting out of the helo and back in. They'd drilled the routine of getting deployed and retrieved until the cadets were all worn out. They'd also worked on hand signals and radio communication.

"Did you fly today?" Caitlin asked, stepping off the last stair as she came in the door.

"Yep. We started helo training. I spent most of it in the water, actually. How was school?"

"Fine," she answered. "I got an 'A' on my Calculus test."

"Great!" Finley replied, hugging her. "And swimming?"

"It was good. He cut me back to every other day because I leave for the tryouts soon. He doesn't want me to get burned out. He said I'll be swimming more there than ever before."

"He's probably right," Finley agreed. "Where's your mom?"

"She was in the kitchen the last time I saw her."

"I still am," Nicole said loudly.

Finley followed the smell of food lingering in the air as she made her way to the kitchen. "How was your day?" she asked, kissing Nicole softly.

"Good, but not as exciting as yours, I'm sure."

Finley grinned. "I do love this part of teaching. I miss being in the air, and the ocean for that matter."

Nicole smiled. "Dinner is almost ready, if you want to shower."

"I'll be quick," Finley replied, hurrying to go wash the saltwater from her skin and hair.

*

Jordy stretched out on her bunk after returning from dinner chow in the mess hall. She was exhausted from spending the entire day jumping out of the helo, swimming with a survivor, and getting hoisted back up as the class repeated their latest drill over and over. She looked at the empty bunk to her right and sighed. It was perfectly made with the blanket tucked tightly, almost as if no one had ever slept on it. She suddenly felt very isolated, despite the fact that the other nine cadets were also in the dorm.

"I snuck this out of the mess hall," Rich said, handing her half of a chocolate brownie as he sat down on the edge of her bunk.

Jordy grinned. "Ericka would give you a hard time if she were still here."

"Yeah, I know." He smiled. "I don't think that woman has ever broken a rule in her life."

"Me either," Jordy agreed, taking a bite of the dessert.

"Have you heard from her?"

Jordy shook her head.

"I'm sure she's just trying to get settled in wherever she is. It's barely been two weeks."

"More than likely, she's at home."

"You think she washed all the way out? Wouldn't they have put her with a cutter unit or administration, or something?"

"I don't know," she uttered.

"When you do finally hear from her, tell her I said hi. Until then, keep your head up. We're in the home stretch," he said, patting her leg before standing and climbing up into his own bunk.

Jordy considered him a friend. In fact, he and Evan both, were friends. At least, they were more like friends than the ones who had neglected to send a single letter. She'd expected that from her parents, who were obviously still upset with her for following her dreams instead of theirs. Her own brother hadn't contacted her either, but then again, he had always followed their rules without hesitation. Whereas, Jordy had pushed the limits on several occasions. Still, she was a little surprised that the couple of girls she'd called friends throughout high school, and part of college, had completely abandoned her. They clearly were nothing like Evan or Rich who would come to her aid with no questions asked.

She'd come to the training center not looking to make friends, and certainly hadn't planned on falling in love with someone, but those grueling weeks of training had broken her down, building her back up again as a stronger, more perceptive version of her former self. Over those same weeks, she had slowly begun to understand the brotherhood code that many service members talked about, which was why she didn't understand how it was so easy for Rich and Evan to accept what had happened with Ericka and simply move on with their training.

She glanced at the empty bunk next to her once more before turning her back to it, as well as the rest of the dorm.

*

By the time Friday rolled around, Finley was ready to have two days off. They'd spent the entire week in the helo and the ocean, drilling the cadets on the rescue maneuvers they'd learned in the pools. Neil was handling morning muster for the weekend, so she had no need to go to the base at all until Monday morning.

As soon as she pulled into the driveway, Nicole was waiting for her. She got out of her Explorer and into Nicole's Mercedes, leaning over to kiss her as she buckled her seatbelt. "What did you tell Caitlin?"

"Nothing. She's at swim practice. I'm supposed to pick her up in an hour," Nicole replied, backing out onto their road.

"This shouldn't take too long. We've already done the paperwork, so they're pretty much going to walk around with me, then hand me the keys."

"Sounds good," she said, manipulating the evening traffic, before turning into the GMC dealership a few miles away. She pulled into a spot near the front.

"I'll see you in a bit," Finley said, getting out. Nicole was barely out of the parking lot before a salesman walked up.

"Can I help you?"

"Actually, I'm looking for Paul. My new Acadia is waiting for me to pick it up," she replied.

"Oh, okay. No problem. I'll have him paged for you. Come on into the showroom."

Finley stood near the receptionist's desk, looking around at the couple of people who were sitting at open tables, obviously working on car deals.

"Senior Chief, good to see you," Paul said, sticking his hand out. He'd done a four-year stint in the Navy right out of high school, before moving on, getting married, and having three children, nearly twenty years ago, all of which she'd found out the weekend before when she went in to purchase her new vehicle.

"You too. I'm sort of in a hurry. I need to get home and hide the new car before my fiancée and daughter get home."

"That's right, tomorrow is her birthday, correct? She's getting your old Explorer."

Finley nodded.

"Alright, well the deal has been completed, so all we need to do is the delivery. It's in the back. Follow me," he said.

Finley walked along, slightly ignoring him as he relived his sailor days while he spoke to her. As soon as they stepped outside in the service area, she saw the new, dark-blue SUV. It had upgraded wheels, chrome accents, and black interior, just like she'd asked for. It wasn't in stock at her local dealership in the dark-blue color, so they'd ordered it from another one and had it shipped over, which was why it had taken so long to get it.

"Here we go!" Paul exclaimed. "All shiny and ready to go for a ride."

"Can we skip the test drive? I already drove the red one you have on the lot."

"I'm sorry, all vehicles have to be test driven."

"Okay, can we just stay in the lot then? I really am in a hurry."

"Sure. We can go behind the service building. There's plenty of room. You can even do a doughnut if you want," he laughed.

Finley gave him an odd look. She'd bought an SUV, not a sports car. Paul handed her the keys and instructed her on where to go. Finley started the truck and accelerated slowly through the service center. When she reached the other side, she smashed the gas pedal to the floor and the vehicle took off. She quickly pumped the brakes, checking them out, before doing a couple of left and right turns. "Everything seems fine to me," she said, pulling back up to the service area.

"Great. Let's do a walk around, sign one more paper, and you can take her home!"

"Excellent," she replied, getting out.

*

Finley walked through the front door of her house and quickly looked out the window, hitting the remote lock on her new keychain as she peered at the new SUV, which was sitting in the neighbor's driveway. The lights flashed and the horn honked, indicating the doors had just been locked. Headlights turned into her driveway a split second later. She quickly rushed up stairs, jumping into the shower because she needed to get the saltwater off her skin, but also to make it look like she'd been home a little while.

"How was your day?" Nicole asked, popping her head into the bathroom.

Finley opened the glass shower door and smiled as Nicole gave her a thumbs up. Their plan had worked. Caitlin hadn't even noticed the SUV next door.

*

The next morning, Finley and Nicole were sitting at the dining table, drinking coffee and green tea, when Caitlin made her way downstairs. She was usually a morning person like both of her mothers, but she used the weekends to catch up on extra sleep, rolling out of bed whenever she felt like it, unless she had plans with Will, of course.

"Good morning, sleepyhead," Finley said. "Coffee?"

Caitlin raised a brow as she passed by her in search of breakfast, which was usually a protein packed sandwich made from two small, whole-wheat pancakes for buns with two egg whites and a turkey sausage patty in the middle. However, since it was the weekend, Nicole had made breakfast for everyone.

"Breakfast is in the microwave," Nicole said.

"Sweet!" Caitlin exclaimed as she pulled the plate of homemade banana, chocolate-chip muffins out.

"I assume you're running with me later," Finley mumbled.

"Why is that?" Caitlin asked, sitting down with a muffin on a napkin, along with her glass of milk.

"Because she ate two of those," Nicole answered with a laugh.

Finley rolled her eyes and sipped her coffee.

"So…" Caitlin looked around. She didn't see any presents or cards.

Nicole gave her a questioning look.

"I need to get ready to head to the base," Finley said.

"I brought home a bunch of work to do, too," Nicole added.

Caitlin stared at the two of them.

"Do you need me to pick you up from the mall on my way home, or are you riding with Will?" Finley asked.

"What?" Caitlin hissed. "Are you two being serious?"

Nicole and Finley looked at each other with odd expressions.

"You both forgot my birthday!" Caitlin snapped.

Finley and Nicole burst out laughing.

"Of course not," Finley said, pulling her into a hug.

"We love you. I'm pretty sure your birthday is a day we'll never forget," Nicole added, walking around the table to hug her as well.

"Where are my presents?" Caitlin questioned, looking around again.

Nicole handed her a card, which Caitlin quickly opened. She and Finley had both written messages inside about their little girl growing up, which made Caitlin tear up.

"Thanks," she said.

Finley smiled as she slid a small box in front of her. Caitlin eyed the box suspiciously, before opening it. Inside, she found a pair of earrings that matched the color of her blue eyes.

"These are beautiful."

"Is that all that's in there?" Nicole asked.

Caitlin looked underneath and found a note that read, *go to the den.* Shrugging, she got up and walked into the next room. A slightly larger box was on the couch. Caitlin sat down and opened that one, finding a new android phone and another note, *go to the kitchen.* Realizing her parents had sent her on a scavenger hunt, she chuckled and rushed back through the dining room to see what she was going to open next.

Nicole and Finley watched as Caitlin tore into the next box, containing a Visa card in her name.

"Awesome!"

"That one comes with rules," Finley stated.

Caitlin saw another piece of paper with writing on it when she removed the card. *Go to the living room.* She added the box to the rest of her gifts and moved to the front of the house. A small box was lying on the end table by the front door. Opening it, she found a set of keys and another note, *look outside.* Caitlin held her breath as she pulled the curtains back. Finley's well taken care of, six-year-old Ford Explorer, had a big blue bow on the hood.

"No way!" she squealed.

"Happy birthday," Finley and Nicole said simultaneously.

"This is the best present ever!" Caitlin exclaimed, wrapping them in one big hug.

"The credit card is for gas. As long as you keep your grades up and continue swimming, we'll pay for your gas and maintenance," Finley stated.

"That's a no-brainer." Caitlin smiled. "When can I get my regular license?"

"We can go right now, unless you want to wait a little longer," Finley said.

"Uh, no. I'm good to go now. Let me change out of my pajamas first, though," she replied, racing up the stairs.

"Do you want to go with us?" Finley asked, pulling Nicole into her arms.

"No, not really."

"She's going to be fine. She drives every time she's with me, and she does a great job. Better than you did at her age," she giggled.

Nicole gave her a sly grin.

"Come on, I'm sure she'd like to have us both there." Finley pulled back slightly with her arms loosely around Nicole's waist. "Nic...she's not Mike and she never will be," she said softly.

"I know," she sighed. "Alright, I'll go. I don't want to miss this special day in her life."

"Okay, I'm ready. Will is so excited. I just talked to her."

"You changed and made a phone call that quickly?" Finley questioned.

"I did both at the same time."

"I see." Finley nodded.

"Did you invite her to have dinner with us?" Nicole asked.

"No."

"Well, call her back. It's your birthday. I'm sure you would like her to celebrate with you."

Caitlin nodded.

"We'll stop by the phone place so they can switch everything to your new phone while we're out," Finley said as Caitlin moved to walk outside and call Will.

"I already did it."

"Seriously?"

"Yes. It's just a Sim Card, Mom. The phone is basically the same, so I put in my email and switched the stuff over with an app."

Finley looked at Caitlin like she'd sprouted a horn out of her forehead.

As the front door closed, Nicole said, "She's way smarter than we are."

"Yeah…" Finley nodded. "When did that happen?" she muttered.

Chapter 23

The following week, Jordy pulled away from the class even further as they went through day after day of drills up in the helo and out in the ocean. She performed them with ease as her training kicked in, but her heart and mind weren't present. Often times, she seemed miles away, simply going through the motions.

On Saturday morning, Finley sat down at her desk after muster had ended and she'd dismissed the class for the day. She scrolled through the contacts on her phone. Finding the person she was looking for, she hit the call button and waited.

"Hey, you!"

The familiar voice of her friend Tracey, made Finley smile. "Hi, back," she chuckled. "How's it going?"

"Not bad. I'm on nights at the moment, so everything is backwards, and Lillian is at sea for another two weeks."

"That stinks."

"Yep. So, I was thinking about you because I've been meaning to call you. Ericka Burney is smart as hell. She's about halfway caught up and she was six weeks behind. I expect her to be at the level of her classmates by the end of the month."

"Really? That's fantastic."

"Are you sure she had no mechanical experience? Where did you find her again?"

"She washed out of rescue swimmer school because she wasn't physically strong enough. I knew she was smart though. I'm glad she's doing well. She wants to be a flight mechanic."

"If she gets a degree, she could wind up being an engineer."

"Yeah, I told her that. I'm pretty sure she's dating a swimmer in my class, so she wants to be close to her."

"Oh...that sounds like a juicy story."

Finley laughed.

"So, how are things on the home front?" Tracey asked.

"Good."

"Are you ready to get back into the action?"

"Probably, when my post is up here," Finley said, thinking about how much she missed the unpredictable days and thrilling adventure of being a rescue swimmer. "I need to finish up my work for the day and head home. Thanks for doing this for me. I owe you big."

"I'm actually enjoying it. Talking with her every day helps me pass the time while Lillian is gone."

"It must be nice working out of the same base."

"Yeah. Since we got married, they can't send us to separate posts. Now, if I could only figure out how to keep her ship in port, though," Tracey laughed.

"Good luck with that," Finley chuckled. "Tell Ericka I said hey the next time you talk to her."

"I will," Tracey said before hanging up.

Finley tucked the phone into her pocket and grabbed the keys from the top drawer of her desk. She thought about the sadness she saw in Jordy's hollow eyes as she walked to her SUV. She dialed another number, before heading over to the dorm.

"Hey," Nicole said. "Are you on the way home?"

"Not yet. Do we have any plans for this afternoon?"

"No. I don't think so. Why?" Nicole asked.

"I'm bringing someone home to meet you and Caitlin."

"Okay…"

"I'll see you in a bit." Finley hung up the phone and stepped into the dorm. "Stand tall!" she said loudly.

The cadets jumped up from whatever they were doing and stood at the end of their bunks at attention.

"Petty Officer Ross," Finley called out, nodding for her to walk over. "Get ready to go off the base. You have a family member here to see you."

Jordy gave her a questioning stare. "Do I need to be in uniform?"

"No," Finley replied. "As you were," she said to the rest of the group, who eyed Jordy suspiciously before going back to what they were doing.

*

Jordy stepped outside, pushing up the long sleeves of her t-shirt. She shoved her hands in the front pockets of her jeans and looked around for the senior chief. She had no idea who was there to see her, but she was certain it was not a family member. In the back of her mind, she wondered if maybe it was Ericka.

A dark-blue SUV pulled up in front of her. She saw the senior chief behind the wheel, wearing sunglasses, as the tinted window on the front passenger door was lowered.

"Get in," Finley said.

"Senior Chief, I'm a little confused. I'm sure my family isn't here to see me," Jordy said as she buckled her safety belt.

"You're right, they aren't. I'm taking you to meet family," she replied, driving off the base. "My family...to be exact."

"Really?"

"Jordy, I could play the fool all day long and pretend I don't see what's going on with you, but I'd be a hypocrite if I did. I know you're struggling with Ericka's departure. I don't want to see you mess up and washout because of this," Finley said, glancing at her. "You see, I was in your shoes once, albeit a long time ago. An instructor pulled me back in line right before I washed out because I almost quit on her...and on myself," she added, pulling into her driveway. She cut the engine and took her sunglasses off. "Come on," she said, getting out.

Jordy looked around at the two-story, traditional-style house that matched all of the others on the street, which had massive, overhanging-style oak trees. She wondered how old the neighborhood was as she followed Finley inside. A beautiful blonde with pretty hazel eyes, who was a few inches shorter than Finley and a little more petite, walked into the living room.

"Petty Officer Jordy Ross, this is my fiancée, Nicole," Finley said. "Nic, this is Jordy, one of my cadets."

"It's a pleasure to meet you," Nicole said, stepping forward, shaking the young woman's hand. She was surprised at how much Jordy reminded her of Finley when she was a cadet. She had dark-brown hair pulled back in a ponytail and brown eyes, but the military demeanor was the same in both of them.

Jordy was about to speak when the sound of footsteps on the staircase drew her attention to what looked like a much younger clone of the senior chief with shoulder length hair.

"This is our daughter Caitlin," Finley said. "And this is Petty Officer Jordy Ross, one of my cadets."

"Oh, cool. Nice to meet you," Caitlin exclaimed, holding her hand out.

"Hi," Jordy replied, shaking hands with her.

"Lunch is ready. Jordy, I hope you're hungry." Nicole smiled.

"I'm always hungry, ma'am," she replied.

"You sound like my girls," Nicole laughed. "They'd eat me out of house and home if I'd let them."

Jordy smiled as she followed Finley and Caitlin into the kitchen to wash her hands.

The dining room table was full of food. An array of various meats and cheeses were on a platter with two kinds of wraps sitting next to it. Another platter full of different vegetables sat on the other side. A few bottles of salad dressing, along with mayo and mustard, were also on the table.

Finley took her place at the head of the table, with Nicole on one side of her and Caitlin on the other. Jordy sat down next to Caitlin, and one by one, they began passing the platters until everyone had what they needed to build their lunch wrap.

"How many weeks do you guys have left?" Caitlin asked.

"Three," Jordy answered. *Three very long weeks,* she thought as she folded her wrap.

"Is she hardnosed?" Caitlin asked, nodding towards Finley.

Jordy grinned. "Tough as nails."

"I've been on a call out with her. Watching my mom save that missing diver was the most exciting thing I've ever been a part of in my life. I hope to one day do what she does."

"Me too," Jordy mumbled, realizing how much of a hero the senior chief was in her daughter's eyes. She wanted to be someone's hero one day, too.

*

As soon as everyone had finished eating, Jordy helped clear the table and offered to wash the dishes, but she was a guest and Nicole wouldn't allow it. She tossed everything into the dishwasher while Caitlin headed upstairs, but came right back down.

"How was swimming?" Finley asked as she, Jordy, and Caitlin went into the den.

"Good. We're only practicing three more days to give me some rest and recovery time before tryouts. We worked on block timing this morning and tomorrow's focus is turns."

"Sounds like a plan." Finley noticed her keys, wallet, and cell phone in her hands. "Are you heading somewhere?"

"I told Will I'd go with her to find something for her mother's birthday. Is that okay?"

"Did you get all of your assignments yesterday?"

"No. Some of them weren't ready. They are supposed to get them to me on Monday."

"Make sure you get them. You're leaving Tuesday."

"I know."

"Alright. Have fun shopping. Tell Will I said hello, and be safe on the road."

"I will. I love you," Caitlin said, hugging her mother. "It was nice meeting you, Petty Officer Ross."

"You too," Jordy replied. "Is she a freshman?"

"Junior," Finley replied.

"At USC?"

"What? No Annandale...high school," Finley laughed. "She just turned sixteen."

"Wow, she looks older."

"Yeah."

"Does she want to be a rescue swimmer? I heard her mention swimming."

"She's interested in it, so maybe. She's in the Air Force ROTC at her school."

"It's pretty cool that she got to go on a call out with you. I'm sure that opened her eyes."

"Yeah, I'd say so," Finley laughed. "Actually, she's a phenomenal swimmer. She's headed to the USA National Team camp tryouts next week and will be gone for ten days."

"You mean like the Olympic team?"

"Yes." Finley nodded. "That's her dream right now, going to the Olympics, and swimming in college, of course."

"She seems like a good kid."

"She is. She works very hard, sometimes too hard," she sighed, knowing her daughter was just as headstrong as she was. "Anyway, do you want to take a walk?" Finley asked, changing the subject.

"Sure." Jordy shrugged.

"We'll be back in a little bit," Finley told Nicole. She gave her a quick hug before walking out the front door with Jordy. "I brought you here to meet them because I want you to see what your life can be like…with the Coast Guard, as well as outside of it."

Jordy nodded. "You have a nice family, Senior Chief."

"Thank you." Finley paused under a large oak tree just off the side walk, about a block from her house, and shoved her hands into the pockets of her ODU pants. "I know you miss Ericka, but if being a rescue swimmer is truly what you want, then you have to make that sacrifice. If you quit on me, you quit on yourself, and vice versa, but either way, you quit on her. She didn't washout because she quit. If anything, she was one of the most tenacious cadets I've ever seen. In fact, she still is."

"What do you mean?"

"Ericka isn't at home sulking, or swabbing the deck of a cutter ship. She's where she's been for the past fifteen weeks…Station Charleston."

"What? How?"

"She washed out of AST Rescue Swimmer school, but not out of the Coast Guard, and certainly not out of 'A' school."

Jordy looked at Finley like a dog who twists its head when a human talks to it.

"I pulled a lot of strings and got her transferred into AMT school. She's training to become a maintenance tech at the moment, but she'll continue on to become a Flight Mechanic."

"Are you serious?"

"Yes." Finley nodded. "She has a long way to go. She started a number of weeks behind the class, but a close friend of mine, who is also a flight mechanic, is tutoring her on the side as a favor to me. Her class graduates in about eight more weeks."

"Wow," Jordy mumbled, completely flabbergasted. "She's been there this entire time?"

"Yes. She basically packed her bag and moved across the base," Finley replied as she crossed her arms and leaned back against the tree. "I told her that I'd tell you when the time was right."

Jordy nodded. "Senior Chief, can I ask you something?"

"Sure."

"Do you go above and beyond for all of your cadets who washout or are about to?"

"I've never quit on a cadet who didn't quit on his or herself first. But, no. I've never transferred a cadet, which is nearly impossible by the way, or brought one home to meet my family. However, I saw something in both you and Ericka that first week that reminded me a lot of myself back when I was here in your shoes. I know what you are both going through, and I want to see you succeed."

"Thank you," Jordy said, realizing the person she'd come to hate for all of the wrong reasons, was more like family to her than her own flesh and blood. With that, came a newfound admiration for the woman standing in front of her. She knew the senior chief was well-respected among her peers for her work, but she wondered how many of them knew this side of her as well.

*

Finley pulled through the base gates, bypassing the rescue swimmer dorm building, before turning off a side road on the opposite side of the base, near the helo hangars. "Come on," she said, getting out of her SUV.

Jordy obliged, having no idea what they were doing as they walked through a side entrance into one of the hangars.

"Wait here," Finley said, stepping back outside.

Jordy stared at the H65-Dolphin helicopter that was sitting in the middle of the large room, halfway disassembled. Parts of it were scattered around here and there. She moved closer to get a better look.

"Go ahead, it won't bite," a familiar voice said.

Jordy turned around so fast, her brain nearly sloshed back and forth. "Oh, my God!" she exclaimed, running over, picking Ericka up off the ground and into her arms.

Ericka wrapped her arms around Jordy's neck, kissing her passionately.

"I don't want to let go of you," Jordy murmured, setting her back on her feet.

"Then don't," Ericka said.

"I still can't believe you're here."

"I'm sorry I didn't write. Things have been crazy for the past few weeks. I'm doing stuff with my class during the day, then working with my tutor at night. One of the other cadets is also helping me, which is great because the Flight Mechanic that is working with me can't be hands on. We talk through Skype over the phone and on a laptop that I'm allowed to use."

"Do you like it? Being over here?"

"Yeah, actually. I've learned so much. I want to be a flight mechanic, but I could possibly become a flight engineer on a C-130. I like the idea of having options. I miss seeing you every day though, and I do miss swimming, but I don't miss the rigorous drills. Speaking of swimmer training, how are things going over there?"

"About the same. I'm so ready for it to be over with."

"I know. Try tacking on another eight weeks!"

Jordy shook her head. "I still have EMT training when this is over, but that's only three weeks, then one final week of advanced Rescue Swimmer training. So, technically, I do have eight more weeks."

Ericka chuckled.

"I still can't believe you're here. I've missed you so much," she sighed.

Ericka looked at the brown eyes staring back at her. "I love you, Jordy. We might be on different pages right now, but I'm not going anywhere."

"I love you, too." She smiled.

"I should probably get back. I'll write to you, but I'll be at your graduation, so I'll see you soon."

"You promise?"

"I wouldn't miss it." Ericka smiled. "Promise me you won't quit. I know being a rescue swimmer is what you've always wanted. You're so close."

"I will never quit. They'll have to drag me out by my hair, kicking and screaming." She grinned, kissing Ericka one last time before reluctantly letting her go.

Ericka walked across the hangar and out the side door without looking back. She knew if she saw Jordy watching her, the tears she was holding back would start to fall.

Jordy had just wiped away a stray tear when Finley stepped inside.

"I need to get you back to the dorm."

"Thank you," Jordy said.

Finley nodded. "I told you both, I'd never quit on you."

*

Nicole was sitting on the couch with her feet up on the coffee table, watching a movie on the Hallmark channel, when Finley returned from taking Jordy back to the base.

"Wine in the middle of the day? What's the occasion?" Finley asked, kissing her check before sitting down next to her.

"This movie," Nicole mumbled. "It's a tearjerker. I thought a glass of wine might keep me from bawling my eyes out."

"Why not turn it off?"

"Absolutely not! I have to know if she dies in the end."

"Okay..." Finley said with a furrowed brow. She moved to get up and Nicole grabbed her hand.

"So, what was that today?"

"What do you mean?"

"You've never brought a cadet home. Is that even allowed?"

"I told my CO she had a family emergency, and I was taking her to see them."

"Senior Chief Morris broke a rule?" Nicole exclaimed.

"How much wine have you had?" Finley laughed.

"This is the only glass, and it's half full. I'm only teasing you. I know how strict you are with rules and regulations. You wouldn't be a Senior Chief if you didn't follow them to a T."

"You're right, and I didn't exactly break a rule. I bent one."

"Good enough. So, back to the point…"

"Jordy is a good kid. She's been struggling ever since I transferred Ericka out. I've been in her shoes. The loneliness and self-pity eat you alive because you're alone, and in your free time, what little you do get, all you do is think. It can become a very dark place. Fortunately, I had an instructor who actually cared and refused to let me quit on myself. She showed me how quitting on myself meant I was really quitting on you and Caitlin. I guess I was paying it forward. I wanted Jordy to see there is definitely light at the end of the deep dark tunnel that she's in right now," Finley said. "In fact, I bent another rule by taking Ericka, the cadet whom I transferred, out of her dorm so that they could see each other for the first time since Ericka washed out of swimmer school a few weeks ago. I'm pretty sure this was something they've both needed."

"You're the most selfless and genuine person I've ever met," Nicole murmured, curling into Finley's side as Finley wrapped her arms around her. "I love you, and I'm so lucky to have you."

"I'm pretty sure I'm the lucky one," Finley whispered, kissing the top of her head.

Chapter 24

On Monday afternoon, Finley decided to cut out early to spend a little extra time with her family before they headed off to the national team camp the next day, leaving Neil to finish out the day with the cadets. They only had three weeks left in their training and were in the classroom for the final time.

Finley noticed Will's car as she pulled into the driveway next to it, but they'd been seeing her around more here and there. She thought nothing of it as she headed inside the house, kicking off her shoes at the door. She padded up the stairs in her socks, pausing as she passed by Caitlin's open bedroom door. Her jaw hit the floor as she saw her little girl, all grown up and lying on her bed topless, making out with Will, who was also naked from the waist up.

"What the hell!" she shrieked.

"Oh, my God! Mom!" Caitlin screamed. "Shit!" she hissed, looking for her shirt as Will rolled away, doing the same.

Finley turned her back to them as they fumbled to redress. "I don't even know what to say to you right now," she growled, crossing her arms in a haste.

"I—" Will started to talk, but Finley clenched her jaw and pointed down the stairs towards the front door. She hurried out of the house.

Finley looked back at her daughter with an icy glare. "Caitlin Finley Morris, what the hell is going on?" she growled.

"I don't know. It just...sort of happened," she mumbled.

"You don't just sort of fall into bed naked with someone and have sex!"

"We weren't naked, and we weren't having sex."

"Well, half of your clothes were off! I'm pretty sure you were headed in that direction. I've had sex enough times to know the steps!" she yelled. "I'm disappointed in you," she sighed.

"Is it because Will is a girl?" Caitlin muttered.

"No. Why would you think that? I don't care if you're gay, straight, bisexual, whatever."

"Then, what's the big deal?" Caitlin huffed.

"You're too young to be having sex...with anyone!"

"Weren't you and Mom doing it at my age?" Caitlin countered.

Finley blew out a frustrating breath and shook her head. "No. As a matter of fact, we were nearly eighteen and graduating soon. Even then, we were too young. You have your whole life ahead of you."

"Mom, I really like Will. I think...I think I love her," Caitlin said.

Finley knew that feeling all too well. She fell in love with her best friend in high school, and here she was seventeen years later, still in love with her, and about to finally get married. She sighed, pulling Caitlin into a hug. "I know what you're going through. You're young, your hormones are racing, and you're in love for the first time."

"What if she breaks up with me over all of this?"

"I doubt that will happen, but if it does, you'll pick up the pieces of your broken heart and move on," Finley replied, letting go of her. "Was this the first time anything has happened beyond kissing?" she asked.

Caitlin nodded.

"Have you talked about having sex?"

"Not really."

"Has Will had sex before?"

"No."

"Well, there's a definite learning curve, I'll tell you that. However, experimenting with the unknown the day before you leave for the biggest week of your life, is probably not the best idea. Know what I mean?"

"Yeah. It was stupid."

"Sex isn't stupid when it's with the right person, and you're in love. When it is meant to be, it will happen. Just be safe about it. Okay?"

"Yes, ma'am."

Finley turned to walk away, but stopped when Caitlin said, "Are you going to tell mom?"

"You know I am. We don't keep secrets."

"Okay," Caitlin uttered. "By the way, why are you home early?"

"Because I wanted to spend time with you before you left," she replied softly, as she headed down the hall to change out of dark-blue, ODU, which she wore on classroom days, or any other day that did not involve the pool or physical fitness.

*

Later that evening, as Nicole packed her suitcase, Finley sat on the edge of the bed. "Nic, I need to talk to you about something. I was going to let it wait until you got back, so it didn't ruin the trip, but you need to know."

"Okay?" Nicole muttered, stepping over to her. "What's going on?" she asked nervously as she looked into the deep blue eyes staring back at her.

"I'm pretty sure the thing with Will isn't just a phase Caitlin is going through."

"Huh?" Nicole scrunched her face in bewilderment.

"I caught Will and Caitlin on their way to having sex this afternoon."

"What do you mean…on their way?" she asked, still a little confused.

"I came home from the base early to spend a little extra time with Caitlin since I can't go with you guys. She and Will were in her bed, naked from the waist up, in the middle of a heated make-out session. I'm pretty sure they were about to have sex."

"Oh, my God!" Nicole exclaimed as the color drained from her face. "Are you serious? What did you say to her?"

"There was a little yelling from both of us, but we had a long talk. I don't believe it was planned. They happened to go a little too far."

"Wow," Nicole gasped, shaking her head.

"She told me she's in love with Will. I think she's a little overwhelmed by all of it."

"Yeah, your first time isn't exactly the greatest," Nicole mumbled.

"My first time with you was," Finley murmured, grabbing her hand.

"Yeah." Nicole smiled, placing her other hand on Finley's cheek. "It was an awakening for me, I know that."

Finley grinned.

"So, where does this leave us with Caitlin?" Nicole sighed.

"She's scared Will might break up with her now."

"Why? Was she pushing her to do it?" she questioned, removing her hands from Finley and folding her arms like an angry mother hen.

"No. They're both virgins. In fact, I don't think she's planning on doing anything like that again anytime soon. I'm pretty sure they were both embarrassed."

"Well, that's good to know." She shook her head, still surprised by what she'd just heard. "At least they were smart enough to come here and not mess around in a parked car."

Finley laughed. "Everyone should do it in a car at least once."

"Maybe when they're in their thirties and a hot mess, but not sixteen and naïve," she chided with a sly grin, thinking about the time she and Finley had gotten busy in the back of Finley's mother's car in the park, nearly three years ago.

Finley stood up, pulling Nicole into her arms for a warm embrace. "I'm going to miss you," she sighed.

"I know. I'll miss you, too," she murmured, kissing her softly.

*

The next morning, Finley dropped off her fiancée and daughter at the airport, and headed to the base. She'd changed from sweats to her full wetsuit and survival harness, before meeting up with the class, who were waiting in one of the helicopter hangars on the other side of the base.

"Are we ready?" she asked Neil.

"Yes," he replied. "The landing crew just arrived on the beach. I'll be out in the patrol boat."

Finley nodded. "I'll see you in a couple of hours."

"Aye-aye, Senior Chief," he said before walking out of the hangar.

Finley turned to the class. "With only three weeks left, you are going to be tested more strenuously than ever before. There's no way you can be fully prepared because when you're called out, you never know what you're going to run into. So, over the next ten days, the best thing you can do is sleep when you get a chance, eat when there is food, and rely on the training you've been through over the past fifteen weeks," she said.

Jordy watched her speak to the helicopter flight crew for a minute, before returning to their group.

"Today's drill is a pass or fail test. We're going to fly you off shore, dropping you two nautical miles from the Sullivan Island Lighthouse. You will then have 50 minutes to swim, in full gear, from the drop off point to the beach in front of the lighthouse. If you take longer than 50 minutes, you have failed, and if you cannot complete the swim, you have failed," she said loudly. "Each of you have a GPS transmitter on your survival harness, so we'll know where you are at all times. Plus, you have a two-way radio for communication. We'll also have a helo in the air and a patrol boat in the water, as a safety precaution. If either of them need to come to your assistance, you have failed," she added. "Load up!"

Jordy rushed into the waiting helo with the rest of her class members. She buckled her safety belt and pulled her helmet on quickly.

Finley did a final check of the cadets. Each one gave her a thumbs up. "Lieutenant...Rescue Swimmer One. We are ready for wheels up. Over."

"Roger, Swimmer One," the pilot replied.

Jordy listened to the chatter on the radio and looked out the window as they flew over the ocean. She was a little nervous, but her adrenaline was pumping at full steam. She figured Rich felt the same way since his foot was bouncing erratically next to her. She reached over, placing her hand on his knee to stop his foot. He smiled and gave her a thumbs up.

"Listen up, we're two minutes out. The seas are less than two feet, so we'll go into a freefall hover when we arrive at the drop point. When you hit the water, pop up with the okay signal, then swim out of the rotor wash. As soon as everyone is out of the helo, you'll hear a loud siren. This is the start of your 50 minutes, so take off. The helo will stay between the swimmers and the beach, to keep you on course. Make sure you look up every few minutes to make sure you are still heading towards the helo in the air."

"Aye-aye, Senior Chief," the class replied over the radio.

"Swimmer One, we are on site for the drop," the pilot said.

"Roger," she said as the flight mechanic slid the cabin door open. "Get into position, when you are cleared and ready, jump. Whoever is next, slide quickly into position and keep moving. Webber, you're first. Followed by Ross, then Parish and McDonald. Let's go!"

Jordy sat on the edge of the open doorway, and pulled her mask down over her nose and eyes. She gave a thumbs and jumped in when she was tapped on the shoulder. In the air, she adjusted her body to the freefall position, and entered the water smoothly. The water was warmer than she'd expected. She quickly gave the 'all clear' signal and swam over to Rich.

"Are you ready for this?" he asked.

"Semper Paratus," she answered, stating the Coast Guard motto: Always Ready.

"My thoughts exactly."

"Are we doing this together?" Evan asked, swimming over to them.

"Once a team, always a team," they said in unison.

*

None of the cadets noticed Finley jump in behind them as the siren wailed, signaling the clock had begun ticking. They hurried off, freestyle swimming as fast as they could through the mostly flat sea. Finley hung back a bit, keeping a close eye on the group. An open water, two-mile swim was a lot more difficult than it sounded.

As she swam, Finley thought about Caitlin and Nicole. Their flight wasn't scheduled to land for a few more hours. She hated not being there to witness Caitlin following her dreams, but Nicole had promised to video as much as she could. She even promised to sneak and do it if they didn't allow recording.

After the first mile, she noticed the pace slowing for some of the cadets. She kept an eye on them as she reduced her strokes in order to stay behind the group. By the time they reached a mile and a half, one of the cadets, Jon Parish, had fallen completely off and was barely swimming. Finley swam over, pulling him to the surface as soon as he went under.

"I've got you," she said as she maneuvered him into the swimmer hold position.

"I can't breathe," he gasped, starting to panic.

"Yes you can. Calm down. Take slow, easy breaths."

"My body is cramping...and...my lungs are burning," he mumbled between gasping breaths.

"You'll be alright," she assured him as she swam him towards the patrol boat. Grabbing her radio, she called for Neil to come over with the boat. Once the cadet was secure in the boat, she said, "Petty Officer Jon Parish, you've failed to complete the Open Water Swim Test. You're finished as a rescue swimmer, but you made it further than most of your classmates. Hold your head up high."

"Aye-aye, Senior Chief," he sighed.

"The class is nearing the finish; do you want a ride?" Neil asked, leaning over to haul her up into the boat.

"No, I'm good," she replied. "Go get him processed out. I'll sign the papers as soon as I get back," she added, swimming away.

*

Jordy, Evan, and Rich collapsed in a heap on the beach, less than ten feet from the waves washing ashore.

"Holy shit," Rich gasped.

"My legs feel like jelly," Evan mumbled.

"Come on, boys! I could go another mile," Jordy joked, barely able to lift her arms.

They'd finally caught their breath enough to move further up the beach, when they noticed another swimmer coming in. Jordy looked around, counting the cadets. There were only nine of them sitting in the sand, plus two other Coast Guard members who were there to escort them back to the base.

"That doesn't look like one of us," Rich muttered as the swimmer walked out of the surf carrying a set of fins. "That's Senior Chief!"

"Get out! She did the swim with us?" Evan moved to get a better look.

Finley waved at the group, who looked half dead, as she meandered up like she'd only swam a couple of laps in the pool.

"Why is everyone sitting around? Stand tall!" she yelled, checking her watch. There was still three minutes left.

The cadets struggled to get on their feet.

"Congratulations to those of you who are standing in front of me. You passed. However, one of your classmates, Petty Officer Jon Parish, failed to complete the test and has subsequently washed out."

The cadets began to whisper amongst themselves.

"Stand tall!" she yelled. "Everyone head up to the lighthouse parking lot. You'll find recovery food, water, and a dry towel. The van will be heading back to base in ten minutes. I suggest you replenish, get hydrated, dry off, and find a seat before you get left. Move!"

Jordy took off, stumbling through the sand on shaky legs with Rich and Evan behind her, as well as the rest of the class.

"I can't believe Jon washed out," Evan said, as he grabbed a bottle of water.

"It serves him right. He's been an asshole to everyone for months," Rich replied with a mouthful of banana.

"I wish I'd have been there to see the look on his face," Jordy muttered, as she squeezed the small packet of peanut butter onto her banana and bit into it.

"I heard he nearly drowned and Senior Chief had to rescue him. Apparently, he cramped up or something," one of the other cadets added.

"Let's go, people! You can gossip when you get back to the dorm this evening. Our training day isn't over yet. Get your snack, get dried off, and get into the van!" Finley yelled, noticing everyone standing around as she walked up from the beach. One of the Coast Guard members who was there helping out, handed her a water and a banana, which she gladly accepted.

A smile crept across Jordy's face when she saw Finley put peanut butter on her own banana, just as she had done.

*

Finley spent the rest of the week working long hours at the base, then going home to her quiet house. It had been nearly three years since she'd had time away from Nicole and Caitlin, and it reminded her of what life was like before she and Nicole had reconciled. Back then, she'd spent many nights alone, sitting by the river, looking up at the stars. Her life had practically changed overnight on several occasions, sending her spinning in different directions, but this last time had turned out to be the perfect adjustment.

As promised, Nicole had sent a few videos each day of Caitlin's training, most of which she had to sneak around to get because recording was not allowed in the facility.

On Friday evening, Finley was sitting in front of the TV, trying to figure out what was going on in the murder mystery show that she'd stopped on while searching the channels. Coming into it after the first ten minutes, made her completely lost. She was about to just turn the TV off when her phone rang.

"Hey, kiddo!" she answered. "How's it going?"

"Oh, my God, Mom! These coaches are awesome!" Caitlin exclaimed as she went on and on about her day. The first two days had been mostly about nutrition and fueling the body, as well as recovery. So, Friday was their first full day in the pool.

Finley sat on the couch with a smile on her face, listening to her daughter talk as fast as a cartoon character. She wished she could've gone along, but it had come up so fast, there was no way she could've taken that kind of time off, especially at the end of Phase Three.

"Here's Mom. I love you," Caitlin said.

"Love you, too. Have fun!"

"Hey, babe," Nicole sighed.

"You sound tired."

"I am. The hours are crazy, and all I do is sit around and work on my laptop. She and one other kid are the only minors, but her mom does nothing but scroll the internet all day. She's a professional dog groomer."

"Professional?"

"Oh, yes. She's a step above the ones at the regular pet stores. She works at a pet salon," Nicole said, dragging out the word salon like a someone who is trying too hard. "I'd rather her be nuts like one of those cheerleader moms. At least she wouldn't bore me to tears explaining the latest Lhasa-Doodle-Retriever style trend."

"What the hell is that?"

"Beats me. I tune her out."

Finley laughed hysterically.

"So, what do you have planned for the weekend?"

"Well, I ordered a prostitute. She should be here soon. Other than that, I'm sitting on my butt in front of the TV."

"Uh huh," Nicole chuckled.

"I'm on muster duty, so I'll be at the base for a bit both days. I'll probably swim some laps while I'm there, but I don't have anything exciting planned. I was thinking of going to see my mom on Sunday. She bought some kind of shelf thing and she asked me to put it together."

"That's good."

"What about you? What's on the agenda for Caitlin?"

"She'll be in the pool all weekend, so I'll be sitting at a side table, working on my computer. At least I'm able to get some stuff done, so I won't be so bombarded when I get back."

"Yeah," Finley muttered. "I miss you."

"I miss you, too."

"I should probably get to bed. It's been a long week. Another cadet washed out."

"That stinks."

"He cramped up during the open water swim. I had to actually rescue him."

"Oh, wow."

"I'm sure the cadets have been celebrating in secret. He was an ass to begin with."

"Do unto others…" Nicole stated.

"I'd like to do unto you," Finley murmured.

Nicole laughed. "Isn't your hooker on the way?"

"Oh, yeah. I forgot about that," Finley chuckled.

"I love you," Nicole said.

"I love you, too. Have a good weekend."

"You too. Enjoy your quiet time off. Relax for a change."

"Yes, ma'am," Finley laughed before hanging up.

Chapter 25

Finley stood in front of the cadets first thing Saturday morning. The large configuration of four rows deep, five cadets to a row, had narrowed down to a single, straight line for their muster formation since there were only nine of them left. It didn't take long for the headcount and inspection since after sixteen weeks of this daily assessment, they knew how to present themselves. All females needed to have their hair up in a tight bun, or cut short and off their collar. The men had to be closely shaven, with their hair cropped short, off the ears and the collar, but not necessarily high and tight like a Marine. Whichever uniform they were supposed to be in that day, including: sweats, physical fitness clothing, and sneakers, had to be in perfect condition with no strings hanging off, and no stains. On the weekends, they mustered in their ODU, which was basically the same uniform Finley and Neil wore when they weren't doing physical fitness or pool drills. The only difference between the two was the rate and rank insignia.

"What happened to your cap?" she asked, looking at Evan.

"I dropped it in the pool and the chlorine did this," he replied.

Finely raised a brow. "Do not show up at my muster again with that ratty thing. Go to the Exchange and get a new one!" she growled, shaking her head.

"Aye-aye, Senior Chief."

"We have two weeks left," she said, stepping back to address all of them. "You should be proud of yourselves for getting this far." She paused, looking at each cadet. "I'm granting you liberty for the rest of the weekend. No alcohol, and you must be back on the base before five p.m. on Sunday night. You also have permission to use one of the base vans."

"Aye-aye, Senior Chief!" they exclaimed as a group.

"Dismissed," she said.

All of the cadets except Jordy rushed towards the dorm to get ready to leave the base. She simply walked along behind them. There was no where she wanted to go, except to the other side of the facility to see Ericka, which was against the rules. Deciding she'd rather train for the upcoming week, not knowing what was in store for them, she headed over to the pool room.

*

As soon as she dismissed the group, Finley went to her office. She'd already been given the files on the incoming cadets for the next class, and figured she might as well give them a look.

She hadn't been at her desk more than ten minutes when her cell phone rang.

"Senior Chief Morris," she answered, recognizing the number was from the base.

"This is Lieutenant Commander Phillips in Operations Command."

"What can I do for you, sir?" she asked. She knew him well enough from all of the training missions she'd flown with her cadets over the last two and half years.

"I thought I saw you come in this morning. Are you still on the base?"

"Yes, sir. I mustered my cadets about a half hour ago. I'm in my office at the moment."

"I need a swimmer," he said, talking quickly. "We have a container ship sixty miles off our coast, taking on water and heavily listing. I have one helo on scene, but we need another bird out there. We have no idea how many survivors are on board at this time."

"I'm on my way," she replied, rushing out of her office.

"6509 is fueled, and waiting outside of hangar two," he stated before hanging up.

Finley was already racing down the hallway towards the pool room lockers, which was where she'd stored her swimmer gear and flight bag. She nearly plowed over Jordy as she rushed inside.

"Whoa!" Jordy shrieked.

"I'm sorry," Finley called, as she quickly opened the locker her gear was in and began stripping.

Jordy stared at the senior chief like she had two heads. "What's going on?" she asked.

"A container ship is sinking off the coast. They need another swimmer on scene."

"Can I go with you?"

Finley looked at Jordy, who was already dressed in her wetsuit. "What are you doing?"

"I was about to work on some training."

"Where is the rest of the class?"

"They took off in the van as soon as you dismissed us."

"Come on," she said, knowing it was a bad idea to bring a cadet on a call out, but at the same time, live action

287

was the best way to learn. Plus, the extra swimmer could be handy if they were dealing with multiple survivors, as well as injuries.

Jordy pulled on her harness and boots, and grabbed the flight bag that contained her mask, snorkel, and fins. Both women jumped into Finley's SUV and rode around to the opposite side of the base where the hangars were located.

*

Jordy stared nervously at the floor of the helicopter as it bounced through a bit of turbulence. She went through the months of training over and over in her head.

"Search and Rescue 6509…Sector Charleston. Be advised, we have a report of twenty plus survivors on board, some with injuries. Over."

"Sector…6509. Copy. We have the ship in sight and are two minutes out. Search and Rescue 6533 is not visible. Over," the captain radioed.

"6509…Sector. Roger. 6533 hit bingo and returned to refuel. They should be back on scene within twenty minutes. Over."

"The ship will be gone in twenty minutes," Finley muttered to herself.

Jordy quickly looked out the window, seeing for the first time, the badly listing ship. Large shipping containers were floating around it, with some half sunken already. "Oh, my God," she whispered, too low for the radio to pick up her voice.

"We're going to get hoisted down together. Once we're on board, listen to everything I tell you," Finley said.

"Aye-aye, Senior Chief," Jordy replied.

"Swimmer One and Swimmer Two, ready for deployment?" the pilot asked.

"Roger," Finley answered, unbuckling her seatbelt. She sat on the floor of the helo, allowing the flight mechanic to attach the hoist clip to her harness.

Jordy got into position in front of her, face to face. She watched Finley attached her harness clips to Finley's D rings, connecting them together.

Finley gave a thumbs up, as did Jordy, and the flight mechanic opened the cabin door.

"Sector Charleston...6509. Deploying Swimmer One and Swimmer Two. Over."

"6509...Sector. Copy."

The flight mechanic tapped Jordy and Finley, then pressed the button to raise the hoist. They swung out of the helo together, dangling thirty feet in the air over the crippled vessel. Jordy looked around, trying to figure out where they were going to land as they began to move lower and lower.

"Put us on top of the cargo," Finley radioed.

"It's shifting all around," the flight mechanic said. "It's too dangerous."

"Just do it!"

"Roger," he replied.

"When we touchdown, we're going to have to climb down and work our way back to the bridge!" Finley yelled.

Jordy gave her a thumbs up, indicating she heard her and understood.

"6509...Swimmer One. Do we know if 6533 left their swimmer aboard?" she radioed.

"Swimmer One...6509, negative. Repeat, negative on the swimmer. He was resuscitating a high injury, low alert survivor."

"They hit bingo because they flew that survivor to the hospital," she said, mostly to herself, knowing the protocol. "Okay, here we go!" she yelled to Jordy as their feet touched the top of a burnt-red colored container. She quickly unhooked Jordy from her harness, then removed the hoist hook, before giving the 'all clear' signal.

The container slid a few inches closer to the one next to it, which was practically hanging over the edge. Jordy dropped to her knees to keep from falling. Finley climbed down first and turned to help Jordy. There wasn't much to hold onto and their rubber dive boots, barely got any traction on the metal surface.

Both on their feet, they made their way around the maze, careful of sliding containers weighing thousands of pounds that could easily crush them or toss them overboard. Finley had been on a couple of container ships over the years, so she had a pretty good idea where to go. Sure enough, she opened the door to the bridge and found the captain, along with four crewmen.

"I'm Senior Chief Morris with the United States Coast Guard. Do you speak English?"

"Yes," he replied, sounding as American as she was.

Thank God, she thought. She spoke enough Spanish to get by, but many of the cargo ship captains were surprisingly, Dutch. A language she knew nothing about. "Do you have a raft on board?"

"Yes, but we can't get to it. The freight in the compartments is shifting all around. I have a man stuck down there."

"Alright. We'll get him." She turned to Jordy. "We have to get these men out of here. We don't have a lot of time. We're going to have to climb up onto a container out away from the bridge, the same way we came down. Do you think you can handle that?"

"Yes," Jordy said as her heart raced. She'd never felt an adrenaline rush like the one she was experiencing.

"If we lose contact or you need to call the helo, use your radio. Your call sign is: Swimmer Two."

"Roger."

"Captain, we're going to get these men off of here first, then come back for you and the injured man," Finley said.

"Okay."

"Let's go." Finley waved her hand for the men to follow her. "Do you speak English?"

"We do," two of them said in shaky voices.

"Can you communicate with them?" she asked, pointing to the other two.

They both nodded.

"Alright. Jordy, I'll lead. You bring up the rear. Keep the group tight."

"Roger," Jordy replied.

The ship listed another degree, sending the container they'd landed on, and the one next to it, into the ocean. Finley began to move around a container, when another came crashing into it. She quickly shoved the man behind her to keep him from getting crushed to death. Re-thinking her plan, she decided to go up over top of the containers, figuring they could jump from one to the other, if needed, to get far enough away from the bridge to safely use the hoist.

Finley lost her footing several times, but finally made it up. The men were in work boots with deck shoe gripping on the bottom, so they were able to scale the side of the container a little easier. Once they were all up, she reached down, pulling Jordy up.

"We need to move fast," she said, grabbing the radio on her vest. "6509...Swimmer One. We have four survivors. Repeat: four survivors. Alert: ten; Injury: zero. Send the sling," she radioed, then gave the signal for the sling in case they hadn't heard her.

"Swimmer One...6509. Roger. Deploying sling," the captain replied.

Finley looked back, checking their distance from the bridge, as the bright yellow sling slowly made its way down to them. She quickly grabbed one of the non-English-speaking guys and slipped the sling over his head and through his arms. She clasped the buckles and gave the 'all clear' signal. "Tell him to keep his legs straight down and be still," she said to the man next to her.

He quickly spoke in a language she didn't recognize, just before the man's feet were lifted off the ground.

Jordy felt the ship rocking again as she watched the sling get pulled into the helo. She silently prayed they had enough time to get everyone off the ship, including themselves, before it sank.

The second and third guy went up into the helo as easily as the first. The fourth guy shook his head when Finley went to strap him into the sling.

"What's wrong?"

He shook his head no and pointed up at the helicopter hovering over them.

"You'll be fine," she encouraged.

He was the other guy who didn't speak English, so he kept shaking his head no.

"I think he's afraid of heights," Jordy said.

The man looked over at the water like maybe he was thinking of jumping in.

"Oh, don't go into the water you dumb shit," Finley growled. She got his attention and put her hand on the top of her head like a shark fin and moved around while chomping her jaw like a shark.

The man's eyes lit up and he quickly tried putting the sling on by himself. Jordy laughed as Finley got him strapped in and sent him on his way.

"Swimmer One…6509. Be advised, the captain is still on board, as is one injured survivor, both are below deck. Unsure at this time if any other survivors remain. Over," she radioed as she and Jordy made their way across the top of the containers and back towards the bridge.

Jordy was starting to feel the wear on her body from all of the climbing and jumping.

"6509…Swimmer One. Copy. Do we know the status on the injury? Over."

"Swimmer One…6509. Negative. Repeat: negative injury status. Over," she answered as she entered the side door. "Captain, is there anyone else on board?"

"No. I checked the crew roster twice. The other helicopter took six men with them," he said as he led her down the ladder to one of the cargo bays where the guy was trapped. The ship had adjusted once again, putting them very close to a forty-five-degree angle.

"We don't have much time," Finley muttered, looking at Jordy.

"He's in here," the captain exclaimed, jamming the door open.

Jordy and Finley both shined their flashlights in the dark room, landing on the man. One of his legs was pinned between two containers that had slid together.

"That container weighs thousands of pounds," Jordy mumbled. "How are we supposed to move it?"

"I don't know, but we're going to try," Finley said. "Look around, see if you can find something to leverage against one of the containers, but be careful. You don't want to get stuck, too."

Jordy searched around while Finley assessed the guy, checking his vitals as best she could without medical equipment. "Will this work?" she asked, coming back with a pipe that had broken off a wall when a container crashed into it.

"Probably, not, but let's give it a try. What's his name?"

"Hans," the captain replied.

"Alright, Hans. We're going to try to get you out."

"Swimmer One...6509. We are five minutes from bingo. Over."

"Answer them for me," Finley said, jamming the pipe between the containers.

"6509...Swimmer Two. Copy. We are trying to free the trapped survivor, Over," Jordy radioed as Finley and the captain used all of their weight, hoping to get some space between the two containers, but they wouldn't budge.

"Damn it!" Finley yelled. Just as she and the captain tried again, the ship listed further. The container behind the man moved slightly. She and the captain wedged the pipe into the space on the opposite side of his leg. "Pull him out!" Finley shouted.

Jordy grabbed the man's arms up under his shoulders from behind and tugged as hard as she could. The man screamed in pain as she yanked him free.

"We have to go, now!" Finley yelled. "You'll be okay, Hans. Hang in there!"

Jordy led the way with the flashlight while Finley and the captain carried the man through the hallway, towards the metal ladder. Jordy climbed up and out first, followed by the captain.

"Here, hold my feet," she said to him as she leaned over the opening, reaching down for the man.

Finley went up the ladder beside him, holding half of his weight against her as Jordy pulled him up. As soon as they were back in the bridge, Finley wanted to sit down and catch her breath, but she had no time.

Beads of sweat poured off Jordy's brow as her heart thumped in her chest. Her upper body burned from using everything she had to pull the man up the ladder.

"Swimmer One...6509. Survivor is freed. We are coming out. Send the basket. Alert: eight; Injury: seven," she radioed as she and Jordy carried the man out the door of the bridge and onto the deck. The ship was listing well over forty-five degrees, threatening to plunge below the surface at any moment as more containers slid off the deck.

"6509...Swimmer One. Copy."

"We have to get him up on top of the containers. There's no way we can get him into the basket down here," Finley yelled as the helicopter moved closer. "I'll go first. See if you and the captain can put him on your shoulders, one each, and lift him up. Use your legs to support the weight."

Jordy looked at the man lying on the deck. He was smaller than average. "We'll give it a try."

Finley scaled the side of the container once again, her booted feet slipping all around, but she managed to pull herself up. "Alright," she said, lying on her stomach, ready to pull the injured survivor up on top of the container.

Jordy got into position with the captain beside her as they stood the man up on his uninjured leg. He was in so much pain, he did nothing but scream and wobble around. She squatted down, putting the left side of his butt on her shoulder, as the captain did the same on the right side. The three of them had their backs to the container.

"On three," Jordy said. "One...two...three!" She pushed up, fully extending her leg muscles. The captain wasn't in anywhere near as good a shape as she was, but he managed to get his side lifted enough to keep them from tipping over.

Finley turned around and flung her legs over the side, before reaching down as they pushed up. She grabbed the man under his arm pits and forced herself back, pulling him up on top of her.

"Holy shit," Jordy gasped.

"No kidding," the captain wheezed.

She helped push the older man up as he struggled to climb the side of the container. Finley had rolled the man off her and had begun assessing his injury since she could finally get a good look at him. It took everything Jordy had, but she was able to climb up, collapsing beside the injured man. "Hans, can you hear me?"

He was lying there with his eyes closed, and his chest was moving rapidly up and down. Finley was sure he'd gone into shock. "We need to move away from the bridge," she said, looking out at the helo. They were five containers away, with the basket on the hook, dangling a couple of feet below the open cabin door. "Swimmer One...6509. We need the litter. Survivor has gone unconscious. Repeat: send the litter. Survivor alert: zero. Over," she radioed.

As Finley and Jordy grabbed Hans, working out a way to carry him away from the bridge, the shipped lurched and began going under the water.

"Jordy, stay where you are and ride down with the ship!" Finley yelled. "It will try to suck you down with it. Grab the captain and swim straight ahead!" The captain was completely exhausted. She knew he would never be able to swim against the undertow by himself.

Jordy froze.

"Rescue Swimmer, don't you quit on me!" Finley shouted, sitting down and pulling Hans' limp body into a swimmer hold. "I can't save them both!"

Jordy took a deep breath and squeezed her eyes closed. She opened them again just as the water rose over the sides, plunging the ship below the water line.

*

Finley held her breath as her lungs burned. She kicked her legs and stroked her free arm fighting her way to the surface, struggling for every inch, while holding the survivor tightly against her, until they broke the surface. Inhaling a huge breath to fully inflate her lungs, she searched around for Jordy.

*

Jordy saw the sunlight, but couldn't seem to get to it. Her body ached and her lungs burned like they were on fire. She held the captain against her as she thrashed around, trying to go up with the extra weight holding her down.

She was so close, but so far away. One breath and it would all be over. The stinging pain in her lungs, the sharp needles all over her body, it would all be gone.

Fight, Jordy! Don't you quit on me! She heard Ericka's voice say in her head.

Finding an extra ounce of willpower when absolutely nothing was left, Jordy broke the surface with the captain still in the swimmer hold under her arm. She gasped for air, coughing and spitting water.

"Oh, thank God," Finley murmured, seeing her pop up.

The ship was long gone, having settled on the ocean floor, some five hundred feet or more below them as the helo hovered above, slowly lowering the litter.

Finley managed to get Hans inside by herself. Then, she gave the 'all clear' signal and swam to the side, out of the way.

"Is he dead?" the captain asked, choking and coughing as he spit out water.

"No, but his breathing is pretty erratic. He's in shock, and I'm sure he swallowed some water," Finley answered as she gave the signal for the basket.

Jordy held onto the captain and treaded water while the flight mechanic changed the apparatus, before sending the hoist back down. Finley helped her load the last survivor inside, then they swam out of the rotor wash together as he was retrieved.

"You did great back there," Finley said loudly. "I'm damn proud of you."

"I learned from the best," Jordy replied.

When the basket came back down, Finley and Jordy climbed in together, breathing a sigh of relief as they were lifted from the water. As soon as they were inside the helo,

Finley went to work on Hans. His breathing was faint, and he definitely wasn't stable. The pilot radioed ahead for a reroute to the nearest hospital.

"Do you think he will make it?" Jordy asked as they landed on the helicopter pad on the roof of Charleston Medical Center.

"I don't know," Finley replied, watching the doctors rush him inside on the gurney. "This is the part that sucks. We do the best that we can do, and move on. Often times, we don't know the outcome." She pointed towards the waiting helo. "Maybe it's better that way," she said as they ducked under the spinning rotor and climbed inside.

Chapter 26

Finley was lounging on the couch on Sunday afternoon, thinking about the events of the day before, and how much she was reminded of Mr. Dunleavy, the man she'd spent all night holding onto as she treaded water for the both of them while drifting aimlessly in the Atlantic Ocean, nearly three years ago. His sailboat had sunk in a nasty storm and the helo was unable to retrieve them before having to return to the base to refuel. Thinking about that dreadful night at sea with Mr. Dunleavy, and the heroic actions she took to save Hans the day before, reminded her of why she became a rescue swimmer to begin with.

She'd had no idea that the container ship rescue had made national, headline news, until her cell phone rang and she heard the tone in Nicole's voice on the other end of the line.

"What were you doing on a sinking ship in the middle of the ocean?"

"My job," Finley replied calmly.

"You're an instructor."

"I'm still a rescue swimmer, Nic."

"You could've been killed."

"But, I wasn't. I'm sitting on the couch in our house right now, talking to you."

"That's not the point. How did you wind up out there?" Nicole questioned, sounding more perturbed as the conversation went on.

"I was on base when I got the call that they needed another swimmer. I ran into Jordy when I went to get my gear, so I brought her with me."

"You had a cadet with you?"

"Yes. She's been through sixteen weeks of training. If she couldn't handle going with me on that call out, then she shouldn't be graduating from swimmer school," Finley growled. "What's going on with you? Why do you sound so mad?"

"How would you feel if you woke up, turned on the news, and saw your fiancée standing on a half-sunken ship in the middle of the ocean?"

"I was doing my job. I saved six men's lives, including one who was badly injured and would've drown. This is what I do, Nic. You know that."

"It's not what you're supposed to be doing right now, though," she sighed. "I thought you didn't go out on calls as an instructor. At least, you haven't for the past two and a half years."

Finley was at a loss for words. She suddenly felt very alone, like everything was crumbling around her all over again. "Nicole, are you with me now because I'm not in the field?"

"What?"

"Answer me, damn it! Did you get back with me because I took the instructor post?"

The other end of the line was silent.

"Damn you, Nicole!" she snapped, standing up and pacing the floor. "Damn you for putting me through this all over again! If you can't handle my job, then you should've let go and never come back to me," she added angrily. "I'm not staying here another three years as an instructor. As soon as my extended post is up, I'm going back to the action and being transferred to a new air station. You knew this. We even talked about where I should request to be sent."

"I don't want to have this conversation over the phone," Nicole said.

"Well, you should've thought about that before you called me," Finley huffed. "If you're going to quit on me...on us, again, you might as well do it now and get it over with."

The phone was quiet for what seemed like a minute. Finley thought she heard Nicole crying.

Finally, Nicole murmured, "I'll see you in a couple of days."

Finley listened to the silence as the line went dead. She pulled the phone from her ear, tossing is as hard as she could against the couch cushions.

*

As the next to last week of training started, everyone on the base had heard about the ship, as well as the heroic rescue. Finley and Jordy both received praise from the commanding officer, executive officer, and command master chief of the base. Upon graduation, Jordy was also set to receive a commendation medal for her act of bravery as a training cadet.

Jordy wasn't sure how to handle all of the attention she'd begun to receive. The only person she was eager to talk to about the rescue with was Ericka, and that was impossible. She wondered if she even knew about it. She smiled thinking about the two-page letter she'd sent her in the mail that morning, describing the entire call out scene by scene, along with how scared she'd been the entire time, but it was Ericka's voice in her head that had kept her going. She knew no matter what, she wasn't going to quit, not on the senior chief, not on herself, and certainly not on Ericka.

She wondered about the man...Hans, and had tried to find out about his condition on Sunday, but no one knew anything. She hoped Finley could give her some insight as she headed over to the hangars in the van with the rest of the class. They were scheduled for drills in the helo the entire week, working mainly to increase their speed and accuracy rate.

As soon as Finley had gone over their drill instructions for the flight, the class began their preflight checklist. Each cadet had a clipboard and paper. They circled around, checking the exterior, then moved to the interior, before signing the paper and handing it to the pilot. If they found something broken, missing, or otherwise having an issue, they were to report it immediately. Finley had tested them on several occasions, sometimes with the most minor anomaly, but these last eight cadets hadn't made it this far because they were lazy and careless. Each of them had worked extremely hard, many times to the point of collapsing with exhaustion, but they kept on going, which was why each and every time she tested them with something new, they each caught it right away.

"Senior Chief, have you heard any news on Hans?" Jordy asked, handing in her checklist, which was all clear.

Finley nodded as she also signed the paper. "In the news yesterday, they said he'd undergone major surgery to try and repair his crushed leg, but the nerve damage was severe. Their unsure if he'll walk again."

"At least he's alive," Jordy murmured, thankfully. "It was in the news?" she questioned.

"National, headline news."

"Really? Did they say anything about us?"

"Oh, yeah," Finley nodded.

Jordy looked slightly stunned. She'd had no idea what to expect in the aftermath of her first call out, but the daring rescue had certainly gained a lot of attention, especially if it had been in the national news. She thought of her family for a brief second, wondering if they'd seen the news, but the notion quickly vanished. If they didn't care to know what she was doing and how she was, then she didn't care if they anything about her at all.

"Here, before I forget. Put it in your flight bag," Finley said, handing her a small envelope.

"What's this?"

"Something from Ericka. I ran into her this morning before muster. I was over here going through the day with our pilot and co-pilot. She was in the hangar working on something with another cadet before class. She was going to mail it, but asked me if I'd give it to you instead."

Jordy shoved the envelope into her flight bag as her eyes twinkled with anticipation.

Finley patted her on the shoulder. "Come on, let's go show these boys how it's done." she grinned, grateful that she had these daily drills to keep her mind off Nicole.

*

Two days later, Finley sat in the Charleston Airport lobby, dressed in her dark-blue ODU, minus the cap, which was lying on the seat beside her. She tried calming her racing nerves, but nothing helped ease the tension between her shoulders. She and Nicole hadn't spoken since their heated conversation, three days earlier. She didn't like the way they'd left things and wondered what was about to come down on her when they hashed it out. She never thought Nicole would make her choose between a life together and the Coast Guard. She loved them both, and each had given her something invaluable. If that was what it came down to, she wondered if she'd make the right choice.

Her eyes caught sight of the flight board as it changed Nicole and Caitlin's flight from incoming to arrived. She knew it would take them a bit to debark the plane and walk through the terminal, but she got up and walked towards the baggage claim area anyway.

"Mom!" Caitlin yelled, walking swiftly towards her.

Finley smiled and wrapped her daughter in a bear hug. "I missed you," she said.

"I missed you, too. Oh, my God, I have so much to tell you," Caitlin rambled.

Finley looked past her to the blonde standing a few feet away. She stepped around Caitlin and walked towards her.

"I shouldn't have put you on the spot," Nicole said. "It scares me when you go on call outs...I never know if you're coming home," she added, wiping a tear as it fell down her cheek. "I was surprised. When you became an instructor, yes, a small part of me was relieved because I wouldn't have to worry for the next three years."

Finley nodded, unsure what to say. "Are we going to do this here?" she muttered, glancing at the other plane passengers mulling about, waiting for their luggage.

Nicole ignored the people around her as she continued. "I know being a rescue swimmer is your job, but it's not just what you do, Finley. It's who you are. I could never take that away from you, and I wouldn't want to try," she said, looking at her with tear-filled eyes as she put her hand on Finley's cheek. "I will never quit on you, or on us…Never again," she sobbed, still staring at Finley's deep blue eyes. "I love you more than anything. I always have and always will."

"I love you, too," Finley said, wrapping her arms around Nicole, kissing her softly.

The people nearby clapped and one person whistled.

Caitlin had no idea what all the commotion was about until she returned to them with the suitcases. She raised an eyebrow, giving them an odd look when she noticed the loving embrace they were sharing in the middle of the baggage claim area. Seeing her mom wipe tears from her face, she moved closer and asked, "What just happened?"

"Miscommunication," Finley said, pulling her into another hug. "I think you have some communicating of your own to do," she added, waving her hand.

Caitlin stepped away from her mom and turned around. Will was a few feet away, looking extremely shy.

"Will!" Caitlin shrieked, rushing over to her.

The two young girls shared a long hug.

"How did you know—"

"Your mom called me. I had to see you as soon as you landed," Will said, cutting her off. "I love you. I thought you should know that."

Caitlin grinned from ear to ear. "I love you, too!"

"Well…" Nicole uttered. "That settles that, doesn't it?"

"I think so." Finley nodded.

"Mom, do you think I could ride home with Will?" Caitlin asked.

"Sure," Finley replied, looking at Nicole, who added, "But come straight home."

"Okay!"

Finley watched as her daughter disappeared through the crowd. She knew at that moment that she was no longer the light in Caitlin's eyes. She wasn't a little girl anymore.

"Are you alright?" Nicole asked, wrapping her arm around Finley's waist.

"Yeah." She smiled, reaching for the suitcases.

Chapter 27

The final week of Rescue Swimmer school was basically paperwork oriented once all of the cadets had finished their final exam: a two-part written test, a water test in the pool simulator, plus an ocean test in the helo, which had taken up all of Monday and Tuesday. Each cadet passed, ensuring that he or she would graduate that coming weekend.

On Wednesday, they went through rigorous physical exams and eye tests, which together, were also known as an annual flight exam. After that, they completed packets of paperwork to get registered for EMT training, which was next on the list, before they could actually go to a post as a Rescue Swimmer. The three-week course would teach them the basic life-saving skills they'd need out in the field.

*

Jordy could hardly contain her excitement once she had everything ready to go the night before graduation. She walked into the dorm, high-fiving the guys. "We did it!" she yelled at Rich. "We fucking did it!"

He whistled loudly.

Evan finished putting together his Service Dress Blue uniform, and joined them in a huddle.

"Eighteen weeks ago, I walked in here with one thing on my mind…graduate. I didn't care about who else was around me or why they were here," Jordy said. "Now, I look at the three of us and I'm so thankful I went through this with the both of you. I have friends for life."

"Once a team, always a team," Rich replied.

"I love you, guys," Evan added.

"Come on, get in here. We all made it through this hell together!" Jordy yelled, calling the other six cadets over to celebrate with them.

*

The next day, Finley dressed in her Service Dress Blue uniform and stared in the mirror at all of the decorations that littered her dark-blue jacket after sixteen years in the service.

"They're going to have to start pinning stuff onto your pants," Nicole joked, standing beside her and brushing away a piece of lint from her shoulder.

"Nah," Finley laughed. "I'll retire at that point."

Nicole grinned. "Do you have your speech ready?"

She nodded. "This was the hardest one I've ever written. This class was special in a few different ways. I hope I've taught them as much as I've learned from them."

"You're amazing at what you do. If you weren't, you wouldn't have all of those adornments on your jacket."

Finley leaned over, kissing her softly, then she turned, pulling Nicole into her arms as she kissed her much harder.

"What was that for?" Nicole asked, not wanting it to end.

"Practice. I'm not sure which one I want to go with tomorrow," Finley teased.

Nicole chuckled. "There won't be much of a reception if you use the second one. I'll be ready to go right to the honeymoon."

"Oh…second one it is then." Finley grinned.

"Have we decided when we're going to tell her?" Nicole asked, changing the subject as she stepped back, putting space between them. They'd received the letter in the mail two days earlier, welcoming Caitlin to the USA National Swim Team.

"I don't know. How about tomorrow? After the ceremony, of course. We've already wrapped up the Team USA swim cap and t-shirt they sent her, along with the welcome letter. Why don't we give her the gift at the reception? My mom will be there, and Will as well. So, we'll all be together."

"That's a good idea actually," Nicole muttered, heading over to her jewelry box to put on the sapphire blue, stud earrings that matched her dress. "She's going to freak out."

"Who's going to freak out?" Caitlin asked from the doorway.

Finley turned to see her daughter dressed in her school ROTC uniform. She too, had an array of ribbons and pins on her jacket, and the name: MORRIS was also etched on her nametag.

"I'm so proud of you," Finley stated, adjusting the rank pin on her lapel.

"Thanks, Mom."

"What about me? Do I pass the test?" Nicole questioned, twirling in her sleeveless and knee-length, dark-blue dress, with a neck-line just low enough to be noticed, yet still subtle. The matching heels brought her up to

Finley's height. Her honey blonde hair hung loosely around her shoulders.

"You look beautiful as always, Mom," Caitlin said.

"Gorgeous," Finley added with a smile, giving her the once over. "We should probably get going."

*

The ceremony hadn't taken as long as most people thought it would, but it felt like hours had passed for those who were up on the makeshift stage, sitting in the middle of the tarmac outside of the main hangar. A bright-red H65-Dolphin was parked behind them, adding to the overall presence.

The commanding officer, Captain Dale Ingram, spoke first, giving a long, monotonous speech, followed by the executive officer, and the command master chief, who both said a few words and moved on. Finley was the last to talk. She stepped up to the podium and began her speech with day one, week one as she went through each phase, slightly reminiscing about how the class learned about teamwork and never quitting, so others may live. She ended on the call out she and Jordy went on, explaining the Coast Guard Motto: Semper Paratus- Always Ready.

Captain Ingram stood up when she'd finished. "Before we continue with the commencement, we must first recognize the outstanding cadet who went above and beyond the duty of a rescue swimmer cadet this past weekend, Petty Officer Third Class Jordy Ross."

Jordy stood at attention, not quite sure what was happening. Finley had told her she was being commended for her heroic effort on the call out, but she'd had no clue what that meant.

"While it is rare for a cadet to go on a call out during the last week or two of training," he continued, "it isn't unheard of, especially when they're needed to help save lives. Petty Officer Ross did just that when she helped save the lives of six crewmen on a sinking container ship." He held up a velvet box containing the Coast Guard Commendation Medal and matching ribbon. It was green with two white stripes and the bronze medal hanging down, was stamped with the Coast Guard logo.

Finley removed the medal from the box and stepped in front of Jordy. "You gave everything you had that day, and we commend you for it," she said, pinning the medal onto the flap of her jacket pocket, just below the three ribbons she'd earned during her short time in the service.

Jordy knew she didn't have to salute Finley, as she wasn't a commissioned officer, but she did it anyway out of respect.

Finley saluted back, before taking her place next to the officers.

Captain Ingram said a few more words, then he was replaced at the podium by the executive officer. The cadets stood side by side across the stage. The captain held a larger velvet box open as he walked next to Finley, who pinned the gold rescue swimmer badge onto each cadet as their name and rank was called out. She shook their hands and congratulated them as she moved down the short line.

Once that process was over, the captain spoke briefly, congratulating the new rescue swimmers, before formally dismissing class 16-20 for the final time.

The cadets all hugged each other, then Jordy walked over to Finley, giving her a strong hug. "I couldn't have done this without you," she said with tears in her eyes.

"If you ever need anything at all, you call me. I will never quit on you, Jordy. I consider you a part of my family."

"Thank you."

"Come with me, there's someone here to see you," Finley said.

Jordy looked out at the small crowd, waving at Nicole and Caitlin. Two other women, also in Coast Guard uniforms, were next to them. Jordy hadn't noticed Ericka standing behind the two women because she was in her uniform as well. Everyone sort of blended in.

"You're here!" she squealed, rushing up to Ericka, lifting her off the ground in a hug.

"I couldn't miss seeing you graduate," Ericka giggled as Jordy set her down. "My class is on liberty this weekend, so I was able to be here."

"That's awesome."

Ericka smiled. "I'm very proud of you," she said, rubbing her finger over the shiny swimmer badge and bronze medal pinned to Jordy's jacket.

"Thank you. I couldn't have done it without you," Jordy replied, looking into her eyes.

Ericka kissed her softly.

"Hey, since you're free tomorrow, would you like to go on a date with me?" Jordy asked as the kiss broke.

"Actually, I was going to ask you the same," Ericka muttered.

They laughed together, realizing they were both asking the other to go with them to Finley's wedding the following day.

"There's someone I want you to meet," Ericka said. "This is AMT1 Flight Mechanic Tracey Pollack, my tutor. Tracey, this is my girlfriend, Jordy Ross."

"Oh, wow!" Jordy exclaimed, shaking hands with her. "It's nice to meet you."

"Likewise. I'm glad you didn't give up on that old goat over there," Tracey kidded, nodding towards Finley, who was talking with her family. "She's one of my best friends. If you know her, you know you are family, and she'd do anything for you."

Jordy nodded, beginning to understand the family bond between people who weren't actually blood related. It felt good to know that someone would always be there for her, no matter what.

"We hate to the cut the celebration short, but we sort of have something going on tomorrow," Finley said, stepping over to them.

"Yeah, yeah," Tracey teased as she and Lillian hugged them goodbye.

Caitlin had already headed over to the parking lot, talking on her phone along the way.

"You're a great influence on those kids," Nicole said, squeezing Finley's hand as they walked towards the SUV.

"What do you mean?"

"Jordy and Ericka. It's good that they have someone like you, a woman, or even a gay woman for that matter, in the position you are in, showing them that they can be who they are and do whatever they want and succeed in life. The integrity that you've instilled upon them during the past eighteen weeks, will be with them forever. I saw so much respect and admiration in the way they looked at you."

"Thanks. That's the most gratifying part about being an instructor," Finley said as she maneuvered her SUV through the streets of Charleston, heading towards their house. She glanced in the rearview mirror at Caitlin, who was busy texting on her phone, more than likely to Will. She'd worn her uniform with as much pride as those who were up on the stage. Whether or not she ever went into the military, didn't matter to Finley, as long as Caitlin held onto the values she was learning while wearing that uniform.

*

The next morning, just before eleven a.m., the sun began to glisten off the river flowing next to Waterfront Park, under a cloudless sky. Finley and Nicole's closest friends and family members were seated in two short rows of white chairs that faced the large fountain near the water's edge.

No music played in the background. The only sound heard as Finley and Nicole walked down the middle aisle with Caitlin as their escort, was the sound of their shoes on the grass.

Nicole was beautiful in her form-fitting, ivory-colored dress that was cut just above the knee in the front, and slightly lower in the back. Her hair was pulled back from the sides, being held by an ivory clip, and her makeup was simple, keeping to a more natural appearance. She had on minimal jewelry, settling for a pair of small diamond earrings, a platinum gold, tennis bracelet, and her engagement ring.

Finley looked very dapper as usual, in her Full Dress Uniform, which had all of her medals dangling from it instead of the customary ribbon rack that was worn on the Service Dress Uniform. The FDU was the most formal of the Coast Guard uniforms.

Caitlin, who was walking with their arms linked through both of hers, had chosen to wear a striking, black pantsuit, with a feminine cut that hugged her young figure. She couldn't remember the last time she'd worn a dress, and wearing her uniform two days in a row seemed boring, so she'd picked out the suit when she and Nicole were in Colorado and had a free day to peruse the mall before leaving.

A friend of Nicole's took pictures as Caitlin hugged both of her parents, before taking a seat in the front row between Finley's mother and Will.

The officiant, another friend of Nicole's from the bank office, began the ceremony with a poem about devotion and everlasting love, before delving right into the vows. Both Finley and Nicole had wanted the nuptials to be short and to the point, focusing more on the celebration afterwards.

Tears slid down Nicole's cheeks as she repeated her vows while sliding the solid platinum band onto Finley's left hand. In turn, Finley stopped her vows to clear her throat, choking back a sob, as she pushed a matching band up against the engagement ring on Nicole's finger.

As soon as the officiant pronounced them as Mrs. and Mrs. Morris, Finley pulled Nicole into a searing kiss. The people in the seats behind them cheered and clapped. Caitlin rushed from her seat with tears on her cheeks as she hugged them at the same time.

The woman with the camera, snapped a few pictures of Finley and Nicole in front of the waterfall and the river. Then, she added Caitlin, and finally Finley's mother as well.

"Thank you all for being here," Finley said loudly. "The after party is at our house!"

Everyone began walking towards their vehicles. Finley spotted Tracey and Lillian, as well as Jordy and

Ericka, who were all in their uniforms. She smiled, seeing Caitlin and Will walking with all of them.

"I love you," Nicole said, pulling Finley into her arms.

"I love you, too, Mrs. Morris." Finley grinned.

"I've waited over seventeen years to hear that."

"Now, you'll hear it forever," Finley said, kissing her.

Epilogue

"Sector San Juan...Search and Rescue 6571. Be advised: we are on scene and deploying swimmer. Over."

"6571...Sector. Copy," the operations officer in dispatch radioed in reply.

"I'm Senior Chief Morris with the U.S. Coast Guard," Finley said. "Keep calm and I'll get you out of here."

The man nodded his head, still slightly in shock after watching his boat sink right underneath him.

"6571...Rescue Swimmer. Survivor is alert: nine; injury: zero. Send the sling. Over," she radioed, before swimming into the rotor wash with him under her arm.

The bright yellow sling slowly made its way down, and she quickly secured him as soon as she could reach it. Swimming back, she gave the 'all clear' signal, and watched as he was lifted out of the water. She floated on her back in the warm, Atlantic Ocean while she waited to be retrieved.

As soon as the hook came down to her, Finley clipped it to her survival harness and gave a thumbs up to Petty Officer Ericka Burney, the flight mechanic on board. When she'd found out there was a new flight mech coming in, she'd never expected it to be Ericka, especially after Jordy had been stationed in Clearwater for her first post, which was also where Tracey and Lillian had been re-posted after their latest transfer. Finley knew there weren't two better people for Jordy and Ericka to be working with than Tracey and herself.

*

"What a day, huh?" Ericka said as they exited the helo.

"Yeah, no kidding," Finley replied, looking over at the survivor, who was being tended to by the paramedics as a precaution, before rushing into the hangar to change out of her wetsuit.

"Where did she go?" the man asked, looking all around.

"Who, Sir?" Ericka answered.

"The woman who saved me. She was my guardian angel," he said in broken English.

Ericka smiled. "I'm sure she's gone by now. Her daughter is flying in from college. She just finished her freshman year at the University of Florida," she replied.

"Oh…" he uttered with a nod.

*

Finley stood at the waiting area, bouncing her weight from one foot to the other in her dark-blue Operation Duty Uniform, which she'd chosen to wear instead of the flight suit she usually wore as working uniform. Standing there, nervously awaiting Caitlin's arrival made her think back to four years earlier when she was in a similar position, waiting for her daughter, who was coming to spend the summer with her.

"You look as nervous as a cat in a bathtub," Nicole chuckled.

"I'm excited to see her," she replied.

"Mom!" Caitlin yelled.

Finley spun around to see her daughter walking towards her with a small carry-on suitcase and Will by her side. She rushed over, wrapping her arms around Caitlin. "I think you've grown since the last time I saw you," Finley said.

Caitlin laughed. "Mom, I'm eighteen. I'm pretty sure I'm done growing."

Finley grinned.

Nicole wiped away tears and pulled Caitlin into her arms. "I've missed you so much!" she cried.

"I missed you, too, Mom," Caitlin said. "I thought you were going to stop crying every time you saw me?" she teased, pulling out of the hug.

Finley bit her lip to keep from laughing.

Nicole furrowed her brow, pinning Finley with a stare. "Who tears up every time she gets off the phone with Caitlin?" she questioned, wiping the last tear from her face.

Finley ignored her as she hugged Will.

"How was the flight?" Finley asked.

"Fine. We can't wait to relax for the next two weeks," Caitlin replied.

"Why only two weeks?" Nicole questioned, also hugging Will.

"I'm headed to training camp with the USA National Team. Summer Regionals start at the end of the month," Caitlin said. She'd just won the NCAA Swimming National Championship with the University of Florida earlier this year, and now her focus was solely on Team USA, especially with the Olympics eighteen months away. "I still can't believe you and mom live here. It's so beautiful," she exclaimed, watching the scenery as they drove through the streets of San Juan. Large cruise ships were docked at terminals near the tourist area, which they drove past on their way to the condo Finley and Nicole were renting right outside of the Coast Guard base.

Finley smiled. "You sound like your mother. If it were up to her, we'd probably stay here permanently. She practically lives on the beach. Look at how tan she is."

Caitlin chuckled. "I plan to work on my tan, too," she said squeezing Will's hand and smiling at her.

"How are things going with you, Will?" Finley asked.

"Good. I'm happy to finally have some time off. When Caitlin goes to training camp, I'm going home to see my family."

Finley nodded, pulling into the parking lot for their building. She and Caitlin each grabbed a suitcase, and Will grabbed the carry-on bag.

"Do you think you brought enough shit?" Finley mumbled, lugging the bag into the elevator.

"Well, you can't leave your shit behind when you move out of the dorm, Mom," Caitlin exclaimed, causing Finley to laugh. "Will and I are moving in together when we go back to school," she added.

"Oh, really?"

"Yes. We're going to get a studio apartment."

"What about the dorm? Don't you get to stay there because you're on an athletic scholarship?"

"Yes, but after one year, I've had enough of it. Besides, we want to live together, not with other people, right?" she said, looking at Will, who nodded and smiled.

Finley understood her point. She couldn't imagine being separated from Nicole back when they were that age, but at the same time, they had been expecting a baby.

"I wish I'd known you were only coming for two weeks. I would've taken more time off," Nicole said.

"Me too," Finley added. "We barely get to see you as it is."

"You two are a mess," Caitlin chuckled. "I was just with you for the holidays. I can't wait to see you as grandparents," she said, shaking her head.

"What's that supposed to mean?" Finley asked, crossing her arms.

"Not right now, or any time soon for that matter. I have way too much crap on my plate to worry about changing diapers," Caitlin muttered, carrying one of the bags down the hall to the spare bedroom.

Nicole sighed in relief as Will followed her with the other two suitcases. "She just about gave me a heart attack," she uttered.

"Unless Will sprouted a penis, we have nothing to worry about," Finley stated.

Nicole laughed, shaking her head as she wrapped her arms around Finley's neck.

"Do you want to do anything tonight?" Finley asked.

"Besides you?" Nicole murmured.

Finley grinned, before kissing her passionately.

About the Author

Graysen Morgen is the bestselling author of *Falling Snow*, *Fast Pitch*, *Cypress Lake*, *Never Let Go*, the Bridal Series: *Bridesmaid of Honor*, *Brides*, and *Mommies*, as well as many other titles. She was born and raised in North Florida with winding rivers and waterways at her back door, and the white sandy beach a mile away. She has spent most of her lifetime in the sun and on the water. She enjoys reading, writing, fishing, coaching and watching soccer, and spending as much time as possible with her wife and their daughter.

Email: graysenmorgen@aol.com
Facebook.com/graysenmorgen
Twitter: @graysenmorgen
Instagram: @graysenmorgen

Other Titles Available From
Triplicity Publishing

For a Moment's Indiscretion by KA Moll. With ten years of marriage under their belt, Zane and Jaina are coasting. The little things they used to do for one another have fallen by the wayside. They've gotten busy with life. They've forgotten to nurture their love and relationship. Even soul mates can stumble on hard times and have marital difficulties. Enter Amelia, a new faculty member in Jaina's building. She's new in town, young, and very pretty. When an argument with Zane causes Jaina to storm out angry, she reaches out to Amelia. Of course, she seizes the opportunity. And for a moment of indiscretion, Jaina could lose everything.

Never Let Go by Graysen Morgen. For Coast Guard Rescue Swimmer, Finley Morris, life is good. She loves her job, is well respected by her peers, and has been given an opportunity to take her career to the next level. The only thing missing is the love of her life, who walked out, taking their daughter with her, seven years earlier. When Finley gets a call from her ex, saying their teenage daughter is coming to spend the summer with her, she's floored. While spending more time with her daughter, whom she doesn't get to see often, and learning to be a full-time parent, Finley quickly realizes she has not, and will never, let go of what is important.

Pursuit by Joan L. Anderson. Claire is a workaholic attorney who flies to Paris to lick her wounds after being dumped by her girlfriend of seventeen years. On the plane she chats with the young woman sitting next to her, and when they land the woman is inexplicably detained in Customs. Claire is surprised when she later runs into the woman in the city. They agree to meet for breakfast the next morning, but when the woman doesn't show up Claire goes to her hotel and makes a horrifying discovery. She soon finds herself ensnared in a web of intrigue and international terrorism, becoming the target of a high stakes game of cat and mouse through the streets of Paris.

Wrecked by Sydney Canyon. To most people, the *Duchess* is a myth formed by old pirates tales, but to Reid Cavanaugh, a Caribbean island bum and one of the best divers and treasure hunters in the world, it's a real, seventeenth century pirate ship—the holy grail of underwater treasure hunting. Reid uses the same cunning tactics she always has before setting out to find the lost ship. However, she is forced to bring her business partner's daughter along as collateral this time because he doesn't trust her. Neither woman is thrilled, but being cooped up on a small dive boat for days, forces them to get know each other quickly.

Arson by Austen Thorne. Madison Drake is a detective for the Stetson Beach Police Department. The last thing she wants to do is show a new detective the ropes, especially when a fire investigation becomes arson to cover up a murder. Madison butts heads with Tara, her trainee, deals with sarcasm from Nic, her ex-girlfriend who is a patrol officer, and finds calm in the chaos of police work with Jamie, her best friend who is the county medical examiner. Arson is the first of many in a series of novella episodes surrounding the fictional Stetson Beach Police Department and Detective Madison Drake.

Change of Heart by KA Moll. Courtney Holloman is a woman at the top of her game. She's successful, wealthy, and a highly sought after Washington lobbyist. She has money, her job, booze, and nothing else. In quiet moments, against her will, her mind drifts back to her days in high school and to all that she gave up. Jack Camdon is a complex woman, and yet not at all. She is also a woman who has never moved beyond the sudden and unexplained departure of her high school sweetheart, her lover, and her soul mate. When circumstances bring Courtney back to town two decades later, their paths will cross. Will it be too late?

Mommies (Bridal Series book 3) by Graysen Morgen. Britton and her wife Daphne have been married for a year and a half and are happy with their life, until Britton's mother hounds her to find out why her sister Bridget hasn't decided to have children yet. This prompts Daphne to bring up the big subject of having kids of their own with Britton. Britton hadn't really thought much about having kids, but her love for Daphne makes her see life and their future together in a whole new way when they decide to become mommies.

Haunting Love by K.A. Moll. Anna Crestwood was raised in the strict beliefs of a religious sect nestled in the foothills of the Smoky Mountains. She's a lesbian with a ton of baggage—fearful, guilty, and alone. Very few things would compel her to leave the familiar. The job offer of a lifetime is one of them. Gabe Garst is a police officer. She's also a powerful medium. Her work with juvenile delinquents and ghosts is all that keeps her going. Inside she's dead, certain that her capacity to love is buried six feet under. Anna and Gabe's paths cross. Their attraction is immediate, but they hold back until all hope seems lost.

Rapture & Rogue by Sydney Canyon. Taren Rauley is happy and in a good relationship, until the one person she thought she'd never see again comes back into her life. She struggles to keep the past from colliding with the present as old feelings she thought were dead and gone, begin to haunt her. In college, Gianna Revisi was a mastermind, ringleading, crime boss. Now, she has a great life and spends her time running Rapture and Rogue, the two establishments she built from the ground up. The last person she ever expects to see walk into one of them, is the girl who walked out on her, breaking her heart five years ago.

Second Chance by Sydney Canyon. After an attack on her convoy, Marine Corps Staff Sergeant, Darien Hollister, must learn to live without her sight. When an experimental procedure allows her to see again, Darien is torn, knowing someone had to die in order for this to happen.
She embarks on a journey to personally thank the donor's family, but is too stunned to tell them the truth. Mixed emotions stir inside of her as she slowly gets to the know the people that feel like so much more than strangers to her. When the truth finally comes out, Darien walks away, taking the second chance that she's been given to go back to the only life she's ever known, but she's not the only one with a second chance at life.

Meant to Be by Graysen Morgen. Brandt is about to walk down the aisle with her girlfriend, when an unexpected chain of events turns her world upside down, causing her to question the last three years of her life. A chance encounter sparks a mix of rage and excitement that she has never felt before. Summer is living life and following her dreams, all the while, harboring a huge secret that could ruin her career. She believes that some things are better kept in the dark, until she has her third run-in with a woman she had hoped to never see again, and gives into temptation. Brandt and Summer start believing everything happens for a reason as they learn the true meaning of meant to be.

Coming Home by Graysen Morgen. After tragedy derails TJ Abernathy's life, she packs up her three year old son and heads back to Pennsylvania to live with her grandmother on the family farm. TJ picks back up where she left off eight years earlier, tending to the fruit and nut tree orchard, while learning her grandmother's secret trade. Soon, TJ's high school sweetheart and the same girl who broke her heart, comes back into her life, threatening to steal it away once again. As the weeks turn into months and tragedy strikes again, TJ realizes coming home was the best thing she could've ever done.

Special Assignment by Austen Thorne. Secret Service Agent Parker Meeks has her hands full when she gets her new assignment, protecting a Congressman's teenage daughter, who has had threats made on her life and been whisked away to a Christian boarding school under an alias to finish out her senior year. Parker is fine with the assignment, until she finds out she has to go undercover as a Canon Priest. The last thing Parker expects to find is a beautiful, art history teacher, who is intrigued by her in more ways than one.

Miracle at Christmas by Sydney Canyon. A Modern Twist on the Classic Scrooge Story. Dylan is a power-hungry lawyer who pushed away everything good in her life to become the best defense attorney in the, often winning the worst cases and keeping anyone with enough money out of jail. She's visited on Christmas Eve by her deceased law partner, who threatens her with a life in hell like his own, if she doesn't change her path. During the course of the night, she is taken on a journey through her past, present, and future with three very different spirits.

Bella Vita by Sydney Canyon. Brady is the First Officer of the crew on the Bella Vita, a luxury charter yacht in the Caribbean. She enjoys the laidback island lifestyle, and is accustomed to high profile guests, but when a U.S. Senator charters the yacht as a gift to his beautiful twin daughters who have just graduated from college and a few of their friends, she literally has her hands full.

Brides (Bridal Series book 2) by Graysen Morgen. Britton Prescott is dating the love of her life, Daphne Attwood, after a few tumultuous events that happened to unravel at her sister's wedding reception, seven months earlier. She's happy with the way things are, but immense pressure from her family and friends to take the next step, nearly sends her back to the single life. The idea of a long engagement and simple wedding are thrown out the window, as both families take over, rushing Britton and Daphne to the altar in a matter of weeks.

Cypress Lake by Graysen Morgen. The small town of Cypress Lake is rocked when one murder after another happens. Dani Ricketts, the Chief Deputy for the Cypress Lake Sheriff's Office, realizes the murders are linked. She's surprised when the girl that broke her heart in high school has not only returned home, but she's also Dani's only suspect. Kristen Malone has come back to Cypress Lake to put the past behind her so that she can move on with her life. Seeing Dani Ricketts again throws her off-guard, nearly derailing her plans to finally rid herself and her family of Cypress Lake.

Crashing Waves by Graysen Morgen. After a tragic accident, Pro Surfer, Rory Eden, spends her days hiding in the surf and snowboard manufacturing company that she built from the ground up, while living her life as a shell of the person that she once was. Rory's world is turned upside when a young surfer pursues her, asking for the one thing she can't do. Adler Troy and Dr. Cason Macauley from Graysen Morgen's bestselling novel: *Falling Snow*, make an appearance in this romantic adventure about life, love, and letting go.

Bridesmaid of Honor (Bridal Series book 1) by Graysen Morgen. Britton Prescott's best friend is getting married and she's the maid of honor. As if that isn't enough to deal with, Britton's sister announces she's getting married in the same month and her maid of honor is her best friend Daphne, the same woman who has tormented Britton for years. Britton has to suck it up and play nice, instead of scratching her eyes out, because she and Daphne are in both weddings. Everyone is counting on them to behave like adults.

Falling Snow by Graysen Morgen. Dr. Cason Macauley, a high-speed trauma surgeon from Denver meets Adler Troy, a professional snowboarder and sparks fly. The last thing Cason wants is a relationship and Adler doesn't realize what's right in front of her until it's gone, but will it be too late?

Fate vs. Destiny by Graysen Morgen. Logan Greer devotes her life to investigating plane crashes for the National Transportation Safety Board. Brooke McCabe is an investigator with the Federal Aviation Association who literally flies by the seat of her pants. When Logan gets tangled in head games with both women will she choose fate or destiny?

Just Me by Graysen Morgen. Wild child Ian Wiley has to grow up and take the reins of the hundred year old family business when tragedy strikes. Cassidy Harland is a little surprised that she came within an inch of picking up a gorgeous stranger in a bar and is shocked to find out that stranger is the new head of her company.

Love Loss Revenge by Graysen Morgen. Rian Casey is an FBI Agent working the biggest case of her career and madly in love with her girlfriend. Her world is turned upside when tragedy strikes. Heartbroken, she tries to rebuild her life. When she discovers the truth behind what really happened that awful night she decides justice isn't good enough, and vows revenge on everyone involved.

Natural Instinct by Graysen Morgen. Chandler Scott is a Marine Biologist who keeps her private life private. Corey Joslen is intrigued by Chandler from the moment she meets her. Chandler is forced to finally open her life up to Corey. It backfires in Corey's face and sends her running. Will either woman learn to trust her natural instinct?

Secluded Heart by Graysen Morgen. Chase Leery is an overworked cardiac surgeon with a group of best friends that have an opinion and a reason for everything. When she meets a new artist named Remy Sheridan at her best friend's art gallery she is captivated by the reclusive woman. When Chase finds out why Remy is so sheltered will she put her career on the line to help her or is it too difficult to love someone with a secluded heart?

In Love, at War by Graysen Morgen. Charley Hayes is in the Army Air Force and stationed at Ford Island in Pearl Harbor. She is the commanding officer of her own female-only service squadron and doing the one thing she loves most, repairing airplanes. Life is good for Charley, until the day she finds herself falling in love while fighting for her life as her country is thrown haphazardly into World War II. Can she survive being in love and at war?

Fast Pitch by Graysen Morgen. Graham Cahill is a senior in college and the catcher and captain of the softball team. Despite being an all-star pitcher, Bailey Michaels is young and arrogant. Graham and Bailey are forced to get to know each other off the field in order to learn to work together on the field. Will the extra time pay off or will it drive a nail through the team?

Submerged by Graysen Morgen. Assistant District Attorney Layne Carmichael had no idea that the sexy woman she took home from a local bar for a one night stand would turn out to be someone she would be prosecuting months later. Scooter is a Naval Officer on a submarine who changes women like she changes uniforms. When she is accused of a heinous crime she is shocked to see her latest conquest sitting across from her as the prosecuting attorney.

Vow of Solitude by Austen Thorne. Detective Jordan Denali is in a fight for her life against the ghosts from her past and a Serial Killer taunting her with his every move. She lives a life of solitude and plans to keep it that way. When Callie Marceau, a curious Medical Examiner, decides she wants in on the biggest case of her career, as well as, Jordan's life, Jordan is powerless to stop her.

Igniting Temptation by Sydney Canyon. Mackenzie Trotter is the Head of Pediatrics at the local hospital. Her life takes a rather unexpected turn when she meets a flirtatious, beautiful fire fighter. Both women soon discover it doesn't take much to ignite temptation.

One Night by Sydney Canyon. While on a business trip, Caylen Jarrett spends an amazing night with a beautiful stripper. Months later, she is shocked and confused when that same woman re-enters her life. The fact that this stranger could destroy her career doesn't bother her. C.J. is more terrified of the feelings this woman stirs in her. Could she have fallen in love in one night and not even known it?

Fine by Sydney Canyon. Collin Anderson hides behind a façade, pretending everything is fine. Her workaholic wife and best friend are both oblivious as she goes on an emotional journey, battling a potentially hereditary disease that her mother has been diagnosed with. The only person who knows what is really going on, is Collin's doctor. The same doctor, who is an acquaintance that she's always been attracted to, and who has a partner of her own.

Shadow's Eyes by Sydney Canyon. Tyler McCain is the owner of a large ranch that breeds and sells different types of horses. She isn't exactly thrilled when a Hollywood movie producer shows up wanting to film his latest movie on her property. Reegan Delsol is an up and coming actress who has everything going for her when she lands the lead role in a new film, but there one small problem that could blow the entire picture.

Light Reading: A Collection of Novellas by Sydney Canyon. Four of Sydney Canyon's novellas together in one book, including the bestsellers Shadow's Eyes and One Night.

Visit us at www.tri-pub.com

67227858R00189

Made in the USA
Lexington, KY
05 September 2017